ALSO BY THE AUTHOR

THE PULPIT IS VACANT

FRANCES MACARTHUR

DEATH
OF A
Chameleon

Frances Macarthur.

ISBN: 1463527179
ISBN-13: 9781463527174

ACKNOWLEDGEMENTS

I would like to thank my proof readers Leela and Margo and also Jean for her comments and advice.

Thanks to Anne who pointed out mistakes in police protocol.

Thanks too to all my friends who purchased Book 1 and gave me the confidence to have Book 2 published. Keep with the support, folks. There are 7 novels in the Davenport series so far!!

Thanks to Irene and Marilyn who drummed up buyers for me.

Above all, thanks to my very patient husband, Ivor who has managed without my help to understand the offside rule in football when I have been too busy writing to watch with him!!!!!

CHAPTER I

Tall, dark and extremely handsome, David Gibson knew that he was attractive to women. The trouble was that he was also short-tempered and a control freak at work though meek and subservient at home.

He was now at work.

"Geena, get in here now!" he shouted down the corridor. He could easily have walked down to the office but this would not have occurred to him.

Geena, the school auxiliary, ran up the corridor, wondering what she had done now. She found all the staff at Bradford High School very pleasant to work with except David Gibson and it seemed that it was always she who got his work to do. She was beginning to understand why. He could bully her and knew it.

"What's wrong Mr Gibson?" she asked a bit breathlessly. She must try to lose some weight; she really must. Her navy skirt had ridden up her thighs again, her blouse buttons were straining and she was always conscious of her appearance when she was with this man.

"I asked for two hundred timetables, not twenty. There are more than twenty in the third year for goodness sake, woman."

He stood there with his dark grey suit open and showing a grey and white striped shirt, looking so smart it made her feel shabbily dressed though she was not.

"I didn't know it was for the third year. Sorry."

"If you'd had a look, it said, 'Third Year Timetable' at the top. Use your common sense, woman, and bring me the other copies as soon as they're done."

"I'm doing something for Mr Snedden just now."

She tried not to be browbeaten by this man. Bullied at school, she had vowed never to let it happen again.

"Well stop it. Work for the Senior Management Team takes precedence over any other member of staff. 'Precedence' for your information means priority."

She wanted to tell him that she wasn't stupid but found herself scuttling back down the corridor to the room where the photocopier was housed - like a scared rabbit, she thought disgustedly. It wasn't till she had removed Alex Snedden's poetry sheet from the machine that she realised that she had come away without the timetable sheets.

She ran back up the corridor. David Gibson was standing in his room, facing the open door, holding out the sheets. The look on his face would have skinned a peach at twenty yards.

Geena took the sheets and left.

On her way back to the reprographics room, she passed the head teacher, Christine Martin. Tall, blonde and dressed smartly in a black suit and white blouse, she was so different in personality from David Gibson and in looks, as he was dark haired though also tall.

"Are you OK, Geena? You look a bit flustered."

"No it's just hot today."

Geena did not want to tell tales. It was the usual story. Someone bullied other people and no one wanted to be the one to report it in case it made the bullying worse. Whoever would have thought you would be bullied as an adult in a school!

Christine Martin was thoughtful as she went into her own room. She had a fair idea of what David Gibson was like to office staff, young staff and women in particular. She knew he hated having a women head teacher but he could not bully her and she was going to have to think of a way to stop his bullying without having someone 'tell tales'. Geena had come from his room; she had seen that and the poor girl had looked really flustered and on the verge of tears.

She looked at the timetables for staff and noticed that all the management team were free next period.

She had had an idea.

When the bell rang for the end of period five, she stood at the door of her room and caught Stewart Wilson who had come from teaching Maths and Phyllis Watson who had come from Modern Languages. Asking them to come into her room, she went along to David Gibson's room and asked him to join them.

"I'm really busy Christine," he said.

"Yes so are we all but this is important. Come now."

She knew that he would be fuming at being told what to do but she didn't care.

When they were all seated, she began.

"I've decided to move your rooms round. I want David, as senior depute, nearest to my room so that when I am out of school, he is nearest to the office and the rest of the school. Stewart you are next in seniority so you change rooms with Phyllis and Phyllis you will have David's room. The rooms are all the same size, so no problem there.

Naturally David objected.

"It'll take me ages to transfer all my things."

"Fine Christine," chorused the other two. They liked their head teacher and knew that the change made sense.

Christine got up to signal that the short meeting was closed. David had no option but to get up too. Sensing that he would stay behind to try to undermine her decision, she walked briskly out with the other two and went into the office, asking her secretary to get one of the primary head teachers on the phone.

Frustrated, David went back to his room. He took his anger out on Phyllis who having decided that there was no time like the present to transfer her things, arrived at his door shortly afterwards with an armful of books. She was a woman in her mid-thirties, had mousy fair hair which always looked straggly but she was a figure of respect among her pupils who knew she was strict but had a good sense of humour.

"For goodness sake! Can't you see that I'm busy, Phyllis?"

"I won't disturb you at your desk. This is just stuff for a cupboard. Oh good, here's an almost empty one!"

So saying, she removed a few folders from the cupboard and set about arranging her books in it.

David fumed inwardly. It was no use trying to boss Phyllis about. She simply didn't respond and went on her own merry way regardless of what he said and how he said it. It infuriated him but he was at a loss as to how to get any control over her. This was an unusual event for him as women usually either worshipped him or obeyed him or both, usually both.

Christine slipped back into her room, having had a brief chat with Jean Hobson at Southview Primary about a meeting she was giving for all the local primary school teachers the following week. Bradford High was hosting the meeting and Christine needed numbers for catering.

She was quite pleased with herself. She would now be able to hear if David raised his voice to anyone. The walls were very thin between the rooms, this being a comparatively new school and built cheaply.

She noted down the numbers given to her in her diary and decided to pay a visit to the English department to see Alex Snedden about the 5-14 teaching programme which he was running with the primary schools. She was still there when the bell heralding the end of school for that day rang so she didn't see David Gibson almost erupt from his room, snarl at some pupils who got in his way and make for his car, gunning it as he went down the driveway. The janitor, hastily getting out of his way, felt sorry for the man's wife.

"Wonder who rattled his cage," he thought and pitied the wife who would probably suffer when he got home.

But David Gibson was sweetness and light when he walked in the front door of his home.

CHAPTER 2

"Hello? Caroline, are you home?"
No reply. His wife was a beauty consultant and worked in a salon in Bearsden. They had met at a party years ago. He had been instantly captivated by her beauty and sparkling personality. They had gone out occasionally and he had asked her to marry him after only six weeks. She had turned him down. He had wondered if it was because of his somewhat abrasive nature and when they had met up again some years later, he had tried to be more amenable. When he had again asked her to marry him, he had been delighted when she accepted. His new, meek nature must have won her over, he thought and from then on he tried very hard to be meek and thoughtful, so much so that it was now second nature to be a lamb when with his wife while being the lion in the workplace. If he sometimes wished to have a partner who was his equal in intelligence, he quickly dismissed this thought and dwelt immediately on her personality

and looks which he thought made the envy of other men.

Sometime she was home before him but usually he was first. He liked this as it meant that he could get started on preparing dinner. He was going to prepare steak Diane tonight, one of Caroline's favourites.

He was busy in the kitchen when he heard her key in the door. She came straight through into the kitchen, throwing her car keys on the table.

"Hi, David. What a day I've had. A wedding party to be made up, then a double booking. Luckily the second woman wasn't in a rush so we fitted her in later. God, my feet ache."

She sat down on one of the kitchen chairs and kicked off her shoes. She would leave them there when she left and David would pick them up and put them away in her wardrobe later.

"Never mind darling, you've got your favourite meal to look forward to then we're meeting John and June for drinks, remember?"

She wrinkled her nose and David recognised the signs. Sure enough, she gave him a cold look and said, "They're such boring people. You go. I want a quiet night in."

Knowing that it was useless to argue and knowing that if it had been her friends they were going out to meet she would be all sweetness and light, David smiled and said, "Sure darling. I'll go by myself."

This was the pattern of their marriage. They met her friends together and she usually cried off when it was his friends. He had overheard one of his friends call her the ice maiden. They did not like her, finding her shallow and uneducated and were usually delighted when David turned up alone. She made no effort for them and looked cool and bored when with them. With her own circle of friends she was enthusiastic and lively and so, so popular.

"That's your dinner ready now. I've set the table in the dining room."

She preceded him into the dining room. He had set the table to perfection, with candles lit at each end. Her only comment was on the fact that one of the paintings was squint. David moved immediately to straighten it.

They sat at either end of the long table.

"Caroline, that bitch of a head teacher has only gone and told us to change round rooms. She wants me to be in the room next to her, says it's because when she's away I should be the one nearest to the body of the school."

Caroline yawned, showing her perfect, pearly - white teeth and David thought again how lucky he was to have her as his wife. She was beautiful, his goddess. With fair, almost white blonde hair reaching to her shoulders, she looked almost Nordic and she was tall too with a superb figure.

"Did I tell you that Jennifer is going to Dubai on holiday, David?"

The steak, washed down by a bottle of Beaujolais, was followed by fresh fruit salad; no stodgy pudding for Caroline.

The conversation stayed firmly on Caroline's day, her clients, her fellow workers and her feelings on both.

Once the meal was over, she moved off to the lounge, saying over her shoulder, "Coffee in here dear."

David filled the dishwasher and made the coffee. He carried it through and poured it out.

"I'll just go and get ready. Sure you won't come?"

Caroline was already immersed in a TV programme and just replied, "Sure."

As he showered and changed into casual clothes - Caroline had such good taste in men's clothes - he thought for the umpteenth time how fortunate he was to have such a wife as Caroline. He would do anything for her and she knew it.

In the lounge, Caroline yawned again. She was bored, bored with her job, this house and with David. It had been fun at first, moulding him into the perfect husband but he was no longer a challenge and life had become a bit stale. He never argued. She had seen to that but sometimes she would have liked a heated argument. They shared the same views - hers. She had met a man some weeks ago at a party and had really fallen for him. She knew instinctively that she would have fun taming him. They had met only once but the charge between them was electric She was ripe for another affair that would add some spice to her life. Should she phone the friend who had held the party and ask for his phone number? No, that was not her way. She never did the chasing. She was sure he would contact her and after some show of reluctance she would agree to meet him.

When David, the 'doormat' as she called him to herself and to close friends, came into the lounge ready to go out, she blew him a kiss and told him to have a good time.

She had never gone to any of his staff functions - teachers, so boring - and would have been astonished if she had known the reputation he had in school for being bossy and bullying. They in turn would never have recognised Caroline's David.

As he went down the front path to his car, he shrugged off his meek persona and put on the jovial, David- with- friends- at -the -local personality.

CHAPTER 3

It was Monday afternoon, period six. Irene Campbell, the PE teacher at Bradford High was preparing to take her third year class on a short practice cross country run. She was a very popular teacher and the pupils tried hard to please her, all except Neil Fox who was very overweight and had nightmares about PE. He was scared of Irene; he hated her sarcastic tongue which the others loved. They weren't on the receiving end! He sat quietly on a bench inside the gym hall hoping that she might go straight out with the others and not notice him.

He was out of luck.

"Neil. What are you sitting there for? Get into your PE kit and hurry up about it."

"I can't run today Miss. I have a sore leg."

"Is that the same sore leg you have every week?"

He heard sniggers and realised that some of the other boys must be listening.

"No Miss. I twisted my ankle this morning."

"Do you have a note from home?"

"No."

"Right, PE kit on - now! As we're outside you can wear your tracksuit if you have it."

Miserably Neil went into the changing room He absolutely loathed wearing shorts and having the others laugh at his fat legs. He did not have his tracksuit with him.

Mrs Campbell was waiting outside as he came out and together they jogged across the road to the park which was the nearest thing to cross country terrain that they had near the school.

Once they were across the road, she sprinted off, looking slim and healthy in her red tracksuit, her long dark hair tied back with a red scrunchie.

Neil dropped to a trot. He really was not feeling too well this afternoon. He already had a stitch in his side - if only he had eaten less at lunchtime.

It was not long before Irene noticed that he was dropping behind and she stopped to wait for him.

"Neil. You really will have to lose weight, son. Get Mrs Donaldson to give you a diet sheet when you next see her."

Fiona Donaldson was head of Home Economics. He liked her and her subject. He was good at cooking and baking and was expected to do well in the HE exams. She would not laugh at him so he thought that maybe he would ask her for help.

The stitch in his side was getting worse and he stopped.

"Come on Neil. Move it up. The rest are almost out of sight."

Once again she sprinted off. Neil ran a few more yards then there was a blackness. He stumbled and fell.

Looking back, Irene Campbell saw him fall and raced back to him. It was soon clear to her that the boy had fainted. She took her mobile phone out of her pocket and dialled the school asking to speak to her head of department. She asked him to come in his car to the park. There was a road through it luckily and they were not far off the road.

It was not long before the two of them were helping a dazed Neil into the back seat of the car.

Back at school, Neil was taken to the sick room and his mother was rung. The number the school had was her mobile number and luckily she was in the nearby shopping arcade and had her car in the adjacent car park. She was soon at the school.

When she saw the state of her son in his shorts, she was vitriolic in her anger.

"I suppose that PE teacher made him do something he couldn't do - again! His father will be up this time. The boy's ill and it's her fault."

"Mrs Fox. Take your son home and get the doctor if you think he needs medical help," said the school nurse.

Still complaining, Mrs Fox helped Neil to her car.

When Irene Campbell arrived back in school, her head of department who had been informed by the nurse, told her what had happened and warned her that there might be repercussions. He suggested that she inform the senior management team so that they might be ready for any complaints which might come.

Irene took his advice and made her way to the head teacher's room, only to find that Mrs Martin was out of school. The next in line was David Gibson which was unfortunate as he was never sympathetic when dealing with a staff problem. She liked him better than most of the female staff but she still knew his faults.

She knocked on his door.

"Come in."

His sharp voice did not sound inviting.

Irene went in. David was pulling things out of a cupboard and obviously filling a box with them. The staff had heard about the rearrangement of rooms and it had filtered down to them that Mr Gibson was not pleased. She had obviously come at the wrong time - if there was a right time to beard the Gibson lion in his den.

"Irene, what is it?"

Irene told him the story of Neil Fox's collapse and the possibility that his parents might ring or visit the school to complain.

"That's all I need right now. OK I'll deal with it if it happens."

Irene left, feeling about ten years old. He might, she thought, have at least thanked her for warning him. Mrs Martin would have done that she was sure.

She would have been surprised to hear David supporting her when Mr Fox rang the school. He told the irate father that his son needed exercise, that he was fat and unhealthy and that the PE teacher would have been failing in her duty if she had not got him to take PE, which that day had meant running in the park.

Almost stuttering with rage, the father rang off threatening to get his own back somehow. David had heard it all before and it did not bother him in the least. Parents seldom carried out such threats.

He got ready to go home. In the car park he met one of the sixth year girls walking her black labrador dog through the playground. It was a right of way and he often met her. He did not teach her and never had but he smiled at her.

As he drove off, Cathy Cameron, the head girl, thought for the umpteenth time how handsome he was.

CHAPTER 4

Caroline was having lunch in a nearby cafe when her mobile phone rang. It was Jane one of her closest friends, the one whose party she had been at recently.

"Caro. I've had a man on the 'phone asking for your mobile number. He's called James Buchanan. I can't remember him but maybe you do."

"Can't say I remember the name, Jane, but give him my number anyway. I don't suppose he's a mad axe murderer."

"OK Caro. Have to go. See you soon."

"Bye."

Caroline sat back and thought about this. Hopefully this was the man she had fancied strongly.

Back at work the day passed rather slowly. She had no late customers so was allowed to go home quite early. Her boss was very amenable in that way. She was halfway home when her phone rang. She pulled over and switched off the car engine.

"Hello. Is that Caroline?"

She recognised the warm, velvety voice right away.

"Yes. Who's that?"

"You won't know my name, but it's James, James Buchanan. I asked someone for yours and I got your phone number from Jane, the girl who was hosting that party."

"Yes."

Play it cool, girl, she thought. Don't let him know you were hoping he would 'phone.

"What I wondered was, would you meet me for lunch some day?"

He was obviously going to start off slowly.

"Yes that would be nice. I can't manage till next week. How about next Monday?"

"I can't manage next Monday. How about Tuesday?"

He was playing it cool too so he was not going to be a pushover.

They agreed on next Tuesday and arranged to meet not far from Caroline's salon. If anyone from work saw them, she had plenty of excuses. She had done this before. There was no chance of meeting David as he stayed in school for his lunch as he was often on lunch duty. Anyway, he would believe anything she told him should he by some fluke see them or a friend report seeing them.

She turned on the ignition and set the car in motion. She always loved hearing her car engine rev up. It was so smooth. She absolutely adored her red MG sports car. It had cost more than they could really afford but they had economised on David's car, he being happy to settle for his small grey Fiat Uno. Luckily David was well paid as a depute head teacher so he paid the loans for both cars and for their foreign holiday every July. She fancied going to Dubai, having heard about it the other day. It was a nuisance that they had to go away during school holiday times but she had managed the odd weekend away in luxury hotels with her various lovers over the years. She hoped this new one would be as generous as the others.

The car, going at 40 mph had to be slowed down for crossing the Kingston Bridge but soon she could get up to 70 mph on the motorway. She slowed down again through Mosspark remembering the speeding fine she had been given some months ago on this stretch of the road. Soon she was purring along her own avenue and finally slowed right down to go up the driveway. She used her gizmo to open the garage door and drove the car inside. David had to keep his car outside but he seemed not to mind. Maybe they would have a double garage in their next house. She slid out of the car and closed the door. She had to use her key so David was not yet home as if he was at home he usually heard her coming and had the door open for her.

She walked into the kitchen, kicked off her shoes and switched on the kettle. She would make herself a coffee and have a seat in the lounge while she waited for him to come home. She could, she supposed, start the meal. She knew what it was as the salmon was sitting in the fridge but the potatoes were not ready on the hob so David must have left in a hurry today. He usually prepared things before leaving.

Feeling in a good mood, she peeled the potatoes then walked into the kitchen, made her coffee and went into the lounge. She was not in the least interested in the news so she left The Herald untouched and picked up the copy of Hello magazine which she had bought the day before and not got around to reading last night.

She was engrossed in an article about Posh Spice when she heard the door opening.

"Caroline. Sorry darling. Got held up by that bloody janitor complaining again about the rubbish in the playground. What does he think I am, a road sweeper?"

"Really? Poor you."

David swept into the lounge and kissed her on the forehead.

"I won't be long with the dinner. Would you like an aperitif?"

"Yes please. My usual."

David poured her a martini, added ice and a slice of lemon and brought it to her in the lounge before going into the kitchen to start the salmon dish. He was delighted to see the potatoes ready. How kind of her after her tiring day!

Soon they were seated at the dining room table. He thanked her for her help and she graciously accepted his thanks.

Feeling in such a good mood, she might even let him make love to her tonight. It was boring but it kept him happy and she had her liaison with James to look forward to.

CHAPTER 5

David had spent a lot of time on next year's timetable and was proud of the result. He knew that some depute heads had to call in help from the chief timetabler and had been determined that this would not happen to him. Now all that was needed was to hand out copies to the heads of department and then await their comments.

Although a comparatively young deputy at thirty nine, David was of the old school and was not in favour of open management which allowed for input from teachers lower than him in the school pecking order, so he intended to brook no arguments from principal teachers. He put the relevant copies on the desk of the school secretary, telling her to place one copy in the relevant pigeon holes. June Gray thought, as she often did, how unhelpful he was. Even the head teacher did this sort of thing for herself.

David thought he deserved a coffee now so he asked for one to be brought to him and went back to his room. When he left the office, June raised an eyebrow at her assistant and said, "His last slave didn't die of boredom anyway."

Her young assistant, who thought that David was really 'fit' and 'cool', was only too happy to make his coffee and take it along although she was never asked to do this for any other member of the senior management team. Only if a parent or visitor was with Christine Martin would she ask for a tray with coffee or tea to be brought in to her. She went along, patting her hair as she went and glad that she was wearing her new perfume.

At this point Geena arrived in the office, carrying a large pile of hand-outs which she had been running off for the head of Home Economics, Fiona Donaldson. The hand-outs would not fit in Fiona's pigeon hole so, telling June where she was going, she turned to go off to the building which housed HE. Her eye caught the single sheet reposing in the pigeon hole and she took it out. It was difficult for the teachers of PE, Technical and HE to get to the office as often as those in the main block so she would be doing Fiona a favour if she took this missive to her.

It was pleasant to get out of the reprographics' room which was windowless. Smiling, she recalled the conversation she had heard yesterday, "Don't disturb Geena. She's reproducing."

She had to leave the building to get to HE and it was a lovely day so she slowed down to appreciate the warmth of the sun and the gentle breeze. Entering HE she was greeted by the smell of baking. It was clever how the nose could distinguish between baking and cooking! She smelt, rather than knew, that one class had been making scones and was proved right as there were trays of newly baked scones sitting on pupils' tables in Mrs Donaldson's room.

The last HE principal had made scones for the principal teachers' meeting every Friday but young Fiona had refused to carry on this practice, declaring that HE was not a service industry for the school. The PTs of Drama, Music and Technical admired the stance she took. They were not so good at turning down the HT's requests for school shows and scenery and Fiona's fellow teachers in HE still made the costumes. Laura in particular was quiet and calm and took these things in her stride whereas Fiona was prone to fits of temper if she felt put upon.

Christine Martin accepted her caveat about not providing eateries for the staff or for staff functions. She liked Fiona and they were partners in the staff badminton team.

David did not approve of Christine's mingling with the staff in this way and his only social contact with other staff members was at the Christmas night out to which he came alone. He would have been proud to show off Caroline but she was adamant about not socialising with his colleagues whom she was sure would be boring and prosy. She had hated her own schooldays, being deemed flighty and shallow by the staff. Most of the staff at Bradford High brought their partners but David knew that he was popular with the young female staff and most of the men so he had no lack of partners to dance with or men to talk to.

Fiona, smart in her white coat, fair hair pinned back from her face, looked up from inspecting a scone and smiled at Geena who handed over the pile of printed hand-outs.

"Thanks, Geena. That was quick."

"I'm not busy today, Mrs Donaldson. I brought this too. It was the only thing in your pigeon hole."

She handed over the timetable sheet.

"Brilliant. Who wants to think about next year when we're only in May?"

Geena grinned.

"Mr Gibson. That's who."

The older women in the staff did not like David. They were too old to be taken in by good looks, preferring a nice manner which, with the women in the staff, especially heads of department, he did not have. Fiona, although not old, felt this way too.

She had glanced at the timetable. She stiffened.

"There are no double periods, except for the senior classes. How on earth are we expected to do practical work in less than an hour? The man's an idiot!"

The class of first years stifled their giggles. Mrs Donaldson might be good fun on occasion but she would not want them to have witnessed her anger at someone on the staff.

The bell rang.

"Right, girls, collect your scones. Put them in your containers. You can collect them at the end of school. Right, on you go. Quietly now."

The class filed out.

Geena left too to go back to the office to see what they needed her to do now. Fiona looked carefully at the timetable again then she left her room and went to the department staffroom where she knew she would soon find her two colleagues as the next period was a non-teaching one for them all. She sat down and waited. They would be clearing up their rooms as she should be.

In about ten minutes she heard them talking as they approached the staffroom.

"Laura. What do you think of this?" she asked as they came in together. Laura took a look.

"No double periods for S1and S2? How are we going to cope with that?"

"We're not! I'm going to see that mad man Gibson right now."

"Do you think he'll change it?"

"Damn right he will!" stormed Fiona.

She turned and left the room.

"Oh, dear, I wish she'd waited till she calmed down," said Laura, ever the peace-loving one, to an empty room.

David had drunk his coffee and was preparing a sheet for the next year's requisition when he heard a loud knock on his door.

"Come in!"

Fiona marched in, waving the timetable.

"Mr Gibson. This is a dreadful timetable for HE. There are no double periods for S1 and S2. How on earth are we meant to make or bake anything in less than an hour?"

"There are many restrictions on the timetable, Mrs Donaldson. I can't fit double periods into HE for S1 and S2 and that's that."

"But you'll have to."

"Will I?"

Very icy, this tone would have scared lesser mortals. Fiona was not one of them.

"You certainly will."

"We'll see about that."

Fiona left, just managing not to bang the door behind her.

David smiled. He enjoyed wielding power over the staff who would let him.

It would never have crossed his mind that he had made two enemies in a very short space of time.

CHAPTER 6

Fiona had decided to sleep on her argument with David but the next day saw her as determined as ever to fight for her timetable.

In the office at 8.40, she asked June Gray if the head teacher was very busy or out of school that day. June said that she was busy in the morning but if Fiona wanted to see her she would pencil her in for the afternoon. Luckily Fiona had a free period at 2.15 on Thursdays so June fitted her into Christine's diary at 2.25

Thus it was that at 2.20 Fiona was waiting in the office. She wasn't kept waiting for long and was ushered into Christine's room on the dot of 2.25.

"Sit down Fiona. What can I do for you?"

"I'm sorry to be about to cause a problem but Mr Gibson showed me the HE timetable for next session and he's only given us one period slots for S1 and S2. There is no way we can do practical work in such a short time. We've always had double periods."

"I can understand how you feel. Did you ask David if he would alter the timetable?"

"Yes and he just said that the timetable remained as it was and that was final."

"What did you say then?"

Fiona's face reddened.

"I'm afraid I said we'd see about that and went out in a bad temper."

Christine hid a smile. She knew her staff and could have predicted Fiona's reaction.

"Right, Fiona. Leave it with me. I'll get back to you."

Fiona thanked her and left.

Before speaking to David, Christine went off to speak with the PT of Technical who had looked at his new timetable and could tell her that he had double periods for S1 and S2. The story was the same with the PTs of Science and Art who were satisfied with their timetables.

By now it was almost time for the end of school and Christine returned to her room. When she was DHT in her last school, she had done the timetable and all practical subjects had had double periods. She knew that she had factual information to present to her depute. She knocked on David's door but when she went in, he was dressed for leaving so, not wanting to antagonise him, she asked if he would come to see her as soon as was free the next day. David only taught one class in his subject so was able to tell her that he was free at 11.40 after his department meeting. With that she thanked him and went back to her room. David left and made for his car wondering what he would buy for dinner on the way home.

Many women on the staff would have been flabbergasted to know that he not only did the grocery shopping but made the meals most nights too.

Caroline, meanwhile, was looking forward in anticipation to her lunch with James. She hoped that lunch would lead to more exciting meetings. Maybe they would even go on somewhere after lunch. She hummed happily to herself as she worked on her last client who luckily was one of the ladies who did not like to talk during her massage.

Half an hour later, she was getting out of her white overall and into her denim jacket preparatory to leaving for home. As she walked to her car she thought about what she would wear on her date and decided that she must buy something new. Turning the car round, she headed for the nearest shopping precinct. She bought a new, black mini skirt and a modern style lime green top. In spite of being in her late thirties, she carried off the mini very well, having fabulous legs. The shop-girl complimented her on her outfit, looking, Caroline thought, a bit envious of her customer. Caroline was determined that the lunch date would lead to better things so she would dress to entice. Not once did she spare a thought for the meal which David would have prepared for her about an hour earlier. She could have rung him but had not given this a thought either. David would welcome her home, however late and would no doubt apologise if the meal was spoiled.

David was getting worried as he always did when Caroline was late home. No matter how often it happened, he still got anxious. He looked at his watch again. She finished at 5 pm and it was now nearly 6.30. He could have rung her mobile but had done that last week and she had been furious, telling him that it was invading her privacy, treating her like a child.

He heard her key in the lock and, determined to show no annoyance or anxiety, he put a large smile on his face and went to meet her.

CHAPTER 7

Alex Snedden, PT English, had many problems, not least the fact that David Gibson was in his department. Although David never treated male teachers as badly as he did the female ones, he was still often a bit patronising towards Alex, especially at department meetings when he often arrived late or not at all and, having run a department himself, was not averse to criticising Alex's decisions though usually in a humorous way, not appreciating how it belittled Alex in front of his department. Alex still hadn't forgiven him for speaking down to him in front of a class. He had gone in to David's room to give him some important information and David, obviously annoyed at being interrupted, had held out his hand and said, "Give it here." Alex, in spite of a quick temper to match his red hair, had been too much of a professional to retaliate but he would never forget it as he had seen some of the class smirking and knew that he had lost face in front of them.

Alex had lost his assistant principal last June and under normal circumstances he would have expected one of his senior teachers, Jim French, to have applied for and probably got the job. However, Jim French's wife had taken her own life last May, and Jim had remained at the school only until the end of May having decided to take himself and his adopted daughter Jill out of the city, to remove them both from where everyone knew about what had happened.

Now, Alex had had foisted on him one Angus Scott who was the last assistant head of department on the surplus list. Angus was, to put it bluntly, not only useless at his job but a cause of problems. Bearded and stockily built, he had a very short fuse and was, at sixty-two, getting out of touch with teenagers. Only the other day, the young female probationer teacher in the room next to him had had to come between him and a pupil as Angus had lifted his hand to him in the corridor. The young girl, seeing what was happening, had called Angus's name and distracted him long enough for the boy to escape. She had told Alex.

The same probationer had, without being asked, taken on a lot of the duties which should have been Angus's, so was doing for a low salary what Angus was being paid extra for.

Once again David had failed to turn up for today's meeting and the last member of the department, a cynical young teacher of twenty-seven who was too lazy to work for promotion but felt at liberty to make comments, did so now.

"I see his highness hasn't honoured us with his presence again."

This made Alex feel inadequate as if he was failing in his position as head of department.

"Maybe he's with a parent."

This came from Jan, the young female probationer, as usual trying to pour oil on troubled waters.

"Never mind. Let's get on," said Alex and he launched into a discussion on next year's timetable which as usual began the first week of June.

"Why do we have the stupid farce of starting the new timetable in June?" asked Peter, always predictable when the new timetable was brought out.

"Can't you heads of department complain about it?"

"Not everyone thinks it's a bad idea, Peter. However, it's not up for discussion here."

Having realised very quickly that Angus was not an asset - why on earth he had ever been promoted Alex did not know - Alex had decided that he would rather deal with the discipline problems which would come from giving him poor ability classes than fail the better pupils by having them taught by a less than inspiring teacher. He handed Angus a copy of his timetable - first year, second year, poor ability fourth year and Intermediate 1 fifth year. Hopefully many of this already small class would leave at Christmas, having by then reached school leaving age.

At least Peter could keep order in his classroom, in spite of being an unenthusiastic teacher, so he was given a good fourth year class along with his first, second and third year classes. He had an Intermediate 2 fifth year class.

Alex had spent a long time the previous night at home working out the individual timetables from the English master copy he had received from David Gibson but it was worth it to see the delight on Jan's face when she saw that she was being given the top fifth year class of pupils who would sit the Higher exam next May. It was unusual for such a young teacher to be given such a class but Alex knew without false modesty that she was the best they could have except for himself.

David only helped out with one class and he would have third year. Alex himself, like Angus, had some extra free time for administration. Angus spent his in the staffroom.

No one seemed to have any comments. They would be given the list of names for each class as soon as Alex had worked that out.

He was just about to go on to the next item on the agenda when David arrived.

"Glad you could make it."

Alex tried to deliver his comment with humour rather than sarcasm, knowing that David could outwit him in a sarcasm duel.

David sat down and picked up his timetable from the table in front of them. He made no comment as his six periods of English never caused him any problems and he noticed that he had a middle of the ability scale class which suited him fine; little in the way of discipline needed and no high fliers to make him work hard for.

Next item on the agenda was the booklist.

"Does anyone want to put in a request for any particular book?"

"Nope."

"More short plays."

"Could we possibly have 'Whose Life is it Anyway'? It's such a good play, dealing with a person's right to die."

Silence.

If he had seen the responses written down, he'd have known who had said what, thought Alex.

His young cynic liked to hand play books out then sit back and let the class read the parts. As he got all class work done in time, Alex could hardly criticise him.

"Nope," was from Angus who used the same books as he had used in his last school and probably the one before that. Silence was from David who was less than interested in his subject nowadays.

"Certainly, Jan. I've read that play and as you say it's good on a delicate topic and a good stepping stone for discussion and discursive essays."

There being nothing else on the agenda, Alex closed the meeting. He was good at getting through business quickly to pre-empt being told that it was only for half a period by either David who obviously had much more important things to be doing or by Peter who knew his rights and how much free time he should have.

As he tidied up, Alex thought longingly of Jim French who as well as being a reliable member of the department, had also been his friend.

CHAPTER 8

David made his way down from the English base room on the first floor to the administration corridor on the ground floor. It was almost time for his meeting with his head teacher and he wondered what she wanted.

Christine was in the office talking to the staff there.

"Bring tea or coffee in with you, David," she said, going back into her room.

Once they were seated, she lost no time in coming to the point.

"I've been looking at the master timetable which you left for me yesterday David. I'd have appreciated you not handing it out to staff before we'd had time to discuss it. As it is, I've got a query about the allocation of periods for practical subjects."

"Oh I see. I take it that Fiona Donaldson's been to complain already." David's smile was not a pleasant one.

"Does she have something to complain about?" Christine smiled back.

"No she doesn't. That woman just likes to cause trouble."

"I've been speaking with some principal teachers and they talked about their timetables."

David knew what was coming and his face set in hard lines.

Christine continued.

"I wanted to see you about the fact that all practical subjects have double periods for S1 and S2 except HE. Why is that?"

"I had to get extra S1 and S2 periods for RE and PSE."

"So why not take some from Technical, PE, Art and Science?"

"It's not as easy as you make it seem."

"I did the timetable in my last school, David. No one ever said it would be easy but it must be fair."

"Are you asking me to change it?"

"I am."

David was furious and he blamed the HE principal for the extra work he was going to have to put in. Added to this, he was sure that Fiona would tell the staff that she had won in the timetable battle and he found this very hard to swallow.

Christine watched him as he struggled with his emotions. She saw his mouth tighten and his eyes become flinty.

"I'll have a word with all department heads and say that you and I had a discussion about the timetable and decided that HE should not bear the brunt of shortage of S1 and S2 time. You're right, Fiona was unhappy about it but I'll speak to her and I can assure you that she won't speak out of turn."

With this, David had to be satisfied. He knew that Christine had handled the situation well but it made him feel no less hatred for the HE principal.

Hatred.

It was not an exaggeration. David hated easily. He gave love wholeheartedly and hated with equal fervour. It was not a comfortable state of affairs for him or for those whom he loved and hated.

He left the room and went into his own room next door. Christine heard his door slam and his desk drawer bang shut.

It took him some time to alter the timetable and he knew that he should have consulted Christine first as now there were some members of staff who were going to get revised timetables which were not as good as their original ones. Some feathers would need to be smoothed and he was not good at feather-smoothing. He did not leave the building till nearly five o'clock and he met nobody until he was crossing the car park.

"Hello Sir."

"Hello Cathy."

"Sir, You couldn't give me a lift down to the crossroads could you?"

"Jump in."

Cathy got in, delighted, tossed back her long, honey-blonde hair and arranged her mini skirt so that David would get an eyeful of her long, slim legs.

The journey took minutes and soon David was alone again and on his way home.

Although the revised timetable had taken him most of the afternoon and he had stayed on late, he knew that Friday was Caroline's late night at the salon. The meeting with Cathy Cameron had boosted his ego - she obviously admired him - so by the time he pulled up at his own house he was feeling mellower and back in charge of his life.

There was a message on the answerphone from one of his drinking friends, asking him if he would be at the Friday quiz night at the local pub and asking if he would be bringing Caroline. No point in answering the call till he had spoken to her. He doubted that she would come as she was not very good at general knowledge and had, he suspected been ridiculed by some of the regulars last time she had attended a quiz night. Confusing Ayers Rock and Dumbarton Rock had been a real clanger! She would probably take the chance to have a hen night with her own friends.

David did not feel like cooking tonight so he got out some of the take-away menus for Caroline to choose from. He heard her key in the lock and went to meet her, a loving smile on his face.

Caroline was in a good mood as she drove home, unusual for her on a late night. She was planning a night of pampering herself, a long soak in the bath, manicure and pedicure, washing her hair and adding highlights. She would go to bed and imagine how the meeting with James would go.

Last night she had allowed David to make love to her. He had been pathetically grateful. She always had to fake an orgasm, had had to almost all of their married life as after the first few years, she had lost interest in him as a lover. He obviously did not know this and wanted afterwards to talk about how good it had been for him and hear her say how wonderful it had been for her. When he had fallen asleep, she always took a shower to rid herself of him. He wanted a family and thought that she did too. She had told him that she had come off the pill and he believed her. She wanted no children but had no intention of telling him this although no doubt he would accept that too if it ever came to the crunch.

CHAPTER 9

Caroline had had a most enjoyable lunch with James. He had met her round the corner from the salon, away from prying eyes. She was practiced at clandestine meetings and always reached the spot late so that she could slip immediately into the car. He had not asked where she would like to go for lunch but had taken her into the Merchant City where there were some really upmarket restaurants. She was used to being asked where she liked to go but quite liked the masterful touch and wondered if he would be like this in bed. She was determined to get him there, and soon.

James ordered them both a dry martini and then suggested crab mornay, telling her that it was a speciality of the restaurant. Caroline found herself agreeing and they spent a pleasurable hour, talking about their jobs but in Caroline's case, sizing up a potential bed mate. James was a lawyer and kept her entertained with some stories of trials he had been part of. He appeared quite disinterested in her job which annoyed her a bit but she would excuse that if he proved skilful, sexually. She looked at him. Of average height, with fair hair and glasses, he was not her usual choice but there was something about him which had attracted her at the party and did so again now.

They chatted for a while longer and she told him about David and his promoted post at Bradford High School. James informed her that he had been to Glasgow High School and thought that the comprehensive system was failing the brighter pupils.

Soon it was time to get back to the salon. As she slid into the front of his BMW car, Caroline deliberately let her skirt ride up her thighs and was pleased to note him watching her carefully. She let the skirt stay where it was.

They pulled up a street from the salon. Trying not to appear too keen, Caroline thanked him for lunch and moved to open the door only to find him lean over and put his hand on hers, stopping her.

"Caroline. Let's not beat about the bush. We want each other. When can we meet?"

Cool Caroline found herself very uncooly suggesting the next night.

"What about your husband?"

"What about him?" Caroline asked, puzzled. For one wild moment she thought that James was inviting David along too.

James noted her disinterest in David and his mouth firmed into a straight line. This young woman was not going to find him easy to treat so cavalierly. Caroline missed this look but would have been unconcerned if she had as she had never met any man whom she could not control.

"Will he not want to go out with you?"

"Probably, but he doesn't always get what he wants."

James smiled again - a thin smile.

"So, where will we meet or will I pick you up somewhere?"

They arranged that James would pick her up at the corner of her street the next night at 8.00. That would give David plenty of time to be out of the vicinity as he would no doubt go to his usual midweek night at the pub. Caroline did not want to drive as she meant to enjoy the champagne which she was sure would be on offer.

Caroline spent the afternoon smiling to herself as, in between clients, she pondered on what she would wear the next evening. She had some new underwear, flimsy things which would be wasted on David. Reaching home, she put her key in the lock and put a smile on her face.

"Caro, darling, how was your day?"

"OK David. Yours?"

"Pretty shitty. Christine insisted that I alter the timetable and..."

"Tell me later, darling. I must take a shower."

As she was showering, David called in to ask if she was OK with take-away that night and she called back that she was.

Later as he was gathering up the containers which had held the Chinese meal, David asked her if she felt well as she had not eaten much. Caroline said she was OK, just tired and thought back to her lovely lunch with James.

"Will you come to the pub with me tomorrow night?"

"No darling. You know that's not my idea of a good night out. All those boring men and their dowdy wives. I'll probably meet some of the girls for cocktails somewhere."

As always, David accepted her decision.

He never did get to talk about his day at school but there was nothing unusual about that. They watched TV, the soaps for Caroline and then she read some magazines while he watched a current affairs' programme.

They went to bed early that night. Lying in the dark, Caroline thought how the poor sucker never seemed to get suspicious. He had been pathetically grateful for the night of sex which she had granted him last night and had no idea that she had had many lovers during their marriage.

As she turned over, she smiled to herself at the thought of the very different love-making she would be having the next night. She fell asleep with a picture of her conquest's hooded green eyes which were very sexy, thin lips and fair wavy hair. David, as he turned over, was thinking again of what a lucky man he was.

CHAPTER 10

At the interval on Wednesdays, Irene Campbell always met with her first and second eleven hockey teams to discuss arrangements for Saturday's matches. She was waiting for Cathy Cameron to arrive. As well as being head girl she was also captain of the first eleven. It came to 11.15 and there was still no sign of her so Irene told the rest of the first team to be at Shawlands Cross at 8.45. They were playing an away match at Kingspark which was not too far from Bradford High so there was no need for a very early start. She reminded them to take hockey sticks from the store before they left school on Friday. The second eleven were playing at home. She asked one of the first team to let Cathy know the arrangements. Cathy was becoming a bit unreliable. Being head girl and captain of the hockey team was beginning to go to her head, Irene thought. She needed taking down a peg or two. Maybe it had been a mistake for the staff to choose her as head girl in her fifth year. Usually head boy and head girl were taken from sixth year. Gavin Smith the head boy was from sixth year.

As David had suspected, the head of Technical and the head of Art were not very pleased with the alterations to their timetables but David was able to pass the buck by saying that it had been the head teacher who had insisted on the changes. He knew that he was popular with the men on the staff and he enjoyed this popularity. He did not want to lose face with the two men whose timetables were affected and he was only too pleased when they moaned about what they saw as Christine's interference.

Fiona Donaldson was delighted to receive her revised master timetable. She had seen Christine in the office that morning and reluctantly agreed not to mention her 'win' over David. All she said to Laura was that she was glad to get mostly double periods for S1 and S2. She just hoped that Laura's knowledge of David would lead her to the right conclusion, namely that he had been coerced into making the changes.

Alex Snedden was relieved that the week was nearly over. He had had an interview with the head teacher over the fact that Angus had issued his entire second year class with a punishment exercise the day before. A number of parents had phoned the school to complain. Christine had calmed them all down, had agreed that it was unfair, had asked them to back up the teacher this time and promised to speak to him and the head of department. Life was not always fair, she had told them and apart from one mother whose daughter had probably caused most of the trouble, they had agreed.

Alex and Christine had both spoken to Angus but he was unrepentant and quoted the time when he had belted a whole class some years ago.

"Just never do that again Angus," Christine had said in exasperation. "If it happens again, I won't back you up and it'll be you who will be made to look foolish."

Alex had asked him to send any trouble-makers to him in future before things got out of hand and had had a steady stream of troublesome pupils all that day. It didn't help that most of them were pupils he had taught at some time himself and had found no trouble at all. He had kept two second years for most of the last period and when he had sent them back ten minutes from the end of the school day they had asked if they could stay as they had been enjoying his lesson. Only four weeks to go till the holidays but unfortunately the new timetable started next week and that would mean another rant from Peter about the stupidity of a system which expected staff to start with new classes in June.

Stewart Wilson and Phyllis Watson came out of their offices in the administration corridor at the same time. Phyllis had had to reprimand one of her third years and was regaling Stewart with the interview.

"He'd been put out of class and was standing at the window to the side of the door. Sheila noticed that he was pretending to play with himself and she sent him down with a referral form saying that he had been simulating masturbation."

Stewart laughed.

"What did you accuse him of Phyllis?"

"Well I just quoted Sheila."

"And?"

"He said very indignantly, 'I did not do that. I was pretending to wank.'"

They both laughed uproariously and passed on down the corridor. Both were popular figures with both staff and pupils. Phyllis, good natured yet strict with the third and fourth years of whom she was in charge, was reliable in the Modern Languages' department and Stewart was perfect for taking charge of S1and S2. He was a devoted father to four young children and he treated his young charges in a fatherly way. Slightly built, with receding dark hair, he too was a respected member of his department which was Maths. He had a very young department head and he advised and helped her without being patronising. Stewart and Phyllis both got on well with their head teacher and also with David, Stewart liking his forthright nature and Phyllis seemingly totally oblivious to the fact that he tried to put her down at management meetings.

David heard them laughing. He waited till they had gone before coming out of his room. He had not had a good week. Neil Fox's father had come up to the school that afternoon, still angry about how Neil had been treated by the PE teacher and wanting David to reprimand her. David had reiterated that Neil needed to lose weight and that he fully supported the teacher. Mr Fox had left, declaring that he would take matters into his own hands. Then he had seen Fiona Donaldson laughing with Laura in the office and was sure that they were laughing at him over the timetable changes.

Leaving the school, he was once again accosted by Cathy Cameron who wanted to know if she could see him on Monday about her application form for university. She was a beautiful young blonde and David's spirits lifted as they walked out of school together. He suspected that she 'fancied' him. His ego took a boost and when he got into his car, promising to see her at 4pm on Monday, he was smiling to himself.

CHAPTER 11

Wednesday passed slowly for Caroline. The salon was not as busy as usual. Probably clients were waiting till just before their summer holidays to get beauty treatments done. She decided to get a Brazilian waxing done herself; sure that James would appreciate it.

At last it was five o'clock and she drove home. She had told David that she was meeting some friends for drinks at a cocktail bar in town. Luckily she always dressed up for meetings with girlfriends, knowing from future escapades, that this habit could come in handy when she met a man friend instead.

They had their meal. David attempted to tell Caroline once more about his battle with Fiona Donaldson but as usual she was disinterested in his school affairs. She had very little to talk about after the quiet day and of course could not talk about what was on her mind - her date with James.

David filled the dishwasher and cleared the table and they both sat in the living room watching the news on TV and sipping a post dinner sherry. At seven o'clock he went up to change into more casual clothes. Caroline was watching 'Emmerdale' when he came back downstairs. He left soon afterwards, telling her to have a good time and asking when she thought she would be home.

"Probably about midnight, darling. What about you?"

"Oh the usual, around eleven."

"Well don't wait up for me. You'll be tired."

She laughed.

As soon as the door was shut behind him, she ran upstairs, had a shower and changed into the new black, lacy underwear she had bought, taking care not to tear the extra fine black stockings.

She left the house at 8.10, intending to be late. To be on time, showed too much interest. James was sitting in his car.

She opened the door and got in, giving him a quick flash of stockings and white thigh.

"I don't normally wait for women who are late," he said tartly. "Don't be late again."

Caroline found herself apologising and promising to be on time from then on. She was annoyed with herself but explained away her uncharacteristic meekness by telling herself that she wanted the evening to start well, not with an argument.

After about forty minutes' driving, James pulled up in front of a small hotel.

He came round and opened the door for Caroline and together they entered the foyer.

"A room please," said James to the receptionist. "Double bed. One night only."

"Will you be having breakfast sir?" she asked.

"No."

Caroline was embarrassed and annoyed. James had as good as told the girl that they were having an affair. Other single men friends, and she seldom had a fling with married men, always pretended that they would want breakfast and had stayed the night themselves, ordering breakfast for two, she imagined.

Worse was to come.

"Name sir?"

"Smith."

"How do you wish to pay?"

"Cash."

Caroline stood there feeling cheap. She saw the look the receptionist gave her as James handed the money over.

As they walked up the stairs to the first floor room, she said angrily, "You might as well have taken out an advertisement, James. She knows now exactly what we're here for."

"So what? It *is* what we're here for," he retorted.

At this moment if she had had her car outside, Caroline would have left. She felt let down but this changed when he folded her into his arms the minute he had closed the room door. She felt her knees weaken with his kisses and when he pressed her shoulders they sank down, leaving her kneeling on the floor.

She looked up at him and was about to get to her feet, telling him that he had made her go literally weak at the knees when she saw his face and realised what she was in for.

He unzipped his trousers.

Never had Caroline been treated like this. Every time she tried to move her face, he had caught her by the hair and pulled her back. He seemed to be excited by her obvious reluctance. At last it was over. Caroline stood up and was about to leave when he said in a sensuous voice.

"Now it's your turn my darling."

Strong arms pulled her over to the bed. He tore at her clothes. When she was dressed only in her suspender belt and stockings, he undressed himself and soon she was moaning in delight.

As they lay together in the rumpled bed, she waited for the endearments and compliments which usually followed.

He slapped her firmly on the backside.

"Right. Up you get. It's after ten o'clock. You'd better get back home."

"But I've told David I won't be home till about midnight."

"Do you want to start all over again then?" he asked with a cruel smile.

"No I don't and that won't happen again another time."

"Caroline, my darling, you take me on my terms. Not yours. So, will we make arrangements for another date? It's up to you."

Caroline was in a quandary. Things had not gone as planned. She felt dirty and used but she also felt exhilarated. It had been fantastic in the long run. She wanted to see him again. Next time she would be prepared and would initiate things to go her way.

They walked down to the foyer. The same receptionist smiled at James and sent Caroline a knowing look. Back in the car, she told James that the next time she would pay for the evening. There would be no more 'Mr Smith'. James laughed.

"Certainly, Caroline, you can treat me the next time."

He dropped her off where he had picked her up.

"By the way, don't have waxing done again. I like my women with pubic hair."

He drove off.

Caroline walked home.

She had been used and treated like a whore, made to feel cheap in front of that girl and now she had offered to actually pay for their next venture.

What was she thinking of? There had been no champagne, not even one drink and no meal. On the other hand, sex had never been so good, so exciting.

Maybe she would meet him one more time.

CHAPTER 12

It was Saturday morning. David woke early at seven o'clock as he always did. He sat up on one elbow and looked at his sleeping wife. She turned over onto her stomach, moaned and turned back onto her back. She really was beautiful, he thought, even in the morning without make up. In fact, he preferred her without make up. He slipped out of bed being careful not to wake her as she got really irritable if woken up early at the weekend.

Caroline had actually woken when she turned over as she was still quite sore after the antics of Wednesday night but she pretended to be asleep until David had left the room and gone into the bathroom. She rose quietly and surveyed herself in the full length mirror. Her pyjamas were of the baby-doll variety and she could see that some bruising had come out at the top of her legs. She opened her jacket and winced at the sight of a really ugly bruise on one breast. She must be more careful in future as even David would surely ask questions if he saw such bruises. It had been OK during the week but he might have wanted to make love to her this morning. She got back into bed and closed her eyes as she heard the cistern flush but David was on his way downstairs to get his breakfast before showering. She must have fallen asleep again as the next time she woke it was after nine o'clock. She got up and opening the curtains, looked out to see that David's car had gone. He would have gone for the papers. She got up and had her shower, rubbing some arnica into her bruises. She dressed in her town clothes as it was always her habit to shop at weekends and was downstairs by the time David returned.

David asked what she wanted for breakfast and prepared the toast and tea she asked for before going into the living room to read his paper. He always got The Telegraph on Saturdays as it had a general knowledge crossword in it and he liked that kind of crossword being no use at the cryptic variety.

At Shawlands Cross, it was 8.50 and Irene Campbell was getting annoyed. Cathy Cameron had not yet turned up.

"Did someone tell Cathy the arrangements?"

"Yes Miss," said one of the first team, "and I know she got her hockey stick because I saw her with it after school."

"Well, we've got a reserve so we'll just have to go without her."

"Here she comes, Mrs Campbell."

Irene turned round and saw Cathy approaching, not looking very concerned about the fact that she was late.

Realising that they would all be late if they didn't get going right away, Irene decided to leave commenting until after the game.

It was a lovely May morning. They were taking part in a summer hockey tournament and this was to be their second last fixture. The team played very well; so did the opposition and it was only a late goal from Cathy which gave them the winning score. The ball slammed into the back of the net and about a minute later the final whistle blew.

They got dressed in the changing room, chattering excitedly, and when they were ready, Irene called them together for the post match discussion. Cathy was ready to bask in the praise which she felt was her due for scoring the winning goal. She was to be disappointed.

"Right, girls. Well done. Cathy, you may have scored the winning goal but the star of the show for me was Mary. Her pass to you from the left wing was spectacular. I know how hard it is to pass from the left, Mary and that was some pass. Mary, girls, is always an example of an unselfish team member. She always passes at the right time, unlike some of you who tend to hog the ball. Cathy, there was another chance for a goal earlier but you selfishly kept the ball and lost it."

Cathy looked down at the floor.

"While we're on the subject of selfish people Cathy, you forgot to come to the lunchtime meeting on Wednesday and you turned up late today. If it was not for the fact that we have only one match to go, I would drop you from the team, captain or no captain."

Irene smiled.

"Ok girls, lecture over. Well done. We only need a draw next week to win the tournament."

So saying, she walked off towards the bus stop and the team followed her, most of them talking about the game and hoping that the second eleven had done as well in their game at home.

One of the other girls tried to cheer Cathy up, thinking that she would be a bit upset at being reprimanded in front of the team.

"No problem, Iris. I deserved that. It was lucky that Mrs Campbell didn't drop me for the last match."

"It was nice for Mary to get some praise, wasn't it," commented Iris who was a pleasant girl. "Out on the left wing she seldom gets a chance to score goals but Mrs Campbell was right. She does set goals up quite a lot. I can see that from behind you all."

"Yes. You're right."

Turning to her left where Mary was walking along with her own chum, Cathy called over, "Well done Mary and thanks for setting that last goal up for me. Mrs Campbell is right. You *are* an unselfish player."

They got off the bus at Shawlands Cross. Irene had one last instruction for them.

"Remember and bring your hockey sticks in on Monday girls. I need them for taking to the primaries next week. Thanks again and have a good weekend."

Irene walked off with one of the girls who lived quite near her and the rest left for their own homes.

Cathy walked home. She was seeing Mr Gibson on Monday at the end of school to go over her UCAS form. He was in charge of S5 and S6 so dealt with these forms. Cathy could probably have gone to university at the end of fifth year but had enjoyed being head girl and knew she would be again. She knew that Mr Gibson would be nice to her and after all who cared what Mrs Campbell thought of her if he liked her as she suspected he did

CHAPTER 13

Sunday passed without incident for all the characters who were soon to be involved in the forthcoming drama.

David and Caroline passed the day quietly. Both rose late and breakfasted well. David went out to get the Sunday newspapers, buying The Observer for himself and The Sunday Mail for Caroline. Naturally she finished the tabloid before he was halfway through the broadsheet. She went up to their bedroom and used her mobile to ring Jane to have a chat about her date with James. Omitting the less than wholesome part of the encounter, she told Jane how exciting it had been and that she would be meeting him again – soon, she hoped.

James had come along to Jane's party uninvited with one of her male friends so Jane knew little about him but she now knew enough, having been asked by her boyfriend to warn her friend that James had the reputation for being what Mark called over-zealous in bed. He had heard this in confidence from his sister whose friend had dated James - briefly. Mark had wrapped up the more blunt terms used by his sister, as being a decent bloke he did not like to use coarse language in front of his girlfriend. Mark's sister had refused to let him confront James. Her friend was married after all.

Caroline pooh-poohed what Jane told her.

"Don't worry about me Jane. I can look after myself."

For a fleeting second she remembered the look on James's face when she had complained of going home so early and he had offered to start all over again. For a moment he had looked cruel but that was her imagination she was sure. He was a respected lawyer for goodness sake! She did not know one important fact about James Buchanan, namely that he only ever bedded married women, women who could not make public his treatment of them.

Later in the day, David and Caroline donned tracksuits and went for a jog round the local park. Glasgow was famous for its parks and this one had tennis courts still, unlike the other nearby one which now had no amenities. They stopped to watch a game between two teenage boys who were really quite good then left the park. Once home they showered, changed their clothes and went for a quick drink at their local pub.

David spent the evening at the computer while Caroline, after dinner, soaked herself and her bruises in the bath. She had never allowed David into the bathroom while she was bathing and knew he would never break this rule and therefore see her bruises which were already beginning to turn yellow. She would show these bruises to James when they next met and warn him to be less rough the next time.

Fiona Donaldson spent the late morning at church where she was an elder, going on to her golf club to meet her husband and teenage son for lunch. There they met some friends unexpectedly and were invited back for the rest of the afternoon. Their son went home. On the way home he was passed by the Gibsons. He did not know them nor they him. They were in Caroline's car. Either she drove when they were both together or they took a taxi, Caroline refusing to be seen in David's cheap car.

The Fox family were having their usual enormous Sunday brunch and were discussing what they should do about the dreadful way Neil had been treated at PE. Mrs Fox was in favour of reporting it to the education authorities but Mr Fox wanted to be the one to show that "bastard of a deputy head" that he couldn't treat him and his son so badly. Neil wanted nothing done in case Mr Gibson took it out on him at a later date.

Geena Carmichael was painting her toe-nails and chattering to her flatmate. They had shared this flat for the last two years, almost, and they told each other everything. Neither had ever had a serious boyfriend. Geena felt she was too fat for any man to take her seriously and her flatmate felt that she was not clever enough to keep a man's interest for any length of time. They had planned to visit a pub in Shawlands and would sit near to James Buchanan who would have agreed with both of them that they were too fat or not clever enough for him

James Buchanan had attended church in the morning and played squash at his club in the afternoon, soundly beating the two men who had challenged him. He had a few drinks with one of them afterwards in a nearby pub then had gone home to his expensive new flat in Newlands. At around eight o'clock he rang Caroline on her mobile.

"Hello Caroline. James here."

"Hello Nancy."

"Is your husband there?"

"Yes."

"Right, phone me back when you get the chance."

"OK Nancy. I'll do that."

Caroline switched off her mobile. David looked up from The Telegraph. He had been trying to finish off yesterday's crossword.

"Is something wrong with Nancy?"

"No. She just wants to borrow something to wear for a date on Wednesday. I'll go up and look it out while I remember."

David went back to the crossword and Caroline ran upstairs.

In the safety of their bedroom, she rang James.

"Hi. It's me, Caroline."

"Hi. Are you free tomorrow night?"

He was keen. She liked that.

"I am as it happens. A friend called our date for the pictures off."

Better to let him know that she had a social life beyond him.

"I'll pick you up at the same place as last time. 7.30 pm."

"Fine but remember I'm choosing the venue this time and arranging the room."

At the other end of the phone James smiled. It was a thin, predatory smile.

They hung up.

In her home about a mile from the school, Cathy Cameron was washing her hair using the juice of a lemon to bring out the shine. Makeup was not permitted at school but she would take some with her and put it on in the girls' toilets before she went to see Mr Gibson the next day. She was planning to bowl him over this time.

CHAPTER 14

Monday morning saw the start of the new timetable. Peter, coming in minutes before the bell rang, was even more disgruntled on this morning than he usually was. Now he did not have any S1 class on his timetable. Well he had one which was on his timetable as S1 but he would not see these youngsters until August. They were still in primary school. He had now a fifth year class where there had been none for the last month, these pupils having left after sitting their certificate exams. He felt it was stupid to have to start next year's work with this class who had been fourth years as some would no doubt be in Jan's Higher class having done better than they were expected to do and some would come down to him from her having not done so well. This new timetable was ridiculous given that some of the new fifth year would not even turn up.

He ran upstairs, remembering that now he had a register class too as he had been given S2 for the new session whereas he had had extra free time recently, his fifth year register class having left after their exams.

His room was next door to Jan's. As she always was, she was in her room although she now had no register class till August when the new pupils came up from primary. He noticed that she had books out on the desks already for her first period class. He and his cronies made fun of her behind her back, calling her 'teacher's pet'.

Cathy Cameron had decided to return to school in June unlike some of her fellow fifth years. She got bored at home and only had a job lined up for July, helping in her aunt's newsagent's shop. She had asked for English to be put on her timetable again as although she felt confident about most of her subjects, she felt sure that she had not got a good pass in English and would have to repeat it to get a Grade A. She had hoped that Mr Fraser, she called him Peter to herself, would be taking the Higher class. She found him attractive though not as attractive as Mr Gibson. She had had Mr Snedden last year and had found him rather boring and certainly not worth turning her charm on. She had looked at her timetable this morning when it had been handed out at registration - nice to be in the only S6 class - and discovered that it was the young teacher Miss Stevenson who was taking the Higher English class. Maybe they could have some fun with her, try teasing her, pretending not to understand, especially any sexual references. She had tried that with Mr Snedden last year when he talked about Hamlet's love of his mother but he had not risen to the bait. Some of last year's class were to be in the same class again and she was sure she could get them to back her up although she was not very popular with her peers. The girls envied her her looks and the boys wanted to go out with her but felt that they would be knocked back. They did not know why none of them were ever successful, but suspected that she set her sights higher, on some male members of staff.

Irene Campbell had just counted her hockey sticks and discovered that one was missing. She was going over to one of the primary schools on Wednesday and needed all of them. One of her team members must have forgotten to bring her stick in this morning. Christine Martin did not like making tannoy announcements which were not urgent so Irene would have to go round some classes today in her free period which was a nuisance. Then she decided that she would find Cathy and get her to go round for her so made her way up to French where S6 had their registration room and with apologies for interrupting, she took Cathy aside and told her what she wanted.

Cathy promised to go round all the members of both teams and make sure that the stick was there the next morning.

The day passed without much incident. Many teachers were disgruntled at finding out that their new fifth year classes were sparse in numbers. Many pupils decided to leave after the exams and then come back in August having changed their minds. It was felt by many staff that any work done now had to be redone when the new school year started though those with common sense simply chose to do something useful but not crucial. In spite of this, most staff were professionals, so tried to go along with what they were expected to do.

Christine Martin heaved a sigh of relief when the bell rang for the end of school that day. There had been few hiccups with the new timetable. She knew that David and her principal teachers had done well to get the new show on the road.

David was about to put on his jacket preparatory to going home when he heard female footsteps pass Christine's door and stop at his and he remembered that Cathy Cameron was coming to see him about her UCAS form. He put his jacket back round his chair and sat down, calling, "Come in !" as there was a knock on his door.

In came Cathy looking fresh and pretty. He did not know that she had spent most of last period getting herself ready for this meeting, missing a period of Modern Studies. This was a new subject for her. She hoped to have passed Higher History and could do Modern Studies as a one-year Higher. If the teacher asked her where she had been she was going to mention Mrs Campbell's request to find all the hockey team members.

"Hello Cathy. Please sit down. Have you brought your practice form?"

David always handed out practice copies which he had had photocopied as there were often mistakes made the first time. Cathy was early with hers but it did not matter. He might as well get one out of the way.

Cathy sat down, arranging her legs carefully. She hoped that David was getting a whiff of her expensive perfume. It had cost her two weeks' pocket money. It had better be worth it!

The administration corridor was empty by the time she left. Only the office staff were still at work. Her colour was high.

CHAPTER 15

David turned out the light in his room. He went into the office and said goodnight to the staff there. This was out of character for him but he was feeling elated by his meeting with Cathy Cameron. He had never been unfaithful to Caroline but he was only human and the fact that this lovely young girl had a crush on him was manna to a man whose wife was sparing with her compliments. As he drove home he wondered whether or not he should share what had happened. He decided against it as Caroline would probably laugh and that would spoil things.

He had just started dinner when Caroline arrived home. She went into the lounge, kicking her shoes off in the hall as she went. David picked them up and came into the room, marvelling again at how fresh and pretty she looked even after a busy day at work.

Caroline had had time to think up a plan.

"David. Jane phoned me at work to ask if I could come over tonight. She's having boyfriend problems and wants a girly chat."

"They looked happy enough at the party."

Sometimes David's memory was too good, thought Caroline.

"Yes they were - then - but something must have happened in between then and now. I'll find out what tonight."

Dinner over, Caroline went up to change. It would have to be something casual for meeting a girlfriend but that didn't matter. James had made no comment on the clothes she had bought specially for their date so he didn't deserve being 'glammed up' for.

Remembering that the evening had finished early the last time, she knew that she would be home at a reasonable time so told David that she would not be late, probably around 10 pm. She kissed him on the cheek, picked up her handbag and left.

She arrived some minutes before James this time so was able to parrot his words.

"I don't usually wait for someone who is late."

James laughed. She was certainly feisty. He liked that in a woman.

Caroline gave him directions to a small hotel on the road to East Kilbride. She reminded him that she was in charge this time and asked him to go to the bar and wait for her. She had brought a small overnight case with her and asked for a double - bedded room for one night in the name of Gibson. She believed in keeping things simple and David never asked to see her credit card statement though she always looked at his. She ordered champagne to be sent up to the room. She went up to the room and left her case there, waited for the champagne to arrive, then went downstairs and into the bar. James was talking to another man. She stood beside him for some minutes before he noticed her and introduced her as, "My girlfriend Caroline."

It seemed ages before the man left and James seemed quite unconcerned. Quite huffily, Caroline told him the room number and pointed out the stairs which led off from the foyer.

"Try not to let the receptionist see you. I've booked the room in my name only."

Saying this, Caroline left the bar and climbed the stairs to the room. She thought that James would probably take his time in arriving but she was wrong. He arrived almost on her heels.

"I'm all yours darling," were his first words.

She opened the champagne and poured two glasses. They drank them, then Caroline began undressing him, slowly and when he had only his boxer shorts on, she told him to lie down on the bed and watch her.

She stripped very slowly until she had only her underwear on, a lace teddy with stockings. It had lots of little buttons down the front and had cost a lot of money but she came over to the bed, lay down beside him and invited him to tear it off. Needing no second telling, James did just that, and then whipped off his shorts. Sensing that he was about to take the lead, Caroline pushed him backwards onto the bed and straddled him.

Remembering that last time he had slapped her on the bottom, she slapped him on the thigh and got up. She had brought spare underwear, more serviceable this time, and soon she was dressed and ready to leave.

"Now I want us to leave separately James. You go first and by the way, don't use after-shave next time. I like my men to smell natural."

Caroline had copied everything he had said and done the first time and was feeling very pleased with herself. James walked over to the door but instead of leaving, he turned the key in the lock.

Caroline was puzzled. Why had he locked the door? It was 9.35 and she had said she would be home early.

"You have been a naughty girl."

James turned the dressing table chair round and sat down.

"Last time we had my turn and then your turn. We've had your turn and very good it was too. Congratulations. Now it is my turn. Come over here."

"Sorry James. I have to be home soon. David is expecting me early. Please give me the key."

"I said come over here. Now."

In spite of herself, Caroline found herself obeying him.

"Now, although I enjoyed your turn, I have to tell you that you are going to be punished for telling me what to do. As I said, you have been naughty and naughty girls are punished. I want you to bend over my knee. You are going to have your bottom spanked."

Caroline gave a shaky laugh. He must be joking. He did not laugh however, so she made for the door. Like lightening he crossed the room, grabbed her wrist and pulled her back to the chair. The next thing she knew she was over his knee and looking down at the floor. She felt one hand on her back pinning her down. She felt her skirt being lifted and the next thing her panties were at her ankles. He spanked her hard six times then stood up making her fall to the floor on her hands and knees.

As he opened the door, he turned to her.

"Now don't pretend that you didn't enjoy this evening. We'll meet again. Just one thing. I don't want you having sex with your husband. Promise me. At the moment you are mine alone."

"He was right damn him," she thought. She had never had such exciting sex.

"I promise."

"Sorry I can't run you home tonight. I have a meeting to attend."

He handed her a ten pound note.

"Take this for your taxi fare."

Secretly delighted that he was jealous of David, she kissed him goodbye. When she left about ten minutes later she was so busy making sure that the receptionist was occupied and did not see her sliding the room key on to the furthest part of the counter that she did not notice that James was sitting in the bar from where he could see her leave.

Once outside the hotel, she used her mobile to call a taxi. It came shortly afterwards. When it set off back to Newlands, it was followed by James Buchanan in his car.

David was almost beside himself with worry but Caroline knew how to handle this. She got angry, asking if she was a child to be expected to arrive home early. David, who had spent the last hours or so worrying about her, was contrite and when she gave him a kiss he felt grateful that he had been forgiven. The lounge curtains had not been closed. Unfortunately.

James, sitting outside in his car, saw the kiss. His lips turned upwards in a cruel smile.

CHAPTER 16

It was a wild, wet Tuesday as David drove to school. He usually arrived there early, as the others in the management team did, preferring that to staying on at night if anything needed doing that could not be done in school time. This morning he was late. It had been difficult to get Caroline up this morning after her late night. He also was in charge of doing the please takes slips for teachers who had to take classes for absent colleagues this week as Stewart who usually did it was away on a three day course to learn how to do the timetable.

David arrived just as the school bus deposited its passengers at the stop nearest to the school, on the main road, so he was held up by streams of children crossing the road with the 'lollipop' woman. Seeing him in the car, most of them scurried across as they knew to their cost that he was not a person to keep waiting. David was known as the one who was strict and sometimes unreasonably so whereas Christine they knew was strict but fair as were Stewart Wilson and Phyllis Watson.

As David eventually went up the drive, hooting at pupils who were walking in his way, his mild nature became his school one. He parked the car and marched, rather than walked, into school, pushing aside any child unfortunate enough to get in his way. He got behind Geena just before the door into the foyer.

"Excuse me Geena. Some of us want to get to work."

"Oh sorry, Mr Gibson, I didn't see....."

He had gone, heading for his own room.

She walked into the office and greeted her colleagues there.

"Watch Mr G. He's not in a good mood this morning."

Fiona Donaldson was once again angry with David. She had free time on Monday, Tuesday and Wednesday, none on Thursday and one period on Friday and David had given her two please takes for absent teachers on Monday and now another one today. That took her down to her minimum free time and yet there were only three members of staff off. She reckoned that it was his less than subtle way of getting his own back after the timetable incident. Laura, ever the peacemaker, offered to take the one today as she was off at the same time but Fiona thanked her and declined her help. No doubt his nibs would turn up and see the wrong teacher taking the class. She could not go to Christine again and wondered how she could get her own back this time. She was not one to let things go.

After the morning interval, David went across to PE to speak to the staff there. The primary schools were coming over for visits the following week and he wanted their syllabus for this event. Christine had stressed to all departments the importance of interesting these youngsters as the school had only just escaped closure last June. He walked across the playground - silly to still call it that as no one ever played there these days but huddled in groups inside. Fourth, fifth and sixth had their own common-rooms and the younger ones tended, except for a few avid footballers, to stand in the foyer or round at Art where there was a large vestibule separating them from the Science labs. He met no one in the PE corridor except for Neil Fox who was sitting on a bench outside the staffroom.

"Not again Fox! How are you ever going to shift your excess weight if you never take any exercise? What's the excuse this time eh?"

"I forgot my kit, Sir."

"Right then we'll get you involved in some different exercise. Get along to my room and clear out the two large cupboards. Take the whole lot along to my new room next to Mrs Martin's. Leave all the stuff on the floor then wait for me. I'll find something for you do to fill this period, boy."

The two other DHTs had moved all their things already but David had taken his time to show his reluctance to move rooms.

Neil left, looking dejected in his ill-fitting school uniform, the shirt buttons straining across his chest.

David spoke to the head of PE and popped his head round into the gym to tell Irene Campbell what he'd done with Neil. He then made his way over to the administration block to find more work for the boy to do. No doubt he would tell tales to his parents but David really did not care.

Irene had been annoyed when no one had turned up with the missing hockey stick. She had asked Cathy to hunt it out and there had been no sign of the girl so at lunchtime she went across to the main building, to the sixth year common room only to find out that Cathy was absent. She did not really have time to spare to seek out all her hockey team members so went into the office to ask Christine Martin if she could possibly put a tannoy message out for it. She was going to Southview Primary while one other primary came to Bradford High. The ones coming here had only one period of PE on their timetable and her boss was coping with that.

Christine agreed to put out the message just before the end of school realising that Irene was going to be really stuck to play a short match with only 21 sticks.

At 3.40 she put the announcement across telling whoever had the hockey stick to return it to PE no later than 8.40 the next day.

As usual, on the final bell, the school emptied like a rushing torrent coming down a mountainside as pupils hurried for buses or to the local cafe or homewards.

Phyllis left as soon as school ended. Both she and Stewart had young children. Stewart picked two of his children up from the primary near to his home in Kingspark and Phyllis picked her toddler up from his child-minder on the way home. As both were extremely conscientious people, Christine did not mind them rushing off. They were always early to arrive and never shirked any responsibilities.

Christine herself had to leave sharp today as she was picking her mother up from the airport at about five o'clock. She heard David at the computer and called out, "Bye David."

He called back, "Cheerio."

About ten minutes later, June Grey, busy at her own computer and on her own as her assistant was across the hallway talking to Geena in the reprographics room, heard footsteps in the corridor but when she looked up she had missed seeing who it was.

She heard a knock on the door two along from the office and heard David call out irritably, "Come in." She heard another voice then David saying something in an angry tone then his door closed. Someone spoke and there was a loud thump and clatter. June knew better than to go along as David might have hit someone and he would not want a witness. Neither did she want to get involved in a court case if whoever it was brought a case against him. He had once hit a pupil who had attacked him and the pupil had pressed charges. The Scottish verdict of 'not proven' had been the result that time.

It had gone quiet now, and then she heard a quiet voice saying something she could not make out. Finishing her typing, she got up and went across to Geena for copies and not being in a hurry, shared a cup of coffee with the two women there.

None of them saw the leaving figure

CHAPTER 17

It was early on Wednesday morning and two cleaners were busy at work in the administration corridor. Having finished the head teacher's room and the office, they decided to have a break and went to the janitor's box where they knew they could have an illegal smoke. Cigarette over, they left the janitor to his Daily Record and went back to their work, chatting as they went about last night's TV. It had been no use including the janitor in their conversation as he had been watching football but being widows, the two women had been in charge of their TV remotes and had been watching 'Eastenders'.

"That Peggy Mitchell," said one. "Goes on and on about family and yet look where hers have got to. They're always arguing and falling out."

"Aye and I can't understand Phil always having women fall for him. He's ugly."

Her pal agreed.

"We're lucky having these rooms to do. They're a tidy lot," said the younger one, opening the door to David Gibson's room.

The other one had just gone into the next room when she heard a scream. She turned and ran back to the other room.

"What is it?"

Her friend was standing just inside the room, her face chalk white.

"It's a man. It must be Mr Gibson. He's had his head smashed in. I saw his legs and went round the desk. I'm going to be sick" and she bolted for the toilet at the end of the corridor.

The janitor, having heard the scream, arrived at the door. He took one look at the body then came out, ushering the women in front of him. He locked the door. They went into his box and he poured them a stiff whisky from what he thought was his secret store. While they drank gratefully, he rang 999.

"Hello, there's been a murder," he said, unconsciously parodying the words spoken in most episodes of "Taggart"

They heard him give the school's name and address.

Mrs Martin arrived at that point and the janitor told her what had happened. She congratulated him on how he had handled things and went into her room to await the police and think about arrangements for the day.

In Shawbank Police Station, things were very quiet, most folk having only recently arrived. DCI Charles Davenport and his deputy, DI Fiona Macdonald were enjoying a coffee in the DCI's room when the telephone rang.

It was the PC at the front desk.

"Sir, there's been a murder at Bradford High School. The cleaners found a body."

Davenport hung up and turned to Fiona.

"Fiona, there's been a murder at one of the local schools. Get Salma, Penny and Frank. I'll meet you in the car park."

Fiona went into the general room where she found Frank Selby and Penny Price. Frank, gangly and boyish, his fair hair receding somewhat, was sharing a joke with his colleague. Penny's brown curls seemed to dance and her brown eyes were sparkling as she laughed at what he had said.

"Where's Salma?" Fiona asked.

"The big noise? She's next door typing something on the computer," replied Frank.

The DI realised that he was being funny about Sergeant Salma Din's name and not racist, so she let his comment go but there was something she wasn't going to pass over.

"Call me Ma'am, Frank or DI Macdonald. How often do I have to tell you this? And another point Frank, your uniform - brush your shoes and make sure your tie is straight."

"Sorry ... Ma'am."

"She ignored the rather insolent pause and asked them both to get Salma and meet her and the DCI in the car park.

"There's been a murder at the local secondary school," she told them when they arrived.

They went over to the school, the DCI and Fiona in his car and the others in a police car.

The janitor came to meet them in the foyer. He took them to the head teacher's room. She rose to meet them.

"Mrs Martin, Inspector. Christine Martin. This is dreadful."

"DCI Davenport, Mrs Martin and this is DI Macdonald"

Together they went to David's room next door. The janitor unlocked the door and opened it. Davenport and Fiona went in then he called Christine Martin in and asked her if she could identify the body, warning her that it wouldn't be pleasant.

Christine went in and round the desk. Her face went pale.

"It's David Gibson my senior depute. This is his room."

He thanked her and told her to go back to her room. He had noticed how pale she looked and asked Penny who had arrived at the door to get her a cup of tea.

"There's bound to be tea-making facilities in the office."

"There are, Inspector. Tea on the shelf next to the sink and milk in the fridge round the corner," said Christine.

Penny no longer resented being asked to make the tea. She admired her boss tremendously and knew that he was not being sexist.

Davenport turned to his DI.

"Obviously dead, Fiona, though we'll need the police surgeon to confirm that. What happened do you think?"

"Hit on the head with a blunt instrument. Fell and knocked himself again on the desk, no doubt."

"No sign of a weapon."

He looked carefully under the desk. It was a small office.

"The murderer must have taken it with him or her," he conjectured.

"My money's on a man. This murder was brutal and basic, a man's crime," said Fiona.

"I agree."

Davenport turned to the other two who were waiting in the corridor.

"Frank, get on to Martin Jamieson. We want him here immediately. Salma get on to SOC. Tell Vince Parker I want them here as soon as possible. We want them here before early staff and pupils start to arrive. Go into the dead man's room and use your mobiles. Stay there until pupils and staff have dispersed to their rooms."

He knew he could rely on the police surgeon to come as soon as possible and the Scene of Crime Officers was usually quick if they had nothing else on.

It was now almost 8.15.They could not stop people arriving at the school so it was important that things looked normal when they did start to arrive. He had asked his two, uniformed constables to wait in the murdered man's room and, warning the janitor and cleaners to say nothing to anyone and asking the two women to stay in school for the time being, he went into the head teacher's room. Fiona and Salma went with him.

"Mrs Martin, when did you last see David Gibson, your senior depute, you said?"

"Yes there are three deputes nowadays. David is the senior of the three. I said, 'Goodbye' to him before I left yesterday at around 4pm. He called back. I didn't see him, only heard him."

"Was anyone with him then?"

"I don't think so. You could ask June Grey who's the secretary. She was still here when I left."

"Had he any enemies that you know of?"

"Enemies is a strong term, Inspector. He wasn't well liked by some staff. He could be intractable and brusque on occasion. To be honest, I wasn't too fond of him myself but I wouldn't have killed him!"

"Would you give me names of any staff whom he's particularly riled recently, please?"

"I don't like doing this Inspector but you would get this kind of information from other members of staff so I might as well be the one to tell you. He had a run in with Mrs Donaldson, Fiona Donaldson who is head of Home Economics over next year's timetable but it was resolved and *he* disliked *her* at the end of it rather than her disliking him, because she kind of won in the end."

"Anyone else?"

"Well Geena was bullied a bit by him. She's the auxiliary. He tended to be a bit bullying towards female staff. I think the men liked him."

She told Davenport of her idea of changing rooms so that she could hear if David started shouting at anyone. He, of course, hadn't done so since the move.

"So the walls are a bit thin then?"

"Yes they are."

She realised what he was implying.

"I see what you mean. Maybe someone heard something last night. I take it that it was last night and not early this morning."

"We'll learn that from the police surgeon shortly but yes, someone in the office might have heard something. Would anyone be there, either later last night or early this morning?"

"Not this morning. The office staff usually arrive about now but June Grey doesn't usually leave till about 5 pm. Her assistant is only temporary and leaves earlier than that."

"Thanks for your help Mrs Martin. One more thing, can we have a room somewhere?"

Christine wanted to ask him to call her Christine but felt that maybe it would be wrong in this situation. She told him to use Room 6 on the first floor. He turned to his companion.

"Anything you want to ask Mrs Martin, Fiona?"

"Did Mr Gibson have anything heavy on his desk, a paperweight for example?"

"I don't think so. The other two have photographs of their children on their desks but I remember thinking David's desk was always bare. He was extremely tidy."

She gave a start.

"Who's going to tell David's wife?"

"Don't worry about that. One of us will do that when we've finished here. No need to rush. Let the poor woman have a few more hours of not knowing. Perhaps however, you would give me his address."

Christine went into the office. She was rifling through the filing cabinet when a grey haired woman came into the office.

"Hi, Mrs Martin. More trouble? I saw the police car in the car park."

She spotted Davenport and Fiona and looked embarrassed.

"And you are?" said Davenport.

"I'm June Grey, the school secretary. Is anything wrong?"

She looked like his aunt Davenport thought, in her tweed skirt and twinset. He was sure she would try to mother the kids here when she got the chance.

"May I use you room, Mrs Martin?"

"Certainly, Inspector. I've written down the address you wanted."

She handed him a piece of paper. Davenport went into her room and asked June Grey to follow him.

"Mrs Grey. There's been a murder here. Mr Gibson has been killed."

June's hand flew up to her mouth.

"Murdered? David Gibson. When? Who did it?"

"That's what we have to find out. Have you any idea who would have wanted him dead?"

"I know some people who didn't like him but not enough to kill him."

"Who are they?"

Looking reluctant, she bore out what Christine Martin had said about the head of HE and then added,

"There was a parent phoned him last week. I took the call first of course and the man was really angry. I actually overheard Mr Gibson's reply as I was on way up the corridor to see Mrs Wilson and he was not being, shall I say friendly, towards the man and he rang off, abruptly, I would say."

"Could you give me the man's name?"

"Yes it was Mr Fox. His son Neil is in fourth year."

"Any idea what it was about?"

"Yes Inspector. In schools the office gets to hear most of what goes on," she laughed. "Neil is a fat boy who tries to get out of gym. The PE teacher had forced him into doing cross country and he collapsed. The father wanted the teacher disciplined."

"Anyone else?"

June shook her head.

"If you do think of anyone else please let me know."

June went back into the office where Christine was drinking her tea. Other staff were beginning to arrive. Christine greeted them all as she usually did. Some pupils were also arriving.

Charles, leaving the head teacher's room, was pleased to see the SOC team entering the school. He went to meet them and escorted them to David Gibson's room. Penny was standing there but there was no sign of Frank.

The police were at the local schools quite often to give talks or to talk to pupils suspected of having possession of drugs or bringing back truants, so the sight of a policeman or woman in uniform would not be a strange sight but Davenport looked annoyed.

Penny spoke to him.

"Sir, I got Martin Jamieson. He should be here shortly.

"Where is Frank?"

Penny looked sheepish and, he thought, reluctant to answer.

"He's having a cigarette with the janitor, Sir. Outside."

"Get him in here now, Penny and meet me in the office."

Penny went for Frank and the two of them went into the office, joining Davenport, his DI and Salma.

"Selby, I'll give you the benefit of the doubt and assume that you were asking the janitor to give you details about him seeing the body but in future when I tell you to remain somewhere, you remain there. Understood?"

Frank looked mutinous but said nothing.

Salma threw him a sympathetic glance. She was a tall girl and her velvety black hair shone under her uniform cap. Davenport gave them instructions.

"Salma, here is Mrs Gibson's home address. Try there first. Mrs Martin, Mrs Grey, do either of you know if she works and if so where?"

"She's a beauty consultant somewhere in Bearsden," said June. My assistant would know the place. She went to her once. She'll be in soon."

"Right. Salma, wait till you get that address too then take Penny and find Mrs Gibson. Break the news to her and tell her that I'll be at her house later. If you find her at work, take her home if you think that is what she wants. Get a friend of hers to stay with her. Mrs Martin, would you have a staff meeting and inform them of what has happened please."

"Certainly, Inspector. I'll wait till after registration then call the pupils to the hall. My other two deputies can hold them there while I talk to the staff. Do you want to tell them or will I?"

"We can both be there. I'll do the talking if that suits you," Davenport replied.

At that moment, both Phyllis and Stewart arrived in the office and Christine took them into her room and told them what had happened. They agreed, looking shocked, to hold the pupils after registration for as long as it took for Christine and Davenport to talk to the staff. There were to be trips out for all year groups next week, to Alton Towers, so they would discuss that with the children. On no account were the pupils to be told what had happened.

Charles went along the corridor to see what was happening with his SOC team. Someone, probably the janitor, had showed the police surgeon up the corridor and he was also in the room.

School began at 8.45 and at 8.55 Christine Martin put out a message that all pupils should report to the hall once the bell rang for period one and all staff should come to the main staffroom. One of the reasons why their school had been chosen as a possible case for closure was its declining numbers and with the first year not yet here and most of the new S5 and S6 deciding not to return, the pupils would all fit into the hall, comfortably.

Davenport and Christine were waiting in the staffroom at 9 o'clock. Most of the staff looked apprehensive as the last full staff meeting had been the previous year at this time to tell them that the school was not going to close and they wondered if the decision had been reversed.

Christine introduced Davenport and the expressions on faces changed.

"Ladies and gentlemen," said the DCI. "I'm sorry to have to inform you that there has been a murder in the school."

He left a minute for the hubbub of voices to die down then continued.

"The victim is David Gibson."

More gasps.

"My scene of crime team and the police surgeon are at present working in Mr Gibson's room and the whole corridor apart from the office will be out of bounds to you all while they are there. Mrs Martin and I will keep you informed as much as possible. Meanwhile I want to speak to Mrs Donaldson and Miss Carmichael. I've been told that you both have free time this afternoon, ladies."

Davenport found out who the two ladies were as, almost to a man, the staff turned to look at two women and both these women blushed.

"Needless to say, if any of you can throw any light on what has happened you can contact me at any time this afternoon, in Room six."

CHAPTER 18

Having got the address of Caroline's salon from June's assistant who arrived at about 8.30, Salma and Penny went off in the police car to drive to Bearsden. Caroline had not been at home. Frank went with them to the car. He was still seething about being pulled up in front of everyone about leaving the room he had been told to stay in and also about having to call the DI Ma'am or DI Macdonald.

"Ma'am! Makes me sound like a pupil with a teacher years ago!"

"Oh, Frank!" said Penny. "I call her DI Macdonald or Ma'am and you don't hear me complaining."

"But you're female. It's not so easy for a man."

"You're incredible, do you know that? DI Macdonald, and Salma for that matter, have earned their promotion and deserve to be shown respect. Why don't you get your act together and then go for promotion and climb the ladder yourself. If you're not prepared to do well at your job, don't knock others who have."

Frank stared amazed. Penny was always so good natured. He found himself apologising. She made a sound very like, "Humph" and got into the driving seat of the car. Salma threw him another sympathetic look and climbed into the passenger seat. She liked to drive but did not want to get on Penny's wrong side right now.

Penny put the car into gear and drove off.

It was some minutes before Salma risked a cautious, "Do you know where we're going?"

"Yes I do. I've a college friend who lives in the same street."

They drove in silence until they reached Anniesland Cross then Penny said ruefully,

"Sorry, Sarge. You got the brunt of that. He makes me so mad at times."

"Well, what you said was correct and probably you'll have made him think a bit as it's so unlike you to go off the deep end. Now let's forget him and concentrate on the job in hand."

It was not long before they pulled up outside "Serenity". As it was still early in the morning they hoped to find the place quiet and this was the case. A small, auburn - haired woman was at the desk and after hearing that they had come to see Caroline Gibson, she called for her and when she came, left them alone, saying that she had to get one of the treatment rooms ready for her ten o'clock client.

Caroline came downstairs, looking very smart in her white coat. Penny thought that she would prefer a beautician to be less glamorous. Caroline would give anybody an inferiority complex.

Salma took charge.

"Hello Mrs Gibson. My name is Sergeant Din and this is Constable Price Is there somewhere where we can sit down together?"

"Yes of course. What's the problem Sergeant?"

As she was talking, Caroline was leading them through into the back of the salon to a small office which had only two chairs, one behind and one in front of the small desk.

Salma motioned to Caroline to sit down. She sat behind the desk and Salma took the seat in front.

"I'm so sorry Mrs Gibson. I'm afraid I have to break some very bad news."

Salma's voice was gentle.

"It's David isn't it? There's been an accident. What's happened?"

Penny thought she seemed remarkably calm but maybe she just did not understand the severity of the words "very bad news".

"Your husband has been murdered."

Caroline giggled.

"Come on. You're joking. Who would want to murder David?"

Penny, watching her closely, saw the exact moment when Caroline thought of someone who might have wanted her husband dead.

"Mrs Gibson, you've thought of someone, haven't you?" Penny asked.

"No. No I haven't. David was popular with his friends. He didn't have enemies except of course for all the school kids he must have made hate him over the years. I know I hated lots of my teachers - bullies some of them."

"Mrs Gibson. I have to ask you a few questions. Do you want to answer them here or will we take you home and talk to you there?" asked Salma.

"I have my own car and I would rather be at home. Let me speak to my boss and I'll meet you there."

Caroline wanted some time on her own to compose her thoughts. The two policewomen suspected this but there was not much they could do about it.

Thus it was that about an hour later, they were sitting in the Gibson's living room and Salma was repeating what she had said earlier about having a few questions to ask.

"Go ahead, Sergeant."

"When did you last see your husband?"

"Yesterday morning."

"Tuesday morning?"

"Yes."

"Was it unusual for you not to see your husband for a whole day?"

"Not really. I was having a meal out with one of my friends, a male friend from my single days and David was going after school to play golf at Lesmahagow with a friend."

Caroline had decided to stick as far as possible to the truth. She and James had had a meal this time. She would not be telling these women what had happened after the meal! This part she would have to fabricate.

"Did your husband not mind this?"

"Certainly not. He had his friends and I had mine, as well as joint friends."

"So when did you get home?"

"After I had eaten with James, I went to the cinema to see "Mamma Mia". I had told David. He wasn't at all keen to see it and all my friends had already seen it so I went alone."

This was safe as she had already seen the film with a girlfriend two weeks ago.

"What time did you get home?"

"I went to the 8.30 showing so I came out at about 10.30 so by the time I got home from The Quay it must have been about 11.15, maybe slightly earlier as the roads were quite quiet."

"Was your husband in?"

"No but he sometimes stayed overnight with this friend if he had been drinking after the game."

"Would he not have phoned you?"

"Sometime he did but occasionally he didn't so I wasn't worried."

She had had a shower which was badly needed after her night with James and had just been grateful that David had not been waiting for her as she had been in some state.

"What about this morning?"

"I woke up late."

"No message on the answerphone at all?"

"As I said, I was late so I didn't try 1571. Will I try it now?"

"Yes please."

Caroline dialled. There was one message.

She hung up.

"One message. From David's friend, Sam, asking what had happened to him and then saying that he would be in the bar if he eventually arrived. Does that mean that David was ...killed... last night?"

"It would seem so but we have to wait for the police surgeon's report."

Caroline felt herself start to shake. Last night, then this news, was starting to take its toll on her.

Penny noticed.

"Would you like some tea or a drink, Mrs Gibson?"

Caroline was clever enough to realise that she needed to keep her wits about her so asked for tea. Asking if it was OK if she used the kitchen, Penny left to get the tea.

When she came back, Salma was telling Caroline that she would not be needed to identify the body as Christine Martin the head teacher had done that.

"Will you be OK here by yourself, Mrs Gibson? Or is there someone we can get to come and stay with you?"

"I'll phone my friend Jane. Where was David killed?"

"In school."

Caroline wanted to speak to Jane, to get the chance to ask her to keep quiet if she was ever asked about the kind of relationship she had started with James. Jane would surely agree if she told her she had finished with him now.

James would be furious if she landed him in the middle of a murder enquiry and James furious was not something she wanted to see!

After seeing off the two policewomen who told her that there would probably be someone round see her again, Caroline rang Jane then sat down in an armchair by the fire.

Suddenly she wanted David, wanted his protective, unquestioning love.

CHAPTER 19

When all concerned had arrived back at the station, Davenport called a meeting in the Incident Room. He had pinned up a picture taken by the SOC team of the body of David Gibson. With the state of the art cameras, Parker had been able to give him one right away. To the side of the body Davenport always wrote the names of suspects and so far this consisted of Caroline Gibson as husband or wife of a murdered person was always a suspect, Fiona Donaldson, Mr Fox and Geena Carmichael although their motives seemed weak ones for committing murder.

"Right, team, briefly, what we know is that the murdered man is David Gibson, senior depute head of Bradford High School. He was found lying on the floor behind his desk by a cleaner at around 8 am. His room was her last job before she left. Another cleaner and the janitor heard her scream and both arrived on the scene within minutes. None of them touched the body as it was obvious that the man was beyond help. The first cleaner, Linda Brown, touched the door handle and may, she thinks, have leant on the desk when she walked round it having seen David Gibson's feet. The body was identified by the head teacher of the school, Mrs Christine Martin who arrived shortly after the body was found. The janitor had the foresight to lock the door after he saw the body."

"When will you hear from Martin Jamieson, Sir?" This came from DI Macdonald.

"He said he would ring as soon as possible and he was very quick in our last murder inquiry."

"Any thought of a weapon Sir?"

Frank wanted to get back into Davenport's good books and thought the best way was to show enthusiasm for this case.

"I looked under the desk. I left the cupboards to SOC but I figure that the murderer took it with him. I hope Vince Parker gets back to me soon too."

"Or her, Sir. It could have been a woman," chipped in Penny.

Davenport smiled.

"Ever the feminist Penny, even when it might be for the role of murderer. Yes you're right. It could have been a woman, though both DI Macdonald and I thought it more likely to have been a man."

Salma asked the next question.

"Sir, when do you think the murder took place?"

"I was coming to that Salma. It could have been at the end of school yesterday or early this morning. I'm hoping that you and Penny can narrow this down having met with Mrs Gibson."

"Well Sir, she arrived home quite late last night and her husband wasn't there but she didn't worry because he had talked of maybe playing golf and he sometimes stayed overnight with this golfing friend. We asked her to try 1571 and there was a message on it from David's golfing friend wondering why he hadn't come to the golf club."

"Martin Jamieson will confirm times soon, hopefully. Where was she till late last night?"

"Having a meal with a male friend, then at the cinema by herself."

"Right then, I'm going back to the school to interview the two people on the staff who had arguments or runs - in with David Gibson. Salma come with me. You can do one of the interviews."

"What about us Sir?" asked Penny eagerly.

"I'd like you and DI Macdonald to go back to see Mrs Gibson. You've met her already Penny, so that might put her at ease. See if she can throw any light on who might want her husband dead and also see if she has anyone to back up her story of eating with a friend and going to the cinema alone. It's an odd thing to do, go alone to see a film."

"I went to see 'ET' for a second time alone." Fiona Macdonald laughed and Charles grinned at her. Frank began humming the 'Skye Boat Song' and Charles looked at him.

"Sorry Sir. I can't seem to get that tune out of my head."

"Well it's getting on my nerves, young Selby. Try replacing it with some other tunes."

"Yes Sir. Sorry Sir."

Frank threw a conspiratorial look at Penny and she had to turn her face to avoid giggling. Unfortunately in doing this she caught Salma's eye and had to stifle a laugh when she saw that Salma too was trying to keep a straight face.

"Something wrong Penny?" asked DS Macdonald.

"No ma'am, just a tickly throat."

"Frank."

Davenport had a job for the PC.

"Yes Sir?"

"I want you to wait at the school in case Martin Jamieson and Parker report. I've asked them to contact me there. We have Room Six on the first floor. Get two of the other PCs to help you set up the room, telephones and a computer and some large tables. Take over a flip chart and also some pin board stands for the picture of the corpse and future photographs of suspects."

Charles had asked Christine Martin for staff numbers before he addressed them and knew that there were thirty-six teaching staff, three office staff, including Geena Carmichael, the auxiliary, a technical and science assistant plus numerous cleaning staff and two janitors. This murder was going to prove a nightmare unless they got an early lead.

CHAPTER 20

Caroline Gibson was experiencing what was for her a rare moment of guilt. She had been, naturally, given the rest of the day off work and would rather have been there to take her mind off the terrible thing that had happened.

As it was, she had too much time to regret her affair with James, especially the fact that she had probably been with him when David was murdered.

She had called James as soon as she knew that David was going to be away most of the evening and perhaps even the night. She would never have done this with any of the other men with whom she had had an affair. She had always played it cool and let them do the running but somehow James had got under her skin and in spite of being treated badly at times, she had felt so excited when with him that this excitement washed out all thoughts of the cruelty which he meted out to her.

James's velvety voice had sounded quite cool, even asking her if she really wanted to see him again. When she had asked him why he was doubting her, he had referred to the fact that he had seen her kiss David the night before after he had expressly told her to have no sex with her husband.

"James. It was one kiss. Surely you don't object to that," she had said, part of her feeling delighted that he should be so jealous of David but part of her feeling uneasy.

His next words filled her with horror.

"Caroline, you are going to have to choose between David and me. I am not going to share you. You are special to me and I want all of you."

"Do you mean leave David?"

Caroline was dismayed. She actually loved David, in a platonic sort of way. He was so good to her, so kind. She could not imagine life without him.

"Yes that's exactly what I mean. I want to have you all to myself. I don't want to share you with David, friends or work. I'll cater for your every need."

Caroline decided then and there that she would have this one more night with James then she would ditch him. He might makes things unpleasant but if the worst came to the worst she would tell David about the brief affair and throw herself on his mercy. She was sure that David would forgive her and after one more exciting, lust-filled night, she would be ready to go back to her safe, warm relationship with David.

"OK James, let's meet again tonight and we can talk about it then."

They had taken both cars this time and had met in town but instead of choosing a hotel, James said that he would lead her to his flat in Newlands.

When they arrived, they could only get parked round the corner from the flats and he led her down a path surrounded by trees, telling her that when she left to go home she should take the road round and not come this way on her own. She felt warmed by his concern for her safety.

He had prepared supper for them both and there was wine this time. The sex which followed was terrific but Caroline found it impossible to stop thinking of what he might have up his sleeve for later. She was delighted when they had dressed and were sitting in the lounge and he had started nothing.

He asked her when she had to be home and when she said she would like to be home in time for David coming back which would be around eleven, if he didn't stay the night at his friend's, he simply got up to bring her jacket. This was the time to tell him that she had no intention of leaving David for him but it had been such a lovely evening that she decided to have one more night with James and tell him then. He was like a drug, this man. She thought she could stop seeing him then found herself wanting him again.

They kissed at the door and she felt him harden and waited for his next move but he simply ruffled her hair and told her to be careful.

"Remember, don't go down that path; take the road to your car, Caroline."

Caroline did just that though it certainly was the long way round. She had almost reached her car when she heard a rustle in the bushes which fringed the road.

She glanced round and just as she did so someone pounced on her. She screamed.

The person put both arms round her and pulled her into the bushes. She fell backwards and was dragged through more bushes close to what she realised was the pathway she had come down earlier with James.

She tried to get up but it was no use. He was now kneeling beside her and had one hand over her mouth and she felt as if she was choking on the woollen material of his glove. With the other hand he tore at the front of her denim jacket. It had not been fully buttoned up so he got it apart easily and went on to her blouse, tearing the buttons off in his haste. She could see now in the dim light that he was wearing a balaclava helmet and she could only see his eyes. She tried, while struggling, to see what he was wearing so that she could tell the police later, if he left her alive to tell anything. She heard herself whimpering, "Please don't hurt me; I won't tell anyone," and realised that she was only thinking these words as she couldn't make herself heard though his gloved hand.

He was kneading one of her breasts now. It hurt. Then his hand went to her white, denim skirt hem and he dragged the skirt up to her waist. She felt the button at the top come off.

Then it was all over and she was trembling with fear as she wondered what he would do to her now. He had taken his hand from her mouth while defiling her and she saw now one hand go up towards his head covering.

"No, don't let me see you!" she shouted. "I don't want to know who you are. I won't tell anyone I promise. Please don't kill me."

"Why on earth would I want to kill you?" asked James Buchanan removing his balaclava.

"You.... you.... beast. How could you do that to me?"

Caroline was feeling mixed emotions, relief and disgust being two of them. She fought away the thought that she had actually felt quite roused.

"I always get my way. You know that. Surely you didn't think that wishy-washy sex earlier in the evening turned me on!"

He rose to his feet, pulling her up to stand beside him.

"That does it! I was going to finish with you the next time we met but I'm doing it now. I don't want any more to do with a pervert like you."

"No one finishes with me, darling," drawled James. "If you know what's good for you and David, you'll end things with him, not me. Get off home to your meek little pussy-cat. I'll phone you when I want to see you again and, remember, no sex with David or you or he will be in trouble."

He turned and walked off down the path. Caroline got into her car, shaken and feeling dirty, both physically and mentally. Her blouse had no buttons left to do up and she was bruised and grass-stained. She decided to tell David when he got home, make a clean breast of her affair and ask him to defend her from this monster. She wanted David's unselfish, undemanding love. She would never cheat on him again.

No, she thought, she would never cheat on him again as he was dead - murdered. She had told the two policewomen half the truth about last night. Automatically she had not brought James into it apart from saying that she had had a meal with a male friend. James would be OK with this and they would have to say that the meal was in his flat as no restaurant would corroborate them having been there as they had not eaten out. They had after all had some supper there. Even if it meant that she had no alibi, she was not going to tell them that she had been with him for the whole evening. She had discovered to her cost that he could be sadistic and she shuddered to think what punishment he would give her if he became incriminated in this murder.

Now that David had gone, she was left with no protection against James and the thought filled her with dread. She could only hope that he would keep away from her now, worried in case he became involved in a murder enquiry. Involved. Had he been involved? Had he gone to the school when she left him? How would he know that David was still there? Surely David would not have been in school so late if he had been planning a golf game. Yet James had threatened her and David. The questions running through her head made it ache and she took some paracetamol and lay down on the settee.

CHAPTER 21

Irene Campbell drove into the school car park at about 12.35. She had been at Southview Primary School all morning after taking registration for her second year class who had been last year's first years. She had enjoyed her hockey practice with the eleven-year olds who also seemed to have enjoyed their first taste of the game. She had had to take a very old hockey stick, not of the club variety as Cathy had been absent and whoever had forgotten to bring the stick had forgotten again.

Locking her car, she was about to enter the PE department when she was hailed from across the playground by Alex Snedden.

She stopped and waited for him to come up to her.

"You'll never guess what's happened Irene."

"What?"

"David Gibson's been murdered."

"What!"

"David's been killed. One of the cleaners found him dead in his room this morning."

"Killed here?"

"Yes. The police have been here. They're coming back this afternoon to interview Geena and Fiona."

"Why them?"

"Well they've had run-ins with him recently."

"So had Neil Fox's Dad. He came up to complain about me making Neil run and David stood up for me. He told me that Mr Fox had threatened him but he said it was an empty threat."

"If I were you I would ask to see the chief inspector and tell him that, Irene."

Instead of going into the PE block as she'd planned, Irene said cheerio to Alex who was going for his midday swim and went into the main block. She went to the office and asked June if there was anybody she could see about some information for the police.

June told her that Christine had given them Room 6 on the first floor and that she might find someone there.

Irene knocked at the door of Room 6 and a pleasant voice told her to come in.

The room had already been cleared of desks and there were four large tables there instead. A computer had been set up on one. Frank had brought the board with the pin up of

David Gibson's body on it and it dominated the room.

"I'm sorry to interrupt you," said Irene.

"Not at all. How can I help you?" asked Salma. "I'm Sergeant Din by the way." She held out her hand and Irene shook it, liking this pretty Asian girl right away.

"Irene Campbell. I teach PE here. I was out at one of the primaries this morning and have only just got back. I met one of the staff and he told me what had happened and I know someone who threatened Mr Gibson recently."

"Sit down Irene. Is it OK to call you Irene?"

"Of course. Only the kids call me Mrs Campbell."

Salma pulled a large A4 pad towards her.

"What is the name of this person?"

"Mr Fox. He's the father of one of our fourth year pupils."

"Why did he threaten Mr Gibson?"

"Well his son Neil always tries to get out of taking PE. He's fat and lazy and I made him take part in a cross country work out last week. He took ill and his mother came up and took him home and later his father phoned. David took the call and backed me up. I heard later that Mr Fox came up to the school and threatened to take things further. One of my friends overheard him in the admin. corridor on Monday. I don't think that David would be worried as parents often bluff that they're going up to Education Offices and very seldom do."

"Will you give me the name of the person who heard him please?"

"Phyllis Watson. She teaches some French but is deputy head too and her room is two along from David's. The walls are thin."

Salma thanked her and said that her DCI would probably want to see her later in the day.

Irene left.

Salma had just sat down again when Geena came to tell her there was a phone call for someone in the police team. Salma went to the office. It was Martin Jamieson who told her that death had taken place sometime between 3 pm and 9 pm last night. Salma thanked him and rang off. It would be better when they had their own phones installed in Room 6.

Frank arrived quite soon after that with another computer monitor and told her that Davenport would be here shortly.

"He's gone to tell the head mistress that he's back and ask her to tell Geena Carmichael and Fiona Donaldson to come here as soon as possible."

"Head teacher, Frank. Not headmistress."

"Same thing."

"No it's not. She's not head of mistresses; she's head of all the teachers here. Will you never learn that there's equality in most jobs now?"

"You're as bad as Penny. She's always going off at me these days."

"Well we're getting really fed up with your racism and your sexism. It won't do your job prospects any good either."

"Fat lot you care."

"I do Frank. We could be a nice wee team, you and I and Penny if we all got on well and I'd like both you and Penny to get promotion one day."

Looking sceptical, Frank turned away as the door opened and Davenport came in.

"Salma, Geena Carmichael and Fiona Carmichael are coming here shortly. I want you to interview Geena. I'll do Mrs Donaldson. Find out what the trouble was between her and David Gibson and where she was, around say end of school yesterday and this morning."

"Sir, we can narrow that down. Martin Jamieson says the murder was committed between roughly 3 pm and 9 pm."

"Good. Any word from SOC?"

"Not yet, Sir."

"Frank, get on to SOC please. Ask if you can use the office phone. I need to know what the weapon could have been and if there were a number of blows to the head or just one."

"Yes Sir."

Frank left and Salma and Davenport chose a table each and sat down to await the two women.

CHAPTER 22

Penny and Fiona were on their way to see Caroline again.

"What did you think of her last time, Penny?" asked Fiona.

"Well, Ma'am. I think she knew someone who might have wanted her husband dead."

"What makes you say that?"

"When Salma told her that her husband had been killed, she said who would want to murder David and a look came into her eyes as if she had just thought of someone."

"Anything else?"

"I though it a bit odd that she was seeing another man for a meal. I'm not married but I wouldn't have thought that a husband would have accepted his wife having what amounted to a date with another man."

"Did you ask her about that?"

"I said did her husband not mind and she said that they had their own friends as well as joint ones."

"I'm not married either Penny but I wouldn't like my husband seeing other women."

At that moment Fiona's mobile phone rang. It was Charles Davenport to give her Martin Jamieson's timescale.

They had reached the Gibson's house. Penny switched off the engine and they sat in silence for a few minutes.

"Nice house, ma'am. Nice car." She pointed to the open garage. "I don't imagine that she earns a lot. He must have had a good salary."

"Come on Penny. Let's get this over with."

Penny rang the bell.

When Caroline opened the door, it was obvious that she had been crying. She told them to come in and showed them into the living room which was untidy with magazines lying on the floor. A large digital TV sat in one corner and the furniture was minimalist but expensive-looking in black and white. Not a comfortable looking room, thought Fiona who preferred comfort to style. She sat down on the settee, black leather but too firm for her liking. Penny took one of the matching chairs, Caroline the other. She perched on the end looking nervous.

"Mrs Gibson. I'm sorry to have to question you at a time like this but I'm sure you want us to catch whoever did this."

"Indeed I do," said Caroline fervently. "I don't know how I'll cope without David. He was everything to me."

That sounded genuine, thought Penny. At least the first part was! She knew she was getting cynical these days but she remembered how cool Caroline Gibson had been when she had thought that David had had an accident.

"Would you tell us where you were between the hours of 3 and 9 last night," asked Fiona.

"I told this woman and another policewoman that I was at a friend's house for a meal and that I then went alone to the cinema. I went to James's house around 7 pm and I left about 8.30 and went to the pictures. I left there around 11 pm and I got home about half an hour later."

"What about earlier?"

"I was at work in Bearsden till 5.30 pm. Sometimes I get away earlier than that but we were busy yesterday."

"So you were at home from around 6 pm for half an hour? Did you hear from your husband at all during the day?"

"Yes he rang me about lunchtime to say that he was at home as he had come for his clubs because a friend had rung him to suggest a game of golf that evening. David wanted to know if I wanted him to leave something out of the freezer for my dinner."

"So he didn't know about the meal with your friend then?"

Caroline realised that if she kept to the truth as far as possible she would not get caught out.

"I told him that I would ring James and see if he was free that night so not to bother about me."

"Did your husband always arrange the meals in your house, Mrs Stirling?"

"Yes he did. 'Fraid I'm not very domesticated."

Penny, looking at her well- manicured nails, could see that. These hands had not washed, scrubbed or gardened recently.

"And your husband had no objections to you seeing another man?"

"No he doesn't...didn't. We had an open relationship and by that I mean we were open with each other, not that we both had affairs."

Caroline felt herself flush.

"So you went to your friend's house. What's his surname and where does he live?"

"In Newlands, in Dunbar Street, number 34. Top floor. His surname is Buchanan."

"Why didn't he go to the cinema with you?"

"He was tired and wanted an early night."

She would have to call James as soon as they went and tell him what had happened and what she had said to the police. He presumably had gone home after his 'rape scene'.

"What film did you see?" Penny asked.

"I saw 'Mamma Mia', as I said earlier."

"Where?"

"At the Quay."

"I don't suppose you kept the ticket."

"I wasn't thinking that I would need an alibi, constable."

Caroline allowed a little anger into her voice as surely she would be angry if all she had done was have an innocent meal and see a film.

"Thank you Mrs Gibson. We'll get back to you once we have any more news for you. Maybe you have a friend who could come and stay with you overnight."

"I could get Jane. I phoned her earlier but I think I'd rather be on my own."

As she showed the two policewomen out, Caroline was reasonably sure that she had come across as an innocent, distraught woman.

The two policewomen sat in the police car. Fiona spoke first.

"So there was half an hour between her leaving James and the latest time for the murder to have taken place. Could James have managed to get to the school in half an hour?"

"Yes."

"She had half an hour in the house after work. Could she have got to the school?"

"Yes and later especially, if she didn't in fact go to the pictures."

"And if they did it together and there was no meal and no pictures......."

"I think our next port of call has to be to this James."

Watching them from behind her lounge curtains, Caroline saw them drive away and went quickly to the telephone. She thought that James would now be at home. Even if she had had his work number, she would not have dared phone him there.

James answered after a few rings.

"James. It's me. Caroline."

"Hello darling. Wanting to see me again?"

"Listen carefully. You'll probably be getting a visit from the police. David's been murdered."

"Damn the man."

"I said I had seen you, had a meal in your house then gone to the cinema by myself because you were tired. I said that David didn't mind me seeing male friends."

"That's probably true. That milksop would have let you do anything. You need someone to take a firm hand with you."

She shivered.

"As it happens I was on the phone to a colleague after you left and our little meeting. But that's no use as an alibi. I need something for.....when did he die?"

"How should I know? Oh, wait, one of them asked where I was between 3 pm and 9 pm."

"Good girl. So I only need an alibi for 3 till I saw you and for any time after you were supposed to have left me. When am I supposed to have seen you?"

"When I did see you. At 7 pm. I came to your house then. I said I left about 8.30.

"Good. I was in chambers till about 6 pm and it takes me about half an hour to get home from town and I called in at the delicatessen for the stuff for our supper."

He sounded relieved. "I couldn't get to the school, kill him and get back in half an hour surely."

His voice hardened.

"I needn't tell you to keep quiet about the true nature of our relationship Caroline."

It was not a question and she heard his steely tone and shivered again.

She knew that she should have felt relieved that he could prove his innocence because he was the first person she had thought of as a possible murderer especially as he has wanted her to himself. He surely would not have found David at school after 8.30, although he did know which school it was as she had told him that at their first meeting.

But how tidy it could have been - him arrested for David's murder and her free of him for ever.

CHAPTER 23

Salma and Charles Davenport did not have long to wait for the arrival of Geena Carmichael and Fiona Donaldson. The two women came to the door of Room 6 punctually at 2.30.

They looked nervous and Davenport rose from his seat and tried to put them at their ease.

"Hello ladies. Don't worry; we just want to ask you a few questions. Miss Carmichael, will you go over to the table where Sergeant Din is sitting and Mrs Donaldson will you take a seat here across from me, please."

Geena walked across the room. Salma sent her a smile of encouragement.

Geena sat down and nervously cleared her throat.

"Can I call you Geena?"

"Yes please. Everybody here calls me Geena, even the kids. I mean the teachers can't let them do that but I don't need the respect of the pupils."

147

Geena found herself gabbling and stopped, embarrassed.

"Right, Geena. How did you get on with Mr Gibson?"

"Well he tended to bully me. He got annoyed with me and talked down to me but I think he did this with quite a lot of the women in the staff. The younger women seemed to like him. He is...was... very handsome."

"Will you be happy not to have to deal with him again?"

"Yes. I can't deny that but I would never have wished him dead," said Geena.

"Now don't worry about what I'm going to ask you. We have to ask everybody this. What were you doing between the hours of 3 pm and 9 pm yesterday?"

"Is that when he was killed?"

"Yes."

"Well, I was in school till about 5 pm."

"Doing what?"

"Running off sheets for the Physics department."

"Where was that?"

"In the auxiliary's room, across the way from the office."

"Did anyone see you there?"

"Our assistant secretary came over and she and I had a cup of coffee together. Oh, June came over a bit later too and she had coffee as well."

"And June is?"

"The school secretary."

"When was this?"

"I can't say for sure but it was after school finished for the day and not long before I went home at 5 pm."

"You say you went home at about 5 o'clock? Where is home and can anyone confirm when you arrived there?"

"I live in Pollokshaws, in a tenement building just up the road from the '1901' pub, on the corner of Haggs Road. I share the flat with another girl. She wasn't in when I got home. She works in Boots in Shawlands and got home about 6.15."

"And for the rest of the evening?"

"We both stayed in and watched TV. 'Emmerdale', then 'Eastenders' then I did some washing and had a bath. May was still watching something on TV - I don't know what."

"Thanks Geena. That's all. You can go now."

Across the room Davenport was questioning Fiona Donaldson. She had removed her white coat and was smart in a straight, grey skirt and white blouse.

"Mrs Donaldson, how did you get on with David Gibson?"

"I didn't get on with him at all. He was overbearing and rude. He tried to browbeat me and he didn't like it when I didn't roll over and die."

Fiona knew that she was making things bad for herself but she was an honest person and anyway anyone on the staff could have told the Inspector this and it was better coming from her.

"Is there particular incident you can bring to mind?"

"Yes. Just the other day, he tried to give me single periods for S1 and S2 next year and we had a row. He refused to see sense so I went to Mrs Martin. She agreed with me and she got him to change things. She asked me not to crow about it and I agreed but he'd lost face and he wasn't pleased as it meant he had to take some periods from other practical subjects and they would know he had been made to change things."

"Thank you for being so honest. Is there anything else I should know?"

"Well…" she looked sheepish. "I was sounding off about the fact that I thought he had given me more than my fair share of Please Takes....."

"What are they?"

"It's taking the classes of an absent teacher."

"Right and you thought that David Gibson was getting his own back?"

"Yes. Exactly. But although I disliked him I didn't want him dead, just on another planet!"

"Now Mrs Donaldson, I want you to tell me where you were between 3 pm and 9 pm on Tuesday evening."

"I left school sharp at 3.45. I went to Asda and got some messages. Then I went home and made dinner for my family, my husband and son."

"Can anyone verify any of this?

"I didn't see anyone I knew at Asda but my son was in when I got home around 5 o'clock and my husband came in about 6.15 pm as usual."

"And the rest of the evening?"

"I had a church meeting at 7.30 in Shawlands, the large church at the Cross. Plenty of folk can verify that I was there, Inspector. The meeting finished at around 9.30 and I drove straight home."

"Thank you Mrs Donaldson. That's all for now."

Geena had waited along the corridor for Fiona. Both women were relieved that the interviews were over and they tried to remember what they had been asked. Both were relieved to have had alibis for most of the evening although Fiona wished that she had met someone at Asda, as she often did, and Geena wished that her flatmate had had a half day and been at home before her.

Charles and Salma exchanged information about the person they had interviewed, Charles informing Salma that Fiona Donaldson did not have an alibi for the time between leaving the school and getting home about 5 o'clock and Salma telling him that likewise there was gap for Geena too between 5 pm and 6.15.

"I feel that if either of the women had committed the murder, they would have fabricated some alibi for the whole time," said Davenport and Salma agreed, though both realised that this could of course be a double bluff.

The bell rang for the end of school. They waited to let the corridors clear then left via the school office. Davenport confirmed with June Grey that she had indeed been with Geena at the time stated and Salma popped her head round Christine Martin's door to tell her that they were leaving and would be back again tomorrow, early.

As they left the building, they met men coming in with telephone equipment and Davenport's mobile rang. It was Fiona Macdonald to tell him that SOC had rung in with the information that David Gibson had been hit once with a heavy weapon. He had hit his head again against the edge of the desk but it was the first blow which had killed him. Lots of fingerprints had been found on his desk and on the window catches but these would probably turn out to be impossible to identify as many pupils and staff would have touched the desk and the cleaners could have touched the window catches. SOC were going to take the prints of the cleaners in charge of the admin corridor and would get back to Davenport if any unknown fingerprints came to light.

Davenport informed Salma of all this and then he told her to get off home unless she had something to collect from the station as she would be needed early next morning. He himself was going to pick up his young daughter from Southview Primary He liked to pick her up if at all possible which was the reason for her being at a school near his work and not near their home in Newton Mearns.

He sighed as he got into his car. This was not going to be an easy case to solve. There were so many people in school, staff, pupils, cleaners, perhaps even visitors.

David Gibson was going to cause as much trouble dead as it appeared he had done alive.

CHAPTER 24

Thursday morning dawned wet and windy. May had been quite a nice month but June had not started so well. Charles Davenport woke to rain battering at his bedroom window. Looking at his bedside clock he realised that he had half an hour before he had to get up. He thought back to the two interviews the day before. Neither of the women interviewed seemed likely murderers but then what did a murderer look like?

The guilty person in his last murder case had seemed very unlikely too but she had killed twice.

Sighing, he pushed back his duvet and got up. This was going to be a difficult case with so many possible people having the chance to kill the victim. Maybe the fingerprints would eliminate some.

His daughter, when he went into her room, looked vulnerable and peaceful under her Micky Mouse duvet cover.

"Pippa, pet."

He shook her gently.

"It's time to get up."

She grunted and turned over towards the wall. She was not a morning person and although cheerful all day, she was grumpy in the early morning.

"Pet, you'll be late for school if you don't get up now."

It was 7.45 and they needed to leave about 8.30.

He waited till she turned over and got up before going downstairs to prepare breakfast. He would wash and shave while she was eating.

On the way to her school, he remembered to ask what he had been meaning to ask for some time now.

"Pippa, do you know yet what teacher you'll be getting after the summer holidays?"

"Yes. It's the new woman, the one who took over after Mrs French went away."

"Have you met her yet?"

"Yes. Our class swapped teachers with another class for a wee while one day last week and we met her then."

"How did you like her?"

"She seemed quite nice but she's very old."

Davenport knew her well enough to realise that that could mean anywhere from thirty to sixty.

"Older than me do you think?"

"We...ll. Maybe about the same age."

At this point they reached Southview Primary and Pippa got out of the car having first kissed her Dad.

"See you later, love," he shouted after her but she was well away into the playground, smart in her uniform with blonde pony-tail swishing, anxious to have some play time before school started.

Charles drove on to the large station where he was in charge of one section. As he walked in, the constable at the desk told him that someone from the SOC team had been in a few minutes ago and left an envelope for him. Charles thanked him and hurried along to his office, opening the envelope as he went and calling out for Fiona Macdonald to join him.

"Information from SOC," he said as she arrived. "Sit down and I'll tell you what it says."

Fiona sat down. They had developed a friendly working relationship along with a friendly outside work one and she now felt at ease with him.

Davenport read:

"There are three sets of clear fingerprints on the desk on top of some smudged ones and some also on the window catch."

He looked down the missive.

"They were going to test the fingerprints of the two cleaners who do the admin corridor."

He read further down.

"They've matched David Gibson's prints with one set on the desk and on the window catch and one set belongs to Linda Brown, the cleaner who found him so that eliminates two sets but there's still one unaccounted for.. I thought that one might belong to the cleaner who found him. She probably leaned over the desk to see who was lying on the floor after she saw the feet sticking out. That leaves us one clear set and I would bet that the murderer leaned on the desk to look over and see that he was dead. They might have gone round the desk too of course."

"Would the murderer touch the window catch?" asked Fiona.

"I must remember to ask the janitor if he noticed an open window when he did his rounds in the evening. Surely if he had, he would have closed it."

"So if David had opened the window, the murderer might have shut it to prevent the janitor coming in to close it."

"Might be worth asking if anyone was in David's room and noticed the window but it's a long shot."

"So what do you want done today, Charles?" Fiona asked.

"There's the parent to interview, Mr Fox, who was gunning for the deceased. Maybe you would tackle that Fiona. You'll be able to get the address from June Grey, the woman in the office. Go tonight if you're not busy. Save disturbing him at work."

"No I'm free till about 7. I'll visit him about 6. Bridge night tonight."

They had played some bridge together and Davenport knew that she was a steady if unimaginative player. He on the other hand was adventurous and it had taken some time for them to get to know the other's game.

"I'll chat with the cleaner who found the body. I'll ask one of the others to search the ground outside the window. See if we can unearth a weapon."

Irene Campbell had gone from speaking to Salma to the PE department where she went to replace the hockey sticks after collecting them in batches from the boot of her car. To her annoyance, the missing hockey stick was in the cupboard, covered in mud. Whoever had forgotten to bring it in had also neglected to clean it. Never mind, she had realised as she was about to put away the other twenty-one that they all had to be cleaned as it had been quite muddy where she had taken the primary schoolchildren to play. Lifting one bundle of sticks, she walked over to the changing rooms where the showers were and rinsed them in one of the shower cubicles. Replacing them in their cupboard, she did the same with the next bundle and the third and final bundle.

As she returned to the PE staffroom, Cathy Cameron came through the swing doors.

"Mrs Campbell, I couldn't find the stick. I'm sorry. I should have told you but I woke up with a migraine on Tuesday morning and I was off again yesterday."

"It's OK, Cathy; whoever forgot to bring it back in time has sneaked it back. Not in time for me to use with the primaries unfortunately. I had to use one of those old ones with bigger heads."

"That's a pity Miss."

Cathy turned and left the department.

CHAPTER 25

Davenport had realised that he was too late this morning to catch the cleaners so had decided to take Frank with him to see the man whom Caroline Gibson had been having a meal with on Tuesday evening. Penny and Salma could do the ground-searching without him. He had rung the man's home and found him just about to leave for his chambers. James Buchanan had said he would rather see them at his home than at work and he would ring in and tell his secretary that he would be late.

As they approached Newlands, Frank commented on the new flats which came into view.

"If this is where he lives Sir, he must have plenty of money. I heard these were selling at £300,000."

"Yes, this is it I think. This is Dunbar Close so we must be near."

They drove past the Close, house numbers 1-33, and found themselves in Dunbar Street. There were two blocks of modern flats and they stopped outside the first one, number 34.

"Top floor I believe," said Davenport.

As they waited for the lift, he warned Frank:

"It was obvious that he knew we would be coming so Caroline Gibson must have rung him after we left."

"Sign of a guilty person, Sir?"

"No, pretty natural I would think. The only thing I find funny is that her husband was OK with her seeing another man."

"Was he, Sir? We only have her word for that."

"Right Selby, a good point. Let's see if we can find out what kind of relationship it was."

The lift arrived and they rode upwards in smooth silence. When the doors opened, they stepped out into a carpeted hallway. There were only two doors, one had a 5 and the other a 6. They stopped outside number 5 which read Simpson and were on their way to what had to be number 6 when that door opened.

A man stood there. He wasn't very tall but he had a stature that would make him stand out in a crowd. His bearing was very straight and he looked slightly aloof. His dark grey suit looked immaculate as did the pristine white shirt and pale blue tie.

"Hello. You must be Davenport, the man who rang me."

"Yes Detective Inspector Charles Davenport."

It was not often that Charles gave his full title but this man's demeanour made him want to establish his credentials, establish who was in charge here.

They shook hands.

"And this is Constable Selby."

"Please come in."

Buchanan made no move to shake Frank's hand.

They stepped into a hallway, the walls of which were home to some very expensive-looking paintings. Buchanan led them through to his lounge. Everything spoke of wealth and taste. Cream coloured leather sofas and chairs took pride of place and the only other items of furniture were a large digital TV set resting on ebony shelving and a mini bar in the same wood.

Davenport sat down on one of the chairs and Buchanan took the sofa. Frank chose to remain standing, thinking that his stance might put the man off balance, show who was in charge here.

"Now detective inspector, I had better tell you that Mrs Gibson has been on the phone to me so I know why you are here."

"A clever move," thought Davenport, "pre-empting my question."

"Well then you know why we are here and as a lawyer you will know that we want to know when you saw Caroline Gibson on Tuesday evening."

"I arranged to meet her at 7 pm and lead her here and I made her supper and she left again at about 8.30."

"Did she say where she was going?"

"To see a film I believe."

"Would it not have been more normal for you to have gone with her?"

"I certainly did not want to see 'Mamma Mia' detective inspector," said Buchanan. "For goodness sake man, Pierce Brosnan singing! Would *you* want to go? I was tired too after a long day, court in the morning and my chambers in the afternoon, preparing for the next day."

"How long have you known Caroline Gibson?"

"Not long."

"Yet her husband was quite OK about you seeing her?"

"He seems to have been an amenable sort of man. I agree, it does sound odd. If I was married I certainly wouldn't let my wife see other men."

"No you would not I am sure," thought Davenport, seeing the way the man's lips thinned into a narrow line as he spoke those words. What on earth did Caroline Gibson see in him as a companion? There was more to this relationship, he was sure.

Frank obviously thought so too.

"Come on Mr Buchanan. She's an attractive woman. Was it only companionship you shared?"

Frank meant to sound insulting.

James Buchanan flushed with annoyance. His thin lips pursed. He knew that he was being seen as either a liar or a wimp and he liked being neither.

"I had known her only a short time. It might have become more than friendship, given time. I think she was attracted to me, as I was to her."

He could not resist letting them know that he was attractive to women. His vanity would allow nothing less.

"Where were you from 3 pm till 7 pm?"

"I was in my chambers all afternoon till probably about 6. I stopped at the local shop to buy food for the supper I was going to have with Caroline."

"Which shop was that, Mr Buchanan?"

"There is only one shop locally. It's in the street parallel to this one, Killburn Street."

Realising that they would get nothing more from this man at this time, Davenport rose and they took their leave.

As they rode back down in the silent elevator, Frank voiced his opinion.

"No way, Sir. He's a wolf. He'd be the kind to go for sex on the first date."

"I agree with that Frank but we'll be hard pushed to break his story. We'd better concentrate on Mrs Gibson."

"I think she might be more scared of him than of us, Sir."

Davenport was pleasantly surprised at his constable's perspicacity and said so.

"Knowing what we both think, I want you to be the next to speak to Caroline Gibson. See if you can get her to be more forthcoming about her relationship with James Buchanan."

Frank was delighted. Usually it was Penny who got all the praise from this man. He felt so delighted that he smiled at Salma when he met her in the corridor back at the station.

"Sarge, are you going for lunch?"

"Yes."

"Can I join you and I'll let you know what happened this morning?"

Salma was surprised and pleased.

They went into the canteen. It was quite late but there were a few members of staff present to notice Frank Selby lunching with Salma Din. Frank did not seem to notice the stares they were getting

Frank told Salma about James Buchanan and his opinion of him. He told her that he was to interview Caroline Gibson that evening and try to find out the real relationship between her and Buchanan. Salma told him she was delighted for him and told him about her interview with Geena Carmichael

They ate their lunch in companionable silence. Penny, arriving at the canteen, saw them laughing together and backed out, hoping that this might be the beginning of the end of Frank's unfriendly attitude towards his Asian sergeant.

CHAPTER 26

Caroline was dismayed to receive a phone call from James Buchanan but he was very pleasant. His voice sounded like warm treacle.

"I've spoken with the police. You did a good job, Caroline. They asked me about our relationship. I said it was platonic." His voice changed. "You'd better back that up if they question you again."

Caroline stifled a nervous giggle.

"Platonic!" she thought and recalled their three meetings which had been anything but.

"Of course, James. We'd better not see each other again I think."

"On the contrary. It would look odd if a *friend* deserted you in your hour of need."

Caroline was disappointed. She had wanted to end things with him as now that she had no David to run to, she did not think she could handle this man and his demands on her.

"What did you have in mind?"

"Well I have to attend a family wedding in a few weeks' time. I'd like you to accompany me."

"Of course. That would be OK."

James rang off.

Caroline rang Jane and asked her to come over that evening. She knew that she would probably have another visit from the police and wanted to prime Jane on her relationship with James. It would be disastrous if Jane let slip that her relationship had been more than friendly. The police might never question her friend but better to be safe than sorry.

Phone call over, she went and sat in the lounge.

"Who on earth would want to murder David?" she wondered. He had been popular with his friends, would never have cheated on her so there would be no jealous husband. At school - well she knew very little about his relationship with his colleagues and wished now that she had let him talk about his job more.

She stiffened as she remembered her earlier thought.

"James!"

James had wanted her for himself. He had said so. Could he have killed David?

She had met him at 7 pm. Could he have gone to the school before that, had a row with David and struck out at him. She knew from her experience that James could be violent. She did not know how or exactly when David had been killed. She must try to find out. She had thought that the meeting with James was giving her an alibi but now she realised that she could be providing an alibi for him. Earlier, she had dismissed James as it had been too late for him to have caught David still at school after she left him but she had not thought about earlier.

She went into the kitchen and looked for something to eat. There was very little in the fridge as David did the grocery shopping on Thursdays but she found some cheese and made herself a sandwich and a coffee. She was only just realising how good David had been to her.

It was about 5 pm when Jane arrived, having left work a little early pleading a headache. Caroline, not usually very demonstrative, gave her a hug. Jane was her oldest friend, her best friend probably though Caroline was not a woman's woman but right now she needed some support.

"You poor thing. What a shock this must have been!"

"I can't pretend to you, Jane, how things were between me and David. You know I've had affairs but I loved him really and I'll miss him dreadfully."

"Yes," thought her friend, "you'll miss him for his salary, the things he did for you. You'll miss being cosseted."

"When was David killed? When you rang me last night you didn't say."

"I'm not sure but the police asked where I was between 3 pm and 9 pm on Tuesday night and he was found in school somewhere."

"So you've spoken to the police? Where were you at that time? Was it with James?"

"Yes it was. David had said that he'd be golfing so I thought that it was a chance not to miss."

"Would it not be better to tell the truth? You can't hurt David now?"

Caroline shuddered.

"I wish I'd listened to you when you tried to warn me about James, Jane. He's a violent man, exciting but scary and I dread to think what he would do to me if I told the police the truth about our relationship. For one thing it would give him a motive for killing David."

Jane asked her about what had happened when she had been with James and Carolina told her, omitting nothing. They had always shared secrets and it was a relief to tell someone. Jane already knew about the first date as Caroline had shared this with her but she knew nothing of the events of the other two meetings.

"I don't want the police to find out that he was anything except an old friend and nothing more. I'm scared of what he might do to me if I got his name blackened. Please, if they speak to you, bear out what I told them."

Jane was horrified. "No wonder he sticks to married women who won't report him to the police. That last time was rape! I hope you've finished with him now."

Caroline explained that he wanted her to go with him to a family wedding and said that she was sure that nothing would happen between them again, now that she was in a way single.

Jane agreed.

Both of them realised that now that she had lied to the police about their relationship, James had a hold on Caroline.

CHAPTER 27

It was late afternoon on Thursday. Davenport had called his team to the Incident Room to give them the information which he had so far. Before doing that he asked Penny and Salma if their search of the school grounds had unearthed anything. "No, Sir," came the chorus. They had looked carefully at the ground under the window of David Gibson's room and the ground was undisturbed.

"I didn't expect it to. The SOC team is usually very thorough. Right team, here are the facts once again. We know that the victim was killed between the hours of 3 pm and 9 pm on Tuesday 4th June in his office in the school. The body was not discovered until about 8 am on the following morning by a cleaner Linda Brown. Her screams brought another cleaner and the janitor who took a look then locked the door and sent for us.

We know now that death was caused by a hard blow to the head by a blunt instrument. Mr Gibson fell, knocking his head on the edge of the desk. Fingerprints found on the desk we now know belonged to David Gibson himself and the cleaner who found him. Fingerprints, not so clear were found on the window catch. One set of these were David's. According to the janitor there were no open windows when he walked round the outside of the school between 8 and 9 o'clock.

Gibson's wife, Caroline, says she was with a James Buchanan in his flat in Newlands having a meal until about 8.30 when she went to The Quay cinema to see " Mamma Mia" by herself. At 5.30 she was still in Bearsden where she works. It's possible that she could have gone to the school between 5.50 and when she arrived at James Buchanan's flat at about 7 pm. She says that no one saw her at home. She says she received a call at work from her husband to say he was playing golf and it was then that she arranged to see James Buchanan."

"Sir, did her husband know about this *friendship*?"

Penny put some emphasis on the word 'friendship' as if she found this suspicious.

"She says he did, that they had an open relationship and were free to have friends of the opposite sex."

"Wouldn't let a wife of mine have her own friends," said Frank,

"Maybe that's why you have no wife," shot back Penny.

"Don't fight, boys and girls," laughed Davenport.

He went on, "James Buchanan verifies that she arrived at his flat in Newlands with him not long after 7 pm and left again between 8 and 9."

"Where was he, Sir, between 3 and 7." asked Fiona, "and between 8.30 and 9 o'clock?"

"He says he was in his chambers till around 6 pm. He went to a local shop for provisions for the meal. Caroline had rung him on his mobile and they had arranged to meet at 7 pm. Apparently he had to lead her to his flat as she hadn't been there before."

"I checked with his secretary," piped up Frank. "She confirms that he was in chambers all afternoon and left, just as she was leaving, at around 6."

"So they both have no alibi for the period between leaving work and meeting up at his flat," said Fiona.

"That's right. We need to ask at the local convenience store and their neighbours, in case either of them was seen at that crucial time but my guess is that they were having an affair and saw David's absence as a perfect opportunity. Whether they stayed together all evening or she really did go to the cinema is anyone's guess. As it is, they say they were together till 8.30 and that leaves them half an hour to get to the school."

"Surely the janitor would have known if David Gibson stayed on at school as late as that," said Fiona.

"Frank asked him that Fiona and he said that there were no lights on in the admin rooms when he switched the lights off in the corridor. He doesn't know what time that was but he was just about to go to his house for his supper and he usually does that about 9 pm."

"Thanks Sir."

"Also, Gibson had arranged a golf game so wouldn't have stayed on at school as late as 9 pm."

Davenport, who had been pacing the floor, pulling his left earlobe as he did when thoughtful, stopped and faced the others.

"Now, things to do. Fiona you are going to see Mr Fox."

"I rang for his address. June Grey gave it to me. They live in Shawlands, in tenement buildings across from the arcade, on Kilmarnock Road."

"Right, I'm going off to see Linda Brown, the cleaner who found the body. Frank you get off to see Caroline Gibson. See if you can get any more from her about her friendship with James Buchanan and while you're there ask the neighbours if they saw her that night."

"Right, Sir."

Frank got up from the desk top on which he had been sitting.

"Penny, get over to Newlands, the new flats on Dunbar Street. Ask around at the other flats nearby and the shop in the next street. See if and when Buchanan was spotted."

"Yes Sir."

"Salma, would you have another word with the school secretary, June Grey? See if she noticed anyone at all going up the admin. corridor in the afternoon. I can't see someone killing David Gibson in school hours. Too risky. We did ask her earlier but the timing was more vague then. Concentrate her mind on 4 till she left the building.

All of you get off home after that. Meet back here sharp at 8 am tomorrow and we can pool our information."

As they were filing out, DI Macdonald stopped Frank and asked to see him in her room.

Once there she took him to task about his uniform.

"Selby your shoes are a disgrace. Make sure they're brushed before you visit Mrs Gibson."

"Sorry," Frank was gruff.

"Ma'am please, Selby. Now get along."

Fiona was a woman of few words but Frank was left in no doubt about her opinion of him.

He was disgruntled when he caught up with the other two and even Penny's imitation of their boss pulling his ear lobe did not cheer him up.

Fiona waited behind as she wanted to ask Charles if he would come to her for supper on

Saturday and bring Pippa. Although they had been seeing each other socially for about a year now, their meetings had been restricted to the odd game of bridge and some golf matches. They were practising for the police mixed doubles golf championships in September. Charles had only once been in Fiona's house and that briefly for coffee, about this time last year and she had never invited his daughter Pippa. She felt a bit nervous as this was taking their friendship a bit further and after a failed relationship at her last station she was vulnerable about men.

"I'd love that Fiona," said Charles enthusiastically. "She'll love to see your collection of Chalet School books. She still can hardly believe that she's found someone who shares a liking for her favourite author."

"Only on condition that you get your train set up and running and invite me to see it. If you don't show me your childish hobby how do I know you won't tease me about mine?"

On this light-hearted note, Fiona left to collect her suit jacket and Davenport left to inform the desk that all the team would be out of the station for the rest of the day.

"Give me a ring on my mobile if anything interesting happens," he told the officer on duty.

CHAPTER 28

Fiona Macdonald arrived at the tenement block across from Shawlands Arcade just as her doctor who had his surgery in the same block, came out to do his evening visits. He was a lovely man who had attended her mother when she was dying and was also Fiona's own doctor. She had had some depression after the end of her relationship with an inspector at her last branch and the doctor had seen her through that and stopped now to ask her how she was. She told him that she had been fine for some time now. Seeing that he had come out of number 151 and the Fox family lived at 153, she took the chance of asking the doctor if he knew them at all.

"Sorry, I can't help you there. I know the family you mean only by sight. All grossly overweight."

Fiona laughed.

"Succinctly put, doctor. Thanks."

They parted company, Fiona walking on to the next entrance. She looked at the names at the door. The Fox's flat was on the ground floor. She rang the bell and the intercom was answered by a female voice.

"Hello?"

"Police. May I come in, please?"

The close door was buzzed open and by the time Fiona reached the Fox's door it was open and Mrs Fox, short and plump, was waiting on the threshold.

"Mrs Fox?"

The woman nodded.

"I'm DI Macdonald. I'm here in connection with the murder of the teacher at your son's school."

Fiona showed her identity card.

"Come in, please."

Fiona was shown into the lounge where a man was eating his dinner from a tray on his lap while watching something on TV. A teenage boy was holding a dessert plate which contained a huge dollop of trifle. They looked up. Both were wearing tracksuit bottoms, probably for comfort rather than for taking exercise, Fiona thought. They were both were quite fat, Mr Fox hiding it better as he was taller she could see when he and his son got up as his wife introduced them.

"It's the police, Bert. A DI Macdonald."

"Good evening, Mr Fox. I'm here in connection with the murder of David Gibson at Bradford High on Tuesday."

They shook hands. Neil sat back down. His father waved towards another seat and Fiona took it.

Mr Fox went back to his own seat but Mrs Fox remained standing, looking apprehensive.

"So it's true what we heard. What do you want to see us about?" asked the man.

"I believe that you had a row with Mr Gibson recently. Tell me about that?"

"Oh come on, it was only a difference of opinion. You surely don't think I killed the man!"

"I'm not saying that Sir. I just want to know what you argued about."

"My son, Neil had been made to do cross country running when he wasn't well. He collapsed. I wanted the PE teacher reprimanded. Gibson wouldn't do it. He seemed to think she was in the right."

"Wasn't she? Did she know he was ill?"

"He'd told her."

"My boy's fragile, sergeant," chipped in Mrs Fox.

"Anyway we'd discussed it on Sunday and Neil didn't want me to take it further. He thought the other boys would tease him and the teacher might take it out on him."

"So that was the end of the matter then?"

Mr Fox looked slightly flustered.

"Yes it was."

"Thank you Mr Fox. Let's get this straight then. Neither you nor Mrs Fox went up to the school on Tuesday to see the depute head?"

Fiona thought that the boy looked inquiringly at his father but the man's reply was definite.

"No we didn't."

Davenport was in the school. He went to the janitor's box and asked where he could find Linda Brown.

"She'll probably be in the staffroom on the second floor."

He looked at his watch.

"Yes that'll be about right. She cleans in there in the late afternoon."

Davenport thanked him and made his way to the staffroom.

As he approached it, he heard voices and entering the room saw two cleaners busy at their work. He knocked on the door and a nervous voice said, "Come in."

It was with relief that they saw who it was.

"Oh, Sir, we're really nervous being in the school now so we do rooms together," said Linda Brown.

"I just want to confirm one thing with you. Did you touch the desk in Mr Stirling's room?"

She thought for a minute.

"I think I must have. I saw feet and looked over the desk so I must have touched the desk top."

"Did you touch the window catch at all?"

"No. I'd have had to step over the body to do that."

She shivered.

"Was the window open or shut?"

Again she had to think.

"I think the window was shut, Sir."

"Thanks. That's all unless there's anything else you want to tell me. Oh, did you see anyone else in the admin. corridor apart from your friend and later the janitor?"

"No, nobody, Sir."

Davenport thanked her and left them to their cleaning He went down to the admin. corridor and looked in the deputes' rooms. He noted the tidiness of David's room and when he popped a head round the door of the other two offices further up the corridor, he saw that their desks were decidedly untidy and each had a framed photograph on it.

On his way out he asked the janitor again if he had noticed whether or not the window in David Gibson's room was closed on the night of the murder and without hesitation got the reply that it was shut. The janitor added that all the windows of the admin. corridor had been shut. He had checked that again in the morning, after phoning the police.

Frank was sitting in the Gibsons' lounge. He had accepted a cup of coffee as he had thought that that would let him stay longer and maybe get more out of Caroline Gibson.

Seeing a younger man and one whom she could wrap round her little finger, possibly, Caroline smiled and said:

"Now, Constable...Selby did you say?"

"Yes, Selby."

"What can I tell you that I haven't already told the other police officers?"

"I believe that you and your husband had friends that you didn't share? Did he have girl friends?"

"No he didn't," said Caroline with a touch of acerbity. She was not a woman to share her husband with other women and wanted this man to know it.

"So you could have male friends, platonic of course, but David couldn't have women friends," said Frank with only a slight touch of sarcasm. He did not want to rile her yet.

Caroline realised that she had made a mistake here. She should have invented some woman but then no one else would have borne out what she said so maybe she had been right.

"If David had wanted a female friend, I wouldn't have minded at all. I'm sure there would sometimes be women on his team at the pub quiz nights."

"But, you actually went to the flat of this man James Buchanan. Not quite the same thing as being on the same quiz team."

"What are you suggesting constable?"

Caroline put anger into her voice, righteous anger.

"I'm suggesting, Mrs Gibson, that perhaps your relationship turned from platonic to something more sexual. Are you sure that nothing physical happened between you and this man? You *are* a very attractive woman."

Caroline preened and Frank noticed this. He must keep trying to feed her vanity.

"Well he may have kissed me but that was all."

"And you still went to the pictures by yourself?"

"Yes."

"Why didn't he go with you?"

"He had work to do."

"I suppose he wouldn't want to listen to Pierce Brosnan singing," laughed Frank.

"Why not? He sang quite well for an actor," replied Caroline.

It was a small thing. Perhaps Buchanan wouldn't have said to her what he had to them but in spite of this Frank saw it as a chink in her armour.

He pressed forward the point.

"Mr Buchanan was quite scathing about his singing."

"Oh was he? Maybe he did say that. I forget."

She looked flustered now.

"What did you have to eat at Mr Buchanan's?"

This was easy. They had had some pate on toast and some wine, quite a lot of wine in fact.

"Toast with some pate and some wine. He only had short notice that I would be up at his flat."

"You told my colleague that you had a meal."

"Well, meal, supper, it's the same thing?"

"Is it?"

Caroline wondered what James had said. She hoped that she had not made a mistake here. He would be furious with her if she had.

"Thank you, Mrs Gibson. This has been an interesting chat. No doubt someone else will be along to see you again tomorrow or the next day."

As he left, Frank felt quite pleased with himself at leaving her thinking that he was pleased with this visit.

Fiona went off to her bridge evening at the golf club. She had noted Neil's questioning look at his Dad when she had asked if he had visited David Gibson at school on Tuesday night.

Davenport , on the way home to his sister's to pick up his daughter, knew now that the windows in the corridor had been shut so it was impossible for the murderer to have come in or gone out that way.

Frank Selby, making for home, prior to a night at the local pub, was sure that more than friendship had been on offer at James Buchanan's flat and had the meal- supper discrepancy to suggest to his boss.

The three felt that progress had been made. The murderer, on the other hand felt quite confident about being unsuspected.

CHAPTER 29

"Where is Selby?"

Davenport's voice reached Penny and Salma as they entered the Incident Room.

"Don't know Sir." said Penny.

"Maybe he's coming from the canteen." said Salma, hoping that the chief would believe this although, as she had come from there herself, she knew that it was not true. She and Penny exchanged glances.

"Let's get started without him."

Davenport's tone did not bode well for Frank when he did turn up.

Fiona told them about her visit to the Fox's house and how Mr Fox claimed not to have gone to the school again. His wife and son had, he said, persuaded him to leave well alone.

"But the look, Neil threw his Dad told another story, I think Sir. I'm positive he went back at some point."

"Right, we'll pay him another visit. Impress on him the importance of telling the truth if he has nothing to hide."

There was the sound of feet pounding along the corridor and Frank burst in.

"Sorry Sir!"

"I've had enough of your late-coming Selby. See me after the meeting in my room."

Frank looked downcast. He had hoped to make a stir at this meeting with his information about Caroline Stirling and James Buchanan. He had created a stir but for the wrong reason.

He had stopped to clean his shoes to please DI Macdonald and now his DCI was annoyed with him.

"I saw Linda Brown, the cleaner," continued Davenport. "She had touched the desk which we already knew from the fingerprint team but she didn't touch the window catch. The janitor confirmed her belief that the window was shut and the janitor also said that all the windows were shut in the admin. corridor. That rules out someone coming in or leaving through the windows. Now, Selby, anything from your interview with Caroline Gibson?"

"It might be nothing." Frank sounded disgruntled. "But I think they're lying about what happened at their meeting that night."

"Why do you think that?" asked Fiona Macdonald.

"Well she mentioned once that they'd had a meal then changed it to a supper of toast and pate and wine. Buchanan said a supper when we spoke to him, Sir."

"That's right he did. Penny you went into the shop. Did you ask what he bought?"

"The woman told me he bought very expensive pate, champagne pate and one small loaf. She was a bit of a blether, Sir and told me that she had kidded him on about having a new woman and he had been quite dismissive. I got the impression that she didn't really like the man."

"Anyone in the flats see anything that night?"

"No Sir, except for one elderly man walking his cairn terrier at around 8.30. He said he saw no one. I thought that that was interesting Sir as he should have seen Mrs Gibson. I wouldn't have been interested if he hadn't said that he only walked to the square of grass outside the flat which James Buchanan lived in and had stood there for some time while his dog sniffed around. But he doesn't see too well. He peered at me while I was talking to him."

"So Selby, you think there was more to the meeting between Caroline Gibson and Buchanan than supper and a friendly chat."

Frank preferred it when his boss called him Frank. He was not looking forward to the meeting which was to come.

"I do Sir. She's an attractive woman and said quite vehemently that David had no women friends in spite of their open relationship." Frank put some emphasis on the words 'open' and 'David'. So that might mean that David didn't know of her being with Buchanan that night and that although her husband had no other love interest, she might have."

Davenport noticed that Salma was looking keen to speak.

"Salma, what about you? Did June Grey have anything to add to what she'd already told us?"

"Yes Sir. Just before she went to the auxiliary's room for a chat and coffee, she thought that she heard footsteps going up the corridor. She looked up from her typing but had missed seeing who it was. She heard a door being knocked and Mr Gibson saying, 'Come in' then a thud and a clatter."

"And she did nothing?"

"She looked a bit embarrassed when I asked that Sir. It turns out that she thought that Mr Gibson might have hit someone and wouldn't want a witness."

"Did she volunteer who it was that Gibson might have hit?"

"She thought it might have been Mr Fox who might have gone in in an aggressive mood."

"I wonder if Mr Gibson had ever hit anyone before. Check that out Fiona will you?"

Fiona left to telephone the school. A buzz of chatter followed her down to her own room. She returned shortly afterwards to tell them that David

Gibson had punched an abusive parent some time before. The parent had admitted being the instigator of the sparring match and had agreed that the deputy head had merely been defending himself.

"Well," said Davenport, "given the time scale of 3 - 9 pm, it would seem that it is now narrowed to nearer 5 pm."

"Sir, there was something else. Buchanan told us he wouldn't have gone to the film because Pierce Brosnan was singing but when I asked Caroline about that she said he hadn't mentioned that to her and when I said he had to us, she got quite flustered."

Frank offered this bit of information, looking a bit smug.

"Well team, it seems quite likely that Caroline and James had more than supper together. What I don't understand is why they don't admit this as it gives them an alibi."

"But not for later on Sir," said Fiona. "Could the noise heard by June Grey be a red herring and the murder have been committed later, say after June Grey left, even as late as 7.30. Caroline might have heard from David that he was still at school and she might have told Buchanan then one or both might have murdered him. We only have her word about the golf match."

"No. Remember she did 1571 while you and Salma were there and there was a message from his golf pal wondering where he was."

"Sorry Sir so there was."

"Well we might wear Mrs Gibson down with all our visits. I'm going back there now," said Davenport. "The rest of you get your reports written up. Selby, I'll see you when I get back. DI Macdonald, come with me please."

CHAPTER 30

It did not take long for Fiona and Charles to reach the Gibson home. Charles thought that Caroline looked weary and a bit apprehensive when she saw them. They had guessed that she would phone Buchanan after the last interview but they could not have guessed how the conversation had gone.

"James. I think I'd better warn you that I mentioned supper then a meal and I didn't know that you had said that the reason you hadn't come to the cinema was that you didn't want to hear Pierce Brosnan singing."

There had been an ominous silence.

"You stupid bitch!" came the quiet, cold voice. It would have been better if he had shouted at her she thought.

"It's not all my fault. You didn't tell me you had mentioned Brosnan."

"Don't get stroppy with me Caroline. I can see that after this is over we will have to have another punishment session."

She felt goose pimples running up her arm.

"I'll see what I can do to retrieve the situation. I'll say something silly such as I knew that you liked Brosnan so I didn't want to belittle him and I'll say meal then laugh and say that I called it a meal when you rang but changed it to supper as you weren't staying long. Can you possibly remember that?" His voice dripped with sarcasm.

Caroline had said that she could. She could not recognise herself in the meek woman she was with him. How she wished she could turn the clock back to before that party where she had met this awful man.

Now here were the police in her home again.

"Mrs Gibson, will you tell me the name of the man who was playing golf with David on Tuesday night."

Caroline furnished them with the name then came the question she had to remember how to answer.

"Was it a meal or a supper you had with Mr Buchanan?"

"Well he'd suggested a meal at first but then he changed it to a supper when I told him on the phone that I wouldn't be staying long."

"Clever," thought Davenport. "Obviously they've discussed this."

"Although he knew that it was now useless, he asked her about the Pierce Brosnan discrepancy and she said she had no idea why James hadn't mentioned that. "Maybe because he knew I liked him so much," she said, inwardly grimacing at the thought of James being thoughtful like that.

Charles and Fiona left shortly after that, knowing that once again Caroline would probably contact Buchanan with the latest news. They decided to drop in at the school as Charles had declared an interest in finding out if anyone knew any more about the proposed golf match.

They went into the office. Christine Martin was there talking to June Grey. Davenport asked Christine if David had mentioned a golf match that Tuesday and she said he had not. She offered to ask Stewart Wilson who sometimes played golf with him and went along the corridor, returning to say that David had mentioned a game with some friend that evening.

"Oh, Inspector, I forgot," said June Grey looking sheepish. "There was a phone call from a man asking to speak with Mr Gibson but he wasn't in his room so I took a message saying that the golf match would have to be a bit later than planned but could David meet this man in the clubhouse first as he would need a drink before the game."

Davenport thanked her, reassuring her that at times like this it was easy to forget something.

When they left the office after thanking the two women, he spoke what they were both thinking. Had Caroline Gibson known this? Had she told James Buchanan? Had one or both of them taken this opportunity to kill David in school somewhere between 4 pm and 9 pm? Would it have been possible for them or one of them to have slipped past the janitor?

The janitor was in his box, speaking with a workman. Davenport waited till their conversation had finished and the other man had gone off then asked the janitor if he had been out of his box at any time between the time when June Grey had left on the Tuesday night and when he had gone for his supper. It transpired that he had as he had made his rounds outside. Asked if at any other time he could have missed seeing someone enter the school, he said that he had been watching TV and might have missed someone but he did not think so. Asked for the time when he had gone outside he said that he was not sure but that he had definitely been in for 'Eastenders' from 7.30 pm till 8 pm and had gone home at about 9 pm so he was probably outside around 8 pm and 9 pm.

They had reached the school door when the janitor called them back to say that he had remembered that he had seen one of the senior pupils leaving the school quite late. When asked who it was he said he thought that is was the head girl whose name he did not know.

"So Fiona, anyone could have come in at any time from 7.30 pm and 9 pm. though it's more likely to have been from 8 pm to 9 pm. You can see his box from the car park and surely no one would have risked coming in while he was in there."

Fiona agreed and they made the drive back to the station in silence, both busy with their own thoughts.

It was a subdued Frank who joined Salma and Penny for lunch in the canteen. Penny, always forthright, asked what had happened and Frank said that it would have been better if the boss had been angry but that he had been, instead, disappointed and told Frank that apart from his timekeeping, he had thought that he had been turning into a competent policeman.

Penny and Salma spent some time trying to cheer him up, then they went back to their report writing, Penny as usual offering to help Frank write his out before he typed it up.

At 5 pm, Davenport came into the room with Fiona Macdonald to say that both of them were leaving now and that the rest should go once their reports were on his desk. He would read them on Monday morning and they would have a moratorium on the case after this.

"Enjoy your weekend folks. See you on Monday. I'll call you in if anything transpires before that."

He and Fiona walked off down the corridor. A new tune followed them. It was not 'The Sky Boat Song' for once and Charles did not take in the relevance of 'Bonnie Charlie's Now Awa.'

CHAPTER 31

On Saturday evening Charles and Pippa went up to Fiona's flat in Shawlands. Charles drove as it would not be a late night with Pippa there and when he arrived he could not find a parking space in the street. He was about three streets away before he found a space he managed to shoehorn the car into, so they were pretty wet by the time they arrived, having worn light summery clothes it being warm for June. Pippa's pale blue trousers were dark in patches as were the pale grey ones worn by her father.

Fiona welcomed then and gave them both towels to dry their hair. She took Pippa's light jacket and Charles's blazer through to her living-in kitchen and hung them on her pulley. She had put in central heating after her Mum died. She explained now to Charles, "Mum was the kind who put on one bar of the electric fire once she had done her housework, even in the depth of winter.

Dad had an electric towel rail put in just before he died and she never used it. I like heat."

"Ever been somewhere really hot on holiday?" Charles asked as they seated themselves in her lounge. He had only ever been in her kitchen on his one visit here and he looked round now at what he imagined had been her Mum's furniture - piano, glass cabinet, sofa and two easy chairs in a lovat green material, coffee table and highboard with a vase of roses on it. In the warm room, he could smell their scent.

"I went to Greece once in October, to Kos and loved it so went back the following August. That was a mistake. The heat was fierce and I spent most of the time indoors! What about you?" Fiona asked.

"I took Pippa to Minorca two summers ago, shortly after her mum and I separated and we found it too hot too, didn't we pet?"

"Yes. I burn because I'm so fair. Fiona can I see your Chalet School books?"

Davenport laughed.

"Straight to the point, Pippa. No polite chit-chat first."

Fiona laughed too.

"Come on young lady. They're in a bookcase in my bedroom. Take any out that you want to look at. They're in the correct order which should help."

They left Pippa to her favourite books and returned to their discussion about holidays in the sun.

"I'd like to try somewhere exotic and far away where there's a humid heat rather than the burning kind," said Charles, "but I don't know if Pippa is too young for faraway places."

"Had you anywhere in mind?"

"I thought of the Far East, Thailand or Malaysia. I've heard that they're friendly places."

"I've a friend who goes every year to Penang which is an island off the West coast of Malaysia. I could ask her what she thinks about Pippa being too young," Fiona offered.

They went on to discuss their next golf match. They had got through the first round of the South Side police tournament and still had to arrange the next round's game.

At about 8.30, Fiona went through to the kitchen to make supper and Davenport went into the bedroom to see how his daughter was. She was reading one of the books, presumably the one she had been unable to find as Chalet School books seemed to have lost their popularity and were seldom seen in bookshops these days.

"Daddy, do you think Fiona will let me borrow this?" said Pippa.

"I'm sure she will pet. She knows you'll look after the book and she did say you could borrow one at any time, didn't she?"

Still clutching the book, "The Chalet School and Rosalie", Pippa followed her dad back into the lounge. She continued reading while Davenport sat thinking. He would have liked to invite Fiona to come on their next holiday but there was the difficulty of both of them getting the same time off work and also the problem of what their colleagues would think. Maybe it was too soon.

Fiona came in at that moment with pizza and crusty bread, coffee for them and Fanta orange for Pippa, so he shelved his thoughts for the time being.

Fiona was only too happy to lend Pippa the book and she sat and read it for the rest of the evening while the adults discussed the possibility of getting two other bridge players to make a weekly foursome. Fiona had a friend who played and she might be able to get a fourth person to partner her. It would need to be people who would understand if the meeting was cancelled because of police work.

This topic over, talk naturally turned to the case in hand. Fiona thought it unlikely that a teacher could have been responsible unless there were personal matters which they knew nothing about as yet.

"I mean you don't murder a colleague just because you have a disagreement," said Fiona.

"David Gibson was attractive to women yet tried to browbeat them. Maybe he was having an affair with one and yet tried to bully her at school," said Charles.

"Or gave her the elbow for someone else," Fiona put in.

"What about the parent, Mr Fox?"

"Fox? That's a funny name," piped up Pippa from the carpet where she was lying, reading. "I'm glad I'm not called something silly like that."

She went back to her book.

"If he became threatening and David tried to shove him away, he might have pushed him back and David hit his head off the desk, do you mean?" asked Fiona.

"No, that wouldn't do. He hit his head after the blow to the head."

Charles sounded disgruntled.

"Could Mr Fox have lashed out in anger and punched him? Did it have to be that he was hit by a weapon?" asked Fiona. "Fox is quite tall and sturdily built."

"It had to be a weapon. The head was caved in. A punch wouldn't have made so much damage. Martin said he was hit by a swinging weapon, like a golf club," said Davenport.

"Where were David Gibson's golf clubs?" asked Fiona.

"Good question? We've never searched his car. Where is his car anyway?"

They looked at each other. This was something they had omitted to do. It was too late now to disturb the janitor in his free time but disturbed he would have to be tomorrow morning. Fiona offered to do this, knowing that Charles liked his Sundays with Pippa.

Thinking of the time, had alerted Charles to the lateness of the hour for Pippa so he got up to leave, thanking Fiona for a lovely evening.

The rain had stopped and the night was still warm as they walked to the car. Davenport thought once again how lucky he was to have a colleague who was also now a good friend.

CHAPTER 32

Fiona went at about ten o'clock to Bradford High and was lucky to catch the janitor on his way to the shops.

"Just off for the Sunday papers," he greeted her.

"Sorry to hold you up. I just have one question. Have you any idea where Mr Gibson's car is?" she asked.

"Well it's not in the car park. I'd have noticed it."

"Is the car park locked at nights?"

"Yes."

They both thought for a while, then the janitor said that perhaps Mr Gibson had parked his car in a street nearby if he had known he was going to be in school late and did not want to get locked in.

"I wouldn't lock the gates if I saw a car but maybe he thought it would be safer that way, just in case."

"Do you know his car?"

"I think it's a silvery grey car, a small one. Don't know the make. I'm not very interested in cars. I don't drive myself."

Fiona suggested that they take a stroll out of the gates and see if there was any small, grey car parked nearby.

As there were double yellow lines immediately outside the school, they had to walk along the street quite a long way before they spotted a car.

"This is where the PE staff often park while they're away for pupils' matches on Saturdays as they can't get inside the car park," explained the janitor and this gave Fiona hope that this car would indeed turn out to belong to David Gibson.

It was a grey Fiat Uno.

Fiona rang the station on her mobile and asked the constable on duty if he would get her the Gibsons' phone number from the file then she rang Caroline Gibson who confirmed that David had indeed driven a silver grey, Fiat Uno.

"Mrs Gibson. Would David have his golf clubs with him?" asked Fiona.

"I don't know. I expect so. I only know that he didn't keep them at home."

Caroline felt guilty now that she had insisted that David keep his clubs elsewhere as she did not want them cluttering up any cupboard. She was experiencing a lot of guilt these days over how she had treated David.

Fiona asked if there were spare keys for David's car and when she found out that there were, she told Caroline that she would be over shortly to pick them up.

Thus it was that about half an hour later, she was opening the boot of the car to find it empty of anything except the spare wheel. David's car was as tidy as his room in school.

"Where were the golf clubs?" she asked herself.

Feeling that she needed to know the answer to this question and being a golfer herself, she thought that the only other place could be in a locker at his golf club. He might have been intending to collect them en route to his friend's course.

Another call to Caroline Gibson elicited the name of his golf club, the one across the road from Fiona's own. She drove there and after showing her warrant card, was shown where the locker room was. She asked in the pro shop where she could find the club secretary and was given his name and told that he was in the dining room having lunch. She found him there, tucking into pie, beans and chips and he took her into the locker room and opened the locker which he knew from his list belonged to David. Fiona pulled out the bag of clubs. She inspected them knowledgeably - driver, two woods, clubs 3-9, a sand wedge.

No putter.

Where was this necessary club?

Thanking the club secretary who locked the clubs away, she left the locker room and went once more into the pro shop where she asked if anyone had a putter in for repair. The answer was a negative.

She left the building and drove home.

When she got home, she rang Charles.

"Hello Charles. Sorry to disturb you."

"It's OK. Pippa's not up yet. I'm just reading the paper."

Fiona explained where she had found the car and the search for David's golf clubs.

"David Gibson's got a putter missing from his golf bag, Charles. Where could it be?"

"No idea. Could it be in for repair?"

"Tried that. No."

"In the school?"

"Why?"

"No idea."

They were getting nowhere. Fiona apologised for disturbing him and was about to ring off when he told her that he had had a call from one of their opponents in the golf competition asking if they could play one evening next week. Charles had suggested Tuesday and now asked if that suited Fiona. It did.

She rang off. There was no point worrying about the putter right now. Maybe someone at school would have the answer when they interviewed the staff next week.

Fiona drove home, stopping first at Morrison's to buy her Sunday papers. She decided to stock up on her gin as it had got depleted after Saturday night and also get some more soft drinks in case she had Pippa as a visitor again soon. She had not realised that it was just after twelve o'clock and there was still the archaic rule that no alcoholic drinks could be sold till after church hours so she went into the cafeteria and bought a latte.

Buying drinks led on to her buying more shopping and she puffed as she climbed the stairs to her top flat carrying three heavy bags.

As she entered the flat, the phone started ringing. She put down the bags, shut the door and picked up the phone. It was Charles.

"If he had the club in his room for some reason then it might have been the murder weapon."

Fiona had reached this conclusion in the frozen food section at Morrison's.

CHAPTER 33

Frank was early on Monday morning. His talk with his DCI had really upset him and he was determined to make his boss think more highly of him. He had also arrived in a smart uniform and what was obviously a new, white shirt. His old ones had been decidedly grey. Penny was delighted and told him so. Salma just gave him a smile and a thumb's up sign. Since being reprimanded by DI Macdonald he had been much more tidy than usual. Maybe it would not last but he was trying at least.

The team met in the Incident Room at 8.30 am and Davenport told them what had happened when he and the DI had gone to see Caroline Gibson again, how she had explained away why she had said that she and Buchanan had had a meal then changed it to supper. He also told them about the phone call to the school telling David that his golf match was later than planned. The caller had suggested that they met first for a drink.

"It bears out what Mrs Gibson said about the golf match," Davenport told them.

"This means that David could have stayed longer at school. He knew that his wife would be out and perhaps took the chance to get some work done before meeting the friend for a drink," said Fiona.

"He could have let his wife know that he'd be staying on at school," said Penny.

"Or didn't bother as he knew she was out," countered Frank.

"Did he know she was out and who she was with?" asked Salma.

"Yes, so she said," Davenport replied.

"So Sir, he could have been murdered anywhere between the 3 o'clock and 9 o'clock limits," said Salma.

"As you said Sir, surely someone would have heard or noticed something if school was still in, till 3.45," offered Frank. "or even till after the office staff left around 5 pm."

"My money is on it happening between 5 and 6, or between 8 and 9," said Davenport. "Remember that June Grey heard a thud just before she went home."

"So do you think we should concentrate on these times unless anything new comes to light?" asked Fiona.

"Yes."

"There is the possibility that a golf putter could be the weapon," said Fiona Macdonald and went on to tell the others what she had told Charles the previous night.

"Where's it gone?" asked Penny.

"Maybe the murderer took it away," said Frank.

"So it would be an unpremeditated crime then, 'cos no one would know that there was going to be a golf club handy," chipped in Salma.

"Which might point to it being Mr Fox or even Fiona Donaldson," said Fiona.

"Or even Geena Carmichael, though she was in the auxiliary's room with June and the other office worker between 4 and 5 and she has an alibi for later in the evening. She could have come back in between 5 and 6.15," said Salma remembering her interview with Geena.

"Fiona Donaldson could only have done it before 5 pm and there were people in the admin block then," said Davenport.

"But Sir, the people were in the auxiliary's room, across the hallway from the admin corridor so might not have seen her coming in," Penny gave her tuppence worth now.

"Anyone could have come in then," said Frank.

"The janitor saw one of the upper school pupils leaving quite late so presumably he was at his post around 4-5. Quite late wouldn't be later than that surely."

"Didn't he say it was the head girl, Fiona?" asked Davenport.

"That's right." Fiona confirmed.

"Let's have a word with her later today. Penny, you could see her."

He thought for a few seconds then said, "On second thoughts, Frank, you see her. She'll be more likely to talk freely with a young man. Pop in afterwards and tell Fiona Donaldson that I'll be up to have another word with her, probably tomorrow."

As all thoughts on the case seemed to have dried up, Davenport chased them all off to their own rooms. Fiona stopped Frank as he left and complimented him on his appearance. She was fair, he thought. Not having anything pressing to do, he decided to get along to the school right away to see the head girl.

Once there, he went into the office and asked June Grey for her name and having got that, he asked where she was likely to be at that time.

June looked at the clock and at that moment the bell rang.

"10.55. She'll probably be in the sixth year common room in a few minutes. That's on the third floor, across from the library."

Frank thanked her and left the office. It was hard work getting up the stairs with all the youngsters coming down but he made it unscathed and soon reached the common room door. He knocked and went it. There were only a few students there, two girls and three boys.

"I want Cathy Cameron," Frank announced from the doorway.

"Oooh! Lucky you, Cathy. Wish he wanted me," quipped one of the girls.

Frank felt himself blush and wished he had chosen his words more carefully. Honestly these young girls were so forward these days!

One of the girls, the blonde one with legs to her armpits and a mini school skirt to show them off, unwound herself from the old settee on which she was sitting.

"I'm Cathy Cameron," she said, smiling at him.

"Where can we talk in private?" asked Frank, preparing himself for another snide comment.

However, Cathy threw a look at them all and said sternly, "This is serious stuff, guys. Mr Gibson was murdered you know. It's not a joke."

Turning to Frank she said, "I take it that that's why you want to see me? I might have been the last person to see him alive."

On that dramatic note, she led Frank across the corridor to the library. Opening the door she led the way in and finding the librarian tidying up a shelf of books, asked if she could have a word in private with the policeman.

The librarian looked at Frank.

Frank, remembering the protocol, asked her if she would mind staying and, feeling as if the girl was taking charge, sat down at one of the tables and told her to sit down opposite him.

"Cathy. What did you mean by saying that you might have been the last person to see Mr Gibson alive?"

"Well I went to see him about some corrections he wanted me to make on my UCAS form after school last Tuesday. I was with him for about ten minutes, then I went to collect my sports bag from PE and left. He was found the next morning. I guess he would have been leaving shortly after me unless someone stopped him."

Frank thought that this was very logical.

"Did you like Mr Gibson?"

Cathy's eyes filled with tears.

"Yes I liked him. He was so kind to me, to all of us really. He was so good-looking too."

"Did you see the janitor when you left school that day?"

"He was in his box watching TV as he always does. I had to come through to the main block from PE because the other gate was closed."

Frank thanked her and they went back out of the library together. He left her at the common room door and made his way back downstairs, easily this time as most of the children would be in their common rooms or in the playground if anyone ever played these days in senior school. What a difference from the primary school playground! Children seemed to grow up so quickly these days he thought.

Remembering that he had to see Fiona Donaldson and thinking that it would be polite to ask the head teacher, he made his way to the office.

June rang through to Christine Martin and told Frank to go in.

"Hello Mrs Martin. Maybe I should have got your permission first. Sorry. I've just had a word with your head girl."

"OK constable but another time please run it past me first."

She smiled.

"You of all people should know all about Child Protection rules."

Frank told her that he had asked the librarian to stay in the room and then told her that he would like to pay a quick visit to HE to let her PT there know that his boss wanted another word with her the next day. She told him that was fine.

"I'm going over that way myself so I'll come with you."

Fiona Donaldson was preparing soup with a class. They had only just started and she was showing them how to chop vegetables without cutting themselves.

She had one large onion in her right hand and was expertly slicing it with her left. Frank felt tears starting in his eyes as he approached the table.

She stopped.

"Just a quick word to say that DCI Davenport will be coming to see you again tomorrow, Mrs Donaldson. When would be convenient?"

"Better make it lunchtime. I'm very busy tomorrow," she said briskly.

He left, very aware of the inquisitive looks he was getting from her class.

CHAPTER 34

Davenport had spent some time with the assistant chief constable, Solomon Fairchild. As his name suggested, he was a fair-minded man and knew that Davenport would be pulling out all the stops to get a result in this case but he was being leant on from higher up and without names being spoken, Charles knew that Fairchild's immediate boss, Grant Knox, was as usual wanting results the day before yesterday. He had discovered this in his first murder case in his new job.

He had told Solomon all that was being done and that man had said that he would try to keep Knox from holding a press interview and promising them results very soon. Davenport had relaxed and over coffee he told Solomon about the janitor who was an avid crime reader and murder mystery watcher, so had known to lock the murdered man's room so that nothing could be touched or disturbed.

"Thank goodness for Poirot and Miss Marple," laughed his boss.

"And for 'Midsomer Murders'," added Charles.

"Yes. I wouldn't like to live in Midsomer. There are about six murders every week! At least you've only got one to deal with."

They both sobered, wondering if there would indeed be only one murder and hoping so.

Christine Martin had interviews for an acting depute head that morning.

She had only just gone into her room when June rang through to say that a Constable Selby wanted to see her. She agreed to him seeing her HE principal teacher, paid a quick visit to her RE teacher, then prepared her room for the forthcoming interviews. A few minutes later, Stewart Wilson, now senior depute, knocked and came in bringing with him the education officer whom he had met outside in the corridor.

They took their seats and Christine handed them the list of applicants. There were three names on the list, Derek Keith, Head of Chemistry, Mary Turner, Head of Art and Alex Snedden, Head of English.

The interviews went ahead according to plan and then Christine convened a meeting of the panellists.

Derek Keith had been very nervous and had not acquitted himself well but Mary Turner and Alex Snedden had done well. It now came down to which of those two should be promoted to acting deputy head.

Although it was not fair, Christine felt obliged to point out that if Alex got the job, Angus, his deputy would become Acting Head of English. For reasons which she explained to the education officer, she did not want this. The education officer pointed out, rather acidly, that this could not be taken into consideration. He was known for being a 'by-the-book' person. Stewart, knowing the problems which would be caused if Alex got the job, voted for Mary. There was a competent Art teacher who would run the department well. Feeling that she was being unfair to Alex, Christine nevertheless, also voted for Mary who had after all done as well in the interview as Alex and had run her department well for four years. The education officer gave in with bad grace and left shortly afterwards.

Christine went to see the applicants. She told Alex that he had acquitted himself well but said that Mary who had also impressed them had one year more than he had as PT of department. She explained to Derek that although she knew him to be a good PT, his nervousness had betrayed him and she offered to give him some practice interviews in the coming school year. Finally she went over to Art and congratulated Mary Turner, telling her that she would start the following Monday and would be using what had been David Gibson's room, there being no need now to have the senior depute next door to herself. She saw no necessity for another reshuffle of rooms.

"One thing, Mary, you'll have to dress much more smartly for your new job. No smocks."

They both laughed. Mary was not one to take offence easily.

She left it to Mary to inform her most senior teacher that she was being temporarily promoted to PT of Art and Design.

At the same time as this was going on, Irene Campbell was having a meeting with the sixth year members of her hockey team during their PE period while the rest were playing badminton. They were in the changing rooms.

"I've called you girls in to tell you my plans for next year's hockey teams. I've recommended both Cathy and Mary for full colours, Cathy for being captain all year and you Mary, for your contribution to all matches.

Now the second piece of information is this. I've decided to make Mary captain of the first eleven next year. You've had your turn Cathy and although you've been an excellent player and scored many goals, I don't think you really deserve to be captain again. You've let both me and the team down on a number of occasions."

There was a gasp at this. It wasn't often that a fifth year was chosen as captain as Cathy had been but it was a real slap on the face to be demoted after one year.

Cathy was however gracious about it.

"That's OK Mrs Campbell. I was half expecting this and anyway I'm going to give up hockey next year as I really need to study harder than I did this year."

There was another gasp. Even Irene Campbell was surprised.

"Mr Gibson asked if I had too much on my plate this year with being head girl and hockey captain. He said I would be head girl again."

"Well that's your decision, Cathy. We'll miss you of course," said Irene. "Now let's get back to the gym and join the others. Mary, would you come and see me at the end of school today and we'll decide who to move up into Cathy's position in the team."

Irene heaved a sigh of relief. That had gone better than she had hoped. The girls joined their classmates for some badminton. Cathy was first to congratulate Mary.

The next period Irene had her fourth year Intermediate 1 class. On the whole they were likeable if not very sporty and few had the academic abilities to do the Intermediate Two course. All were ready for their lesson except of course Neil Fox who was still fully dressed.

"Neil. What is it this time?"

"My Dad says I don't have to take PE if I don't want to, Miss."

"Oh does he?"

"Yes."

Neil quailed when he saw the disgust on his teacher's face.

"And has your father given you a note?"

"No."

"Well in that case, you can come back after the end of school today for detention. Meanwhile, sit down on your usual bench."

Irene turned to the rest of the class and the lesson began.

CHAPTER 35

It was a week after the murder and the police were at Bradford High School to interview all the staff. It had been arranged with the head teacher that staff would come to Room 6 when they were free. Five large tables had been set up for each of the police team.

The first period brought some science teachers who usually left via a back entrance and kept their cars in a small area near there. Only one had felt it necessary to go to the office first and he had seen nothing untoward. Also that period brought the learning support staff who had begged off sharing classes to get this ordeal over with.

One had left school at lunchtime and had spoken to David Gibson in the office. The other two had hurried into the office and had spoken with nobody. One timidly mentioned, when asked, that David had not been popular with support staff as he openly said they were useless and a waste of money in his opinion. He had always sent away any of them who had dared to come to his class to help. They had not told Alex Snedden; few people, including adults, reported bullies.

Period two, about eight folk appeared. Davenport asked three to go to the main staffroom and come down when one of the other five returned there.

He himself spoke to Alex Snedden and later, Peter Fraser from the same department. All Alex could volunteer was that he had seen David that morning coming in with his briefcase and a golf club. He was surprised when Davenport asked him more about the golf club.

"What club was it, Mr Snedden?"

"I'm sorry. He was too far away to see properly but... wait a minute it wasn't a driver or wood as it didn't have a large head."

Peter liked David Gibson and said he was the only one of the Senior Management Team who supported the EIS and still came to every meeting. He had gone on strike last year with the hoi polloi, as Peter put it rather sneeringly, Davenport thought.

Fiona, talking to Angus, made little headway. He had gone into the office rather later than usual as he had left the guitar, with which he sometimes entertained his classes, by singing them ballads, in his room and needed it for that evening. June Grey had been in the office and he thought that David's door was open but could not be certain of this.

Salma spoke to Jan, the young English teacher, who gave off a youthful enthusiasm for her job when Salma asked her how long she had been teaching. She had stayed late to get some notes typed up for the auxiliary to run off in the morning. She had no computer at home and often stayed late. Asked who she had seen on leaving, she said that the office was empty but the light was still on and she had found June Grey in the auxiliary's room with Geena. She had thought about speaking to Mrs Martin about starting up a Burns' Club but there was no light on in that room, only in the room next to it. She could tell because these rooms had fanlight windows above the doors.

Penny interviewed two teachers from Modern Languages. Both were quite elderly ladies who had gone out of school together without recourse to the office.

Frank had talked to the Head of Technical who moaned the whole time about the school. Its pupils were unwilling to learn and the senior management team gave him little support. He had gone home through the playground to the bus stop on the main road. He had only come to the school as PT in April and had not as yet found anyone willing to give him a lift. Relieved to have got rid of him, Frank then spoke to Irene Campbell whose PT had taken the class they both shared and sent her along to be interviewed as she had no free time that day.

Irene said that unlike most of the women on the staff, she got on reasonably well with David Gibson, though he could be a bit brusque at times such as when she had warned him that Mr Fox might come up to the school. She said that she could be a bit like this too so understood this manner in others. She had partnered David in the school mixed golf tournament last year. Asked by Frank if she had any idea why David might have brought a golf club into school, she had laughed and said he sometimes practised putting in his room.

"He warned me not to tell anyone."

She stopped laughing abruptly as if she had just remembered that he was dead.

"He had a little gadget for putting into. It sent the ball straight back if he got it correct."

Asked about her movements on Tuesday afternoon, she said she had stayed on for a bit getting things ready to take to the primary school the next day. Had she seen anyone, Frank had asked her.

She had gone out to her car which she had parked on the road that day and had seen nothing unusual.

"I saw someone walking into the main school from the playground outside PE. Looked familiar but I can't think now who it was. Probably someone from technical or......." she stopped as if unable to think of who else it could have been.

Frank thanked her and quickly ran downstairs to the admin corridor. He told June Grey that he was going to look in Mr Gibson's room and he did but found nothing which resembled the putting game that Irene had mentioned.

As he walked back down the corridor, Christine Martin came out of her room and he explained why he was there.

"Surely your crime team would have found it," she said.

"Well they were looking for a heavy instrument, not a golf game," said Frank.

"Could he have left it in his old room do you think?"

Christine explained that all her team had changed rooms very recently.

Together she and Frank went along to the room now occupied by Phyllis Wilson. She was in and the three of them searched the room, unearthing the golf game under a small cupboard.

Frank took it with him upstairs to room 6 where all his colleagues had now finished their period two interviews and were having a well-earned cup of tea brought to them by Geena.

He showed it to them and said that it seemed to suggest that David had indeed brought his putter into school at times.

Davenport rang Martin Jamieson and asked if David's head wound could have been caused by a golf putter.

"Swung with venom it might have been but I had thought of something larger than the head of a putter," said Martin in his very precise English.

Period three brought the social subject teachers. There were only three of them and they brought nothing new to light. One of them had seen Angus with his guitar leaving the school. She remembered because he seemed an unlikely candidate for guitar-playing.

Last period in the morning, they met the Maths department, all except Stewart Wilson. They were going to talk with the management team at lunchtime. One of them had met no one but passed the Head of Technical standing at the bus stop.

"I felt a bit mean not offering him a lift but he moans such a lot," explained the young man.

The PT Maths had left quite late, about five o'clock. She had a young family and knew that she would not get time for administrative work once she got home. Her husband, who by arriving at work early could finish early, picked the children up from their child minder and understood her need to have some quiet time in school. She explained all this in a rush. Salma who was the one speaking to her, asked if she had seen anyone at that time.

"Well there was no one in the office but the light was on and the computer was still switched on."

"Did you notice if Mr Gibson's light was on," Salma asked her.

"It was off. I'm sure all the lights were off in the corridor. They usually were. None of the management team stayed on late usually."

"So you expected the lights to be off?"

"Yes so I'm sure I'd have noticed if any were on."

'Mathematical logic,' thought Salma and thanked the young woman for her time. Though, she reasoned, if she expected the lights to be off maybe she had just assumed that on recollection.

At lunch time, after some sandwiches from the school canteen, Davenport and Fiona Macdonald met the management team in the head teacher's room. Davenport told them about the putter and the golf game. He told them that David had been killed by a blow to the head.

"Could he have been struck by the putter?" asked Phyllis.

"It's possible but we're looking for something bigger, I think."

"Could anyone have used his paperweight?" asked Stewart.

"What paperweight? There was nothing on his desk apart from a desk diary," said Davenport.

"Phyllis, don't you remember David's paperweight?"

Stewart looked to his colleague for confirmation.

"Can't say I do."

"It was most unusual, shaped like a wee curling stone with a handle and everything. I commented on it to him once."

Frank was sent to once more search the room but returned empty-handed. Phyllis said it had not been left on the desk when the rooms were changed over.

Davenport asked the three if there was anything else they could add but Phyllis and Stewart always left promptly and Christine had had a meeting in Glasgow and had left at about 2 pm.

Davenport asked Mrs Watson, if she had heard the argument between Mr Fox and David.

"Irene Campbell said you had heard him. When was this?"

"Yes I did - last Monday. Mr Fox was furious at the treatment of his son. He said he wanted Irene reported to the authorities, David got angry too and told him his son was unhealthily fat and needed exercise and that he would back the teacher to the hilt. Mr Fox stormed out of the room saying that he would take things further."

"Did he threaten Mr Gibson?"

"I don't think so, just made vague statement about taking the matter into his own hands."

The team left the head teacher's room and returned to Room 6.

They had seen from the staff lists that they had to see only six more teachers so Davenport said he would return to the station and give Martin another call about the paperweight. He asked Fiona to stay at school and conduct more interviews along with the other four, reminding her that there were also non-teaching staff who could be seen after school.

Nothing further transpired except that two more female staff from HE talked about being almost afraid of David Gibson and one young technical teacher said he found him very fair and helpful.

Fiona Donaldson admitted once again to really disliking David. She repeated her whereabouts on the night of the first murder. The Head of PT told Frank that he had always found David to be fair-minded and supported the department's requests with regard to the timetable as far as was possible with the other restraints put upon him.

The non-teaching staff hardly came into contact with him and they were much later leaving school as their hours were different. One of them, a lab technician, had seen the head girl whose name he did not know as she did not take science, standing at the office window when he left, at around 5 pm. Salma got the impression from his demeanour that the man had been leaving early and thought that she could take the time as rather earlier than that. She made a mental note to talk to the head girl.

All interviews over with apart from two absent teachers who had been absent for more than a week, the team made their way to the two cars. The janitor saw them out then closed the gates.

A lot of interviews meant a lot of report writing for them all. Davenport would probably have done his after speaking to Martin about the paperweight. Whether he had or not, he was not at the station so Fiona asked the others to write up their interviews while they still remembered what their notes meant.

She looked meaningfully at Frank as she said this. She had received some of his less than erudite reports over the last year. He flushed.

"We've a lot of comparing of notes to do tomorrow folks," she said. "Please get in sharp."

Fiona met Charles at Cathcart Castle Golf Club just after 5 pm. He had had time to go home to change out of his work clothes and looked refreshed and smart in his navy golf trousers and white sport's shirt, Fiona had taken a change of clothes to work so had stayed on to get her notes typed. She went into the ladies' locker room and had a quick wash and changed into a pair of dark grey golf trousers and a lemon polo shirt. She looked at her watch. Still five minutes before their tee-off time so she went into the pro shop and bought herself and Charles a Mars Bar each.

They had a good, close game marred slightly by the patronising nature of their male opponent who seemed to feel he had to coach his more nervous, younger partner. It transpired that he was her DCI and she was merely a constable and he seemed to feel that that gave him the right to tell her what to do. As a result she became more and more nervous but it was her putt on the seventeenth which drew the game level.

Charles took great delight in praising her stroke.

It was Fiona who won the game for them on the last hole by sinking a lengthy putt. The young girl seemed almost relieved, her boss magnanimous in defeat.

The four had a quick drink in the clubhouse then went out to their cars. Fiona and Charles sat in their cars till the other two drove off, then got back out and, giggling like teenagers, went back into the clubhouse where they had a pleasant meal together. They had agreed while on the course that they could not face sharing a meal with Mr Bossy and would have gone elsewhere had the other two been staying.

Charles went to see who they were playing next and, coming back to Fiona, used his mobile to phone the man involved. It was agreed that they would play the next game on the following Saturday if their murder case allowed. They had already managed one weekend off in the middle of it which was unusual.

Meal over, they headed once again for their cars, reminding each other to be early at work the next day.

CHAPTER 36

The police team were all in on time the next day but were still all too late to take the call which informed the sergeant at the desk that another body had been found at Bradford High School. The call had come in at 7.12, again from the janitor, who had gone his rounds of PE to check that the filter had been working in the pool and discovered a body at the bottom of it. He informed the desk sergeant that he was sure it was Irene Campbell.

The sergeant had telephoned Charles Davenport at home and he had woken Fiona Macdonald to give her the news. They had agreed to meet at the station prior to going to the school to inform the others. Davenport had rung Martin Jamieson before he left home, apologising for waking him too. Martin was, as always, pleasant about the whole thing.

"This is not your fault," he said. "I shall meet you there."

Remembering some crotchety police surgeons with whom he had had to work in his day, Davenport thanked his lucky stars for Martin and rang his sister to ask if she would come round and get Pippa off to school. This had happened once before and he knew she understood that he had to leave as soon as she got there.

Once at the station he informed his team, leaving Salma in charge while he and his DI went to the school.

Soon he, Fiona and Martin were staring down into the swimming pool. Irene Campbell's body lay on the bottom at the shallow end. Martin had rung the head of the SOC team and he and three of his team were just arriving. They had been warned what to expect and had come prepared with their swimwear. Two went into the pool and they bent down and lifted the body, floating it toward the steps where the other two lowered a stretcher. The body was put on this face down and it was raised to the side of the pool where it was gently lowered to terra firma.

Even Davenport and Macdonald could see the swelling on the back of the head.

"Martin, I need to know if she was dead when she went into the pool or if she drowned," said Davenport, "but you know that, sorry."

Martin swept back the lock of fair hair which was always falling over his forehead. It was so at odds with his immaculate black suit, lemon shirt and dark grey tie that Fiona's hand itched for scissors.

"I shall get off then," he said. "I shall be in touch as soon as possible."

Martin must have had elocution lessons, thought Davenport.

It was now after 8.15.

Once again staff and pupils would be arriving shortly. He asked the janitor to redirect any staff and pupils who were trying to get into PE to the school foyer and asked Fiona to wait and explain to the displaced staff what had happened. He would once again wait for Christine Martin who would know where to send any pupils.

When he did meet her, she was glad to tell him that no pupils had registration in the PE department there being no seats for them there, so there were no displaced pupils to sort out. He went to the foyer and found Fiona with only the PE principal teacher. His other assistant took registration in another part of the school. Fiona had told him and he looked shocked and pale.

"Who on earth would want to kill Irene? She was so popular with the kids and the staff."

Davenport sent him to the office with instructions to have a cup of strong tea. He returned to PE in time to see the covered body being lifted into the back of Martin's van. Inside, the SOC team were inspecting the poolside and taking fingerprints from the four doors which led into it, from male and female changing rooms, he surmised and from where else? He slid through one door and found himself in what was presumably a staffroom. When he went back to the poolside, it was through another staffroom. These two doors and the doors from the changing rooms were all unlocked, probably because the outer door would be locked.

Going back to the foyer he found the janitor and asked him about the outer door.

"It was open when I arrived. I thought it was peculiar as it was too early for even the PE staff to arrive."

Davenport made his way to the head teacher's room and on the way asked the PT, in the office having more tea, who had locked up the previous night.

"Irene was to lock up. I left about 3 pm with my volleyball team. We were playing a school on the other side of town and Mrs Martin let them all leave early to get there in time. Me too. Irene was coping with the fourth year on her own with help from two of the sixth year boys who were free last period. Her class were swimming and my class of Intermediate 2 kids were playing hockey on the disused tennis courts. I know it's not strictly speaking legal but it saved another Please Take for someone."

This was not the time to tell him that what he had done was wrong. The man knew that and no pupil had been hurt.

"Could she have had any trouble with any of the kids in those two classes?" Charles asked.

"Just that big lump Neil Fox. He wouldn't have his swimming gear with him no doubt and would be left sitting on a bench outside the staffroom. I can't think of anyone else, certainly not anyone who would try to drown her."

"Why did you say 'drown her'?"

"Well you said she was dead in the pool."

Davenport thanked him, not wanting to say any more at this juncture. He walked back across to the main building.

Going into Room 6 he picked up the phone and rang the station, asking to speak to Salma Din. When she answered, he told her what had happened and asked her to come to the school with Penny and Frank.

They were all in Room 6 by nine o'clock.

Salma reminded her boss that she was to see the head girl, Cathy Campbell, about her being seen outside the office window around 5 pm or earlier and was told to do that right away then get back for more instructions. Frank pointed out that he had seen Cathy but she had made no mention of being at the office window.

Salma got Cathy's timetable from the office and went to the room where the sixth year were registered. She apologised to the teacher and took Cathy outside.

"Cathy, someone saw you outside the office, at the window at around 5 pm last Tuesday. Would that be right?"

"Yes. I was off ill with a migraine but I'd made another appointment to see Mr Gibson about changes to my UCAS form so I came in but I don't think it was as late as that. Mr Gibson doesn't usually stay very late." She flushed. "I told all this to the young policeman."

Salma asked her if she had liked Mr Gibson and she said yes she had. Salma got the impression that this girl had had a crush on David Gibson. She seemed to know his movements.

"What time did you think it was?"

Cathy thought hard.

"I saw Mr Gibson at about 4.15. I may have stood at the office window to see if he was coming out. He sometimes gave me a lift down the road."

This was said with a mixture of embarrassment and defensiveness. Salma pretended not to notice and thanked her for being so helpful. She wondered how long the poor girl had stood there.

"Are you sure you saw no one while you were waiting?"

"Sure. No, wait a minute. As I came in through the swing doors from the PE end of the school, I caught a glimpse of someone going through the other doors at the HE end."

"Who was it?" Salma asked.

"I don't know. I'm pretty sure it was a man, quite tall, wearing joggy bottoms."

Salma thanked her and went back to Room 6. She reported what she had been told and Frank agreed with it. He had not known that Cathy had waited around outside the office.

"She must have left before June Grey went across for coffee," he said.

"I wonder who it was she saw," mused Davenport. "It could have been the murderer."

"Track suit bottoms, Sir. Unless a member of staff had gone home and come back or changed to drive home, it's unlikely to be a teacher. Most of the men dress smartly," Salma pointed out.

"Mr Fox was wearing track suit bottoms when I saw him and so was his son, Neil," Fiona chipped in.

"Male PE staff would probably be wearing them too," said Penny, not to be outdone.

"The head of PE is quite short. Very stockily built," Frank told them. "You said that Cathy mentioned that the person was tall, Salma. Anyway, he seemed to like Mr Gibson."

Davenport had promised to see Fiona Donaldson that day, so he left them saying that he would be back shortly to discuss their next move.

Fiona Donaldson was in the HE staffroom which was fortunate, along with her colleague Laura who got up to leave as soon as she saw Davenport.

When they were alone, Charles sat down and said that he knew that she had said that she did not like David Gibson. Was it possible that she was protesting too much about this and in fact really liked him. He had found out that some of the female staff found him attractive.

Fiona almost choked.

"Are you thinking that I fancied him and he rebuffed me and I killed him, Inspector?"

"You have no alibi for the time you say you were at Asda, so I have to ask you."

"I've disliked the man from day one. He thinks I'm some kind of inferior being because I teach HE. He probably still calls it Cookery to himself. Mrs Martin was OK with the fact that I wouldn't make tea for the principal teachers meetings but I could tell that he thought I should be forced to. He was a vile individual. Ask anyone how I felt about him. I made no secret of it. I love my husband Inspector. I did not, I repeat not, fancy David Gibson."

Davenport thought she sounded really genuine and he apologised if he had upset her.

Back in Room 6, he told his staff what had transpired.

"I think we'll ask Christine Martin to convene a staff meeting and ask if anyone can help us with this second murder. We really can't afford the time to interview them all individually again."

Christine, when asked, said that she would close the school early and hold a staff meeting in the main staffroom at 3 pm. She had been onto headquarters and had been told to give the police all the help they asked for. This must be cleared up soon before parents started removing their children from a school where there had now been two murders.

"We have only just recently been saved from closing because of our dwindling numbers. The last thing we want is to lose pupils now," she said ruefully.

CHAPTER 37

Totally unaware of what had been happening at the school on this Wednesday morning, Caroline was planning David's funeral. She felt very much alone. David's parents were dead as were her own. David had one older brother but they had not been close, Arthur having been very much the apple of his mother's eye. His father, a quiet, unassuming man had not seemed to notice that David was often left out, nor did they notice that David was always competing for the attention he never got. His mother had been a very dominant influence in the family. Her elder son had taken after her in manner. Caroline had not taken to the elder Mrs Gibson, sensing that she might be a rival for David's affections even though she spurned him so often as Caroline herself had often done.

Jane was the only real friend she had though she had many acquaintances and friends who shared her love of a good time. She had tried phoning

Jane the night before then remembered that she had left for her annual fortnight's holiday in Ibiza.

She had registered David's death in the registry offices in Glasgow. She had never been to Martha Street before and found the inside of the building very old fashioned and meeting with the registrar a bit formal. She knew nobody connected with a church to ask who would do the funeral. She and David had never discussed their wishes about such things as funerals and had never made wills. In their thirties, they had not expected to die.

In despair, she telephoned the police station early in the morning and asked to speak to any one in charge of the case and was put through to Salma Din who had just come in.

Feeling an absolute fool, Caroline explained her predicament and Salma was able to give her some help. She should, in the first instance, contact a funeral parlour. There were one or two in Shawlands, on Pollokshaws Road across from the primary school and they would be in the phone book. Salma was sure that the person in charge would set her straight about church, crematorium and other things. She asked Caroline to make no definite date for the funeral until Davenport spoke to her again.

Caroline did as she was bid and rang the Coop funeral parlour. The woman was very helpful and gave her a time to go along, the next day. Caroline explained that her husband had been killed and she wasn't sure about a date yet but was told to come along anyway.

She had not been off the phone long when James rang. He was on his mobile and was, he said, sitting in his car outside her house. Was there anyone with her or could he come in?

Caroline, scared of a man for the first time in her life, said she was expecting someone but would come out to his car. She was relieved when he agreed. She ran down the path and got into the car.

"How are you, Caroline?"

"Not bad, thanks."

"I thought I'd let you know the arrangements for the wedding."

"Wedding," thought Caroline, for a moment wildly thinking that he had arranged for them to marry. An almost manic giggle rose in her throat. "What about straight after the funeral. Could save on catering if they had both meals at once," she thought.

"Caroline what is the matter? You look bemused."

"I'm planning a funeral and you're asking me about a wedding. What wedding?"

"I said I wanted you to come to a wedding with me. Well, it's at the weekend, Saturday."

"I can hardly start socialising so soon after David's death."

"It's not socialising. As a friend, no one would be surprised at you partnering me. A wedding is hardly a party as such. We could leave after the meal."

Caroline vaguely remembered saying that she would do this.

"Fine, James."

"Right, you had better get back inside. I'll be in touch with arrangements."

He leant over and tweaked one of her nipples through her blouse. It hurt and she squealed. He bent over to kiss her and thrust his hand between her legs pinching the flesh on the inside of one of her thighs. Tears came into her eyes. She drew away from him.

"Now get along. I'll phone you after the police come to see me again as they surely will to check the discrepancy of our eating arrangements on the night of the murder."

Caroline hastily got out of the car and almost ran up the path to the safety of her house. After this wedding, she would refuse to see him again. She went into her bedroom and inspected her leg where a weal was already forming. The man was a brute. How different from her caring, loving David.

She felt alone for the first time in her life.

CHAPTER 38

As promised, Christine Martin called a staff meeting at 3 pm on Wednesday. They all knew what had happened. The bush telegraph had been at work all morning. The buzz of talk stopped immediately Christine and Charles entered

Davenport asked anyone with any information regarding this murder to come to see him in Room 6 today, as soon as possible. There had been a silence after he spoke, then one or two of the women had wept openly.

Fiona Donaldson was especially distraught. She came to see the police team right away, getting Laura to be with her class for a few minutes.

"I feel so bad about this," she said to Fiona who sat her down across from her.

"I said I would meet Irene after school, at the office window. We were going to have tea somewhere together and see a film. It's my husband's chess night at his school and my son was going to have his meal with a friend at his house. When Irene didn't come, I texted her rather than go over to PE. She texted back that she wasn't feeling so good."

Fiona asked if she had kept what she had written and what came back and Fiona brought both messages up on her mobile phone.

The first read;

"Where R U. Getting hungry."

The reply read:

"Can we cancel. Feeling rough."

"If only I'd gone over. I didn't though and I can't change that now. I rang her at home and got the answerphone. I thought that maybe she had gone straight to bed and wasn't answering."

"Maybe just as well you didn't go over, Mrs Donaldson. If it was the murderer who texted you and he or she was still there, you might have been another victim."

Fiona left, still looking grief-stricken and Fiona told the others what she had said. Davenport was still speaking to the technical PT who had passed PE as usual on his way home and said that he had seen Neil Fox coming out at about 4.10. He had assumed he'd been kept back for detention. It was common knowledge that he often was, as he regularly forgot his kit.

Salma, Frank and Penny had seen no one.

"We'd better see young Mr Fox. I'll see Christine Martin and get a teacher to accompany him," said

Davenport, having been informed of the text to Fiona. He left the room and returned shortly with a young man, from the science department who was Neil's first line guidance teacher. Christine had promised to fetch Neil herself and appeared about ten minutes later having had to go, ironically, to PE to collect him from his almost permanent seat on the bench.

"Sit down Neil," said the DCI. The boy sat and his teacher pulled across another chair and sat beside him. As expected, the boy was fat and ruddy cheeked but he was looking nervous, rather than belligerent as Davenport had expected.

"Neil, tell us what happened after school ended yesterday. You were in PE and....."

"I was kept behind for detention as I had no PE kit."

"Why did you get detention for that?"

"I had no note from home excusing me from PE."

"Why not?"

"Mum wants me to take it Sir, so I never ask for a note. I just take the lines or the detention."

"Why won't you take PE? Is it the teachers?"

"No Sir. It's the other boys. They make fun of me Sir. I'm hopeless at football and games. I like HE," he added looking a bit sheepish. "I love cooking and baking."

Davenport wondered why he was taking PE if he hated it so much but for the time being that was irrelevant.

"Will you tell me what happened over there yesterday, please?"

"I went over to PE after school and sat down outside the female PE staffroom to wait for Mrs Campbell but she didn't come. I knocked on her door but no one came. I went to the male staffroom but no one answered when I knocked. I went back and sat down but when no one came, I went into the girls' changing area. There was no one there either, thank goodness."

He grinned.

"I thought that Mrs Campbell must have forgotten about me and gone home though I thought that she would have locked the main door if she had."

"Did you see anyone else?"

"Two of the senior girls were there when I arrived."

"Who were they Neil?"

"Cathy Cameron, the head girl and a quiet, dark haired girl whose name I don't know."

"Did they leave right away?"

"Yes."

"So you left?"

"Yes."

"Thanks Neil. You can go back to your class now."

The technical teacher was asked if he would stay for the next interview and he agreed to do this. It was certainly more interesting than sitting listening to his boss's complaints!

Once again Cathy Cameron was sought, found and asked to come to Room 6. This time Davenport questioned her himself. He found her disconcertingly self- assured for her age.

When asked what she and the other girl had been doing, she said that they had been having PE last period and that she and Mary had stayed behind to ask Mrs Campbell something about the hockey match that Saturday. Mrs Campbell had gone into the pool area and they had come out to the hallway from her room where they had been talking.

"I popped back to get her permission to borrow some sticks for a practice some of us were going to have tomorrow during a free period. Mary waited for me."

"What was Mrs Campbell doing?"

"She was kneeling down with her hand in the pool water. I asked about the sticks, she said yes and I took four and joined Mary. She went for a bus and I walked home"

"Did you see anyone else at PE."

"Yes a fat boy was sitting on a bench there."

"Anyone else?"

"No."

Davenport asked where he might find Mary and Cathy said that she would be at science.

"She's a boffin. Always at science if she can find any free time."

This was said in a derogatory way as if science was not worth time spent on it. Davenport wondered if the half sneer was for science or Mary. Frank was despatched to science and returned with a girl who was the antithesis to Cathy in every way. Mousy-haired and shy, Mary sat down and listened while Davenport asked her about the visit to PE.

"Well it wasn't a visit Sir. We were there already for our PE lesson but Cathy asked me to wait with her to see Mrs Campbell about the team for Saturday."

"Why did you both go? Is one of you captain?"

She flushed.

"Well Cathy is for this term but I am for next year so she suggested we team up for the last week and I could learn the ropes."

"Right, so what happened after you'd spoken to Mrs Campbell?"

"Cathy went back to ask for some hockey sticks and I waited in the hallway, then I went for my bus."

"Are you and Cathy friends, Mary?"

"No Sir...well what I mean is we're not enemies but we share different interests and she's a great hockey player. I'm not."

Davenport asked her if she had seen anyone else at PE and she said there had been a boy sitting there. She had heard a noise from the male end of

PE but had seen no one. Davenport thanked her and both she and the young science teacher left.

"I wonder why Mary was taking over from Cathy as captain." Fiona was interested.

"Maybe they only get the chance for one year. Seems fairer," Penny chipped in.

It being now lunchtime, they all went back to the station, leaving Penny manning Room 6 in case anyone else should turn up later.

That evening, Davenport went to see Mr Fox. He had meant to go on Monday evening but had just not had time.

Mrs Fox answered the door. Her husband was not yet home but should be arriving shortly, she informed him. Charles introduced himself and accepted her offer of a cup of tea and he sat in the lounge waiting for it. There was no sign of Neil.

"Is Neil out, Mrs Fox?"

"No Sir. He's in the kitchen doing some baking. Take a piece of cake Sir. He made it."

It was delicious. The lad had indeed found his niche in the kitchen. Davenport wondered how he got on with the rather prickly Fiona Donaldson. He asked Neil's mother.

"Oh he loves Mrs Donaldson. He would do anything for her."

"Unlike PE?"

She went a bit red in the face and agreed that Neil was not cut out for PE. "I wish he would do some Sir. I refuse to give him notes to excuse him from it so I hope he does get some exercise. Not that I approve of Mrs Campbell bullying him into things like cross country," she added.

"What about his father? Does....."

At that moment he heard a key turn in the front door and Mr Fox came in. His wife called him into the front room.

"Mr Davenport is here to see you Bert. He's from the police. I'll leave you to it." She took Davenport's empty cup and plate and left the room.

"How can I help you Mr Davenport?"

"You mentioned having a heated phone call to David Gibson but you omitted to mention to DI Macdonald that you visited him at school last Monday. You were heard shouting at him. Is there anything else you omitted to mention? Another visit on Tuesday night, perhaps?"

Bert Fox blustered:

"OK so I did go up but not on Tuesday night."

"What did you row about?"

"I will not have my son forced into PE. I hated it at school and I won't have him treated as I was."

"Why did he choose it then?"

"He had to take one subject from a certain column. He tried to get into Art but it was full. I let my wife persuade me that if he only did Intermediate 1 he would have an easy time at PE."

"Can anyone vouch for where you were last Tuesday night, from 6-9 pm?"

Bert Fox looked worried.

"I went out after my dinner. It's my darts' night at the pub. I played a few games then my friend left as he had promised his wife to be home earlier than usual that night. I sat on and had another drink then came home myself."

"When did your friend leave?"

"I think it must have been about 8 pm as 'Eastenders' was just finishing on the TV above the bar."

"So can anyone vouch for you after that?"

"I hope so. I didn't actually speak to anyone in particular but I was there for another half hour at least."

"What were you wearing that night, Mr Fox?"

"What has that got to with anything?" asked the man truculently.

"Just answer the question, please, Sir."

"Probably my tracksuit bottoms with a sweatshirt."

"And what about last night, Mr Fox. What did you do then?"

"Last night? I came home then popped out to get us all fish suppers. I got home early and we decided to have a take away meal. I was wearing a suit," he added somewhat sarcastically. "After that it was darts' night again. Why are you asking about last night?"

"Mrs Campbell, the PE teacher you had such a grudge against, was murdered last night."

The man paled visibly.

"It wasn't me," he stammered. "I didn't like the woman but I couldn't kill anyone. You have to believe me."

Davenport thanked him for his time and left.

CHAPTER 39

On Thursday morning, Fiona Macdonald took a call from Martin Jamieson. He had finished with the body of David Gibson. He had found nothing more and the body could be released for burial. It would appear from first investigations that Irene Campbell had died from a wound to the head, he told her, not from drowning. She had been dead at least ten hours before the body was found, at the most sixteen hours. The swimming pool area was quite cool so the body temperature might have been affected by that. Martin was sorry he could not be more precise. Once again a blunt instrument had been used. The wound looked very similar to the one on David Gibson's head. Irene had been hit on the right hand side of the head, David on the left. This meant that David had been hit by a right-handed person and Irene possibly by a left handed person unless she had had her back to her assailant.

Fiona thanked Martin and went to tell Davenport who was in his office next door. It was a pleasant room. The police station was a new one and the rooms were light and airy. Charles had brought in some plants and had on his desk Pippa's most recent school photograph. Fiona had not personalised her room yet. She was good with plants so would eventually bring some in but had only photographs of her parents, being an only child.

"Better get on the phone to Caroline Gibson. Tell that she can go ahead with the funeral."

"Would you mind if I went round to tell her, Charles?" asked Fiona. "I'd like to see her again and see if I can find out who she thought might have wanted to kill her husband. Penny and I both thought she had someone in mind."

So it was that Fiona was ringing the bell of the Gibson house at 11.30, having phoned first to make sure that Caroline would be in.

Caroline opened the door, a very different Caroline from the one Fiona had seen the last time. She looked almost unkempt, her almost silvery blonde hair greasy and lifeless, her face devoid of make- up, her clothes clean but casual.

She welcomed Fiona and asked her into the lounge where the remainder of scrambled egg on toast was sitting on a plate on the floor by the settee, the food only half touched.

"Mrs Gibson, how have you been? Did you get a friend to be with you like you said you would?"

"I phoned Jane but she was leaving for Ibiza the next day. I don't need anyone, honest."

"How are you managing with the funeral arrangements?"

"One of your officers gave me advice when I rang yesterday. I've got an appointment later today with the Coop Funeral parlour in Shawlands.

"How sad," thought Fiona, "that she had to phone us for help."

Out loud she said, "Have you no family?"

"Both my parents and David's are dead. I'm an only child and David didn't get on with his brother and I hardly know his wife."

Fiona felt a sudden empathy with this woman. She herself had had to arrange her Mum's funeral a few years ago and being an only child, she too had no help with things.

Impulsively she offered her assistance.

"Would you like me to come to the funeral parlour with you today, Mrs Gibson?"

"Oh call me Caroline and I would be very grateful if you would come."

"Just let me ask my boss."

Fiona left the room and called Charles on her mobile. He gave his permission as she had been sure he would.

"Let's have a coffee first," she said to Caroline.

Over the coffee, she asked about James Buchanan.

"I know he's only a recent friend, but he's a lawyer, would he not have helped you?"

Caroline shivered then got up to put on the electric fire, claiming that she was cold. Fiona was finding the room warm and had felt the radiator on the way back into the lounge. It was on. Obviously Caroline was a bundle of nerves and unable to get warm.

"He's very busy and he really is a very recent friend so I didn't like to ask him and he didn't offer."

Fiona told her that she could now have David's body for burial.

The appointment being at 1.30, they left, Fiona offering to do the driving. As she slid into the passenger seat Caroline asked about David's car and was told that it had been found parked outside the school. His golf clubs were at his club except for a putter which had gone missing.

"Do you golf Caroline?" asked Fiona.

"No, I'm not very sporty. The only physical thing we did together was jog occasionally. We really did have separate interests. He went to quiz nights at the local pub; my general knowledge is awful. I liked modern music; he didn't. But we did love each other in spite of this."

Caroline sounded heartfelt and Fiona got the feeling that she was regretting that they had not done more things together now.

"I know it's cruel to ask you Caroline but *were* you having an affair with James Buchanan?"

Caroline desperately wanted to confide in this kind woman but she was even more desperately afraid of James so she replied that she had had a few affairs over the years, that David had forgiven her each time but she had not started an affair with James. Maybe she would have, given time. She thought to admit that might put the police off the idea that they were already lovers...though that word didn't quite fit she thought now and shivered again.

They had reached the funeral parlour. Fiona opened the door and could see that Caroline had to psyche herself up to enter.

The woman behind the desk was very kind and helpful. She knew of a minister who would do the service, a local minister, a woman she had had dealings with many times. With Caroline's agreement, she rang this woman and when she handed the receiver to Caroline the two came to an arrangement whereby the minister would come early that evening to discuss David's funeral. That done, it was agreed that David's body would lie in the parlour until the funeral at Linn Crematorium. Caroline chose the casket and the flowers and was told that later she could write an epitaph for The Book of Remembrance.

On their way back to Caroline's, Fiona asked her about finances and Caroline admitted that

David had done all their banking, Caroline simply spending all her salary on herself.

"I sound awfully selfish and I was," she said tearfully. "David gave me housekeeping, ran the cars and paid for holidays as well as all the direct debits. The only things I paid for were things for myself and holiday spending money."

Fiona went to the little bar in the lounge and poured her a small brandy, telling her that she would have to leave now but said she only needed to phone her and she would come round again. She asked Caroline to let the station know when the funeral would be.

"One of us usually attends the funeral. Would you like it to be me?"

Caroline said she would. She knew that David's brother and his wife and children would attend but she would like someone who was there for her.

Feeling a bit guilty but knowing it had to be said, Fiona asked again if Caroline had any idea of who might have wanted her husband dead.

Caroline managed this time to look totally at a loss and said she had no idea unless David had made someone at work hate him as he had always seemed popular with his friends whenever she had met them.

Fiona told her about the second murder and Caroline said that she had never met Irene Campbell but had heard David mention her name in conjunction with the school's golf competition.

"Do you think the two deaths are connected?" she asked.

Fiona had to tell her that they had not had time to discuss this yet but that personally she thought they must be as two deaths in one school was too much of a coincidence in her opinion.

She asked Caroline where she had been the preceding evening and was told that she was at home and by herself all evening.

"No one rang or called?"

"No."

On this note Fiona left, thinking that Caroline looked relieved rather than shocked at the news of the second murder, even though she had no alibi again and for a longer spell of time.

CHAPTER 40

Fiona went back to the station and told what had happened to the DCI. She told him that Caroline denied having an affair with Buchanan and that she had been at home alone on the evening when Irene Campbell was killed.

"Would it be OK if I attended the funeral Charles? I've got a bit of a rapport with her now and she has no close family."

Davenport was happy with that.

"Let's look at the possible suspects for David's murder before we talk to the others," he said.

"Mr Fox. He disliked Irene Campbell perhaps even more than he did David Gibson. He has only a weak alibi for both nights. On the night of the first murder he was at the pub alone and could have slipped out and gone back and on the following Tuesday, he went out for fish suppers. They live not far from the school so it's possible that he could have hurried there, killed Irene, picked up suppers and gone home."

"Would both murders be premeditated?" asked Fiona

"Well the first one must have been unless the golf club was just available when someone lost their temper but the second one might not have been. There are plenty of items in PE which could have been used."

"What about Fiona Donaldson?"

"We haven't asked her where she was the second time but she was at Asda by herself the night of David's murder."

"So she could have killed him, then done some quick shopping? She admitted to heartily disliking him." Fiona was beginning to form a picture of David Gibson at school and it did not match up with Caroline's David.

"Bit of a chameleon, David," she said.

"What about his wife and James Buchanan?" Charles went on.

"Well they had time to do it either singly or together. They might have wanted rid of him so that they could marry, that is if they had been seeing each other longer than they have admitted and the friendship was more than that."

Charles moved on to the second murder.

"What motive could they have had for Irene's murder?"

"Could they have seen her on the night of the murder and thought she had seen them?"

"Wait a minute, Irene Campbell said she thought that she has seen someone coming in or out of the building, didn't she?"

Davenport rifled through the reports on his desk till he found the one containing Irene's statement.

"…looked familiar," he read out.

"Caroline told me today that she had never met Irene Campbell and Irene wouldn't know James Buchanan surely," said Fiona.

They were getting nowhere so Davenport went to his door and called out along the corridor for the others to come to the Incident Room.

He told them of their four suspects so far and asked if anyone could furnish them with reasons why any of these people would have wanted Irene dead. Frank had been looking through his notes on his interviews.

"Sir, Irene stayed on after school finished last Tuesday. She saw someone going into the main building and assumed it was someone from technical. Could it have been either Caroline Gibson or more likely James Buchanan? I'm sorry I forgot to mention this but I was so excited about looking for the golf gadget."

"Doesn't matter Frank, you're telling us now."

As usual, Davenport was magnanimous towards his staff even though he already knew all this.

"Caroline told me today that she had never met Irene Campbell," said Fiona for the second time.

"Sir, is there any possibility of Irene and David having an affair?" Penny asked.

Fiona told them that Caroline had told her of past affairs and wondered if David had also had some in this open marriage.

"Yes but would Caroline get so revengeful as to want to kill them both when she wanted the road clear for her affair with Buchanan, assuming she was having one. Would she not have been content with David occupied with someone else?" Davenport poured cold water over this idea.

"I see Buchanan killing David to leave him free access to Caroline then killing Irene who saw him," said Salma.

Frank agreed with Salma. She threw him a smile.

"What about Irene Campbell's husband?" Fiona asked. "If she and David had been having an affair he could have killed David then his wife."

"It's a possibility. We'll need to check his whereabouts for both Tuesdays."

"Do you think that it was the same murderer then Sir not a copy-cat killing?" asked Penny.

"What do you all think?" Davenport threw the question open.

Frank thought it was more likely to be the same murderer, so did Salma. Penny wondered if it was possible that maybe Mr Fox wanted Irene dead and had copied the style of James Buchanan.

This was getting them nowhere.

"Keep all these possibilities in your heads folks. Keep an open mind." He thought suddenly of what Cathy Cameron had said and reminded them that Irene had been kneeling down at the edge of the pool.

"This means that she had her back to her murderer probably so the murderer could have been right handed both times. Does that eliminate anyone? Think back to Mr Fox, James and Caroline and Fiona Donaldson."

"Fiona Donaldson's left - handed Sir. I can picture her the other day showing the kids how to slice an onion and she held the onion in her right hand to cut it with her left."

"Good for you Frank. Well spotted. Anyone else?"

Nothing else was forthcoming so it was agreed to get Bert Fox, Buchanan and Caroline Gibson in for fingerprinting and find out which was their strong hand.

Fiona told them that Caroline had looked relieved to hear of the second murder even though she had no alibi at all for that evening.

Davenport told them to get back to their room but it being lunch time Salma, Frank and Penny made their way to the canteen. Fiona went into her own room and started writing up her time with Caroline Gibson.

When he had the room clear, Davenport rang James Buchanan's chambers. He was lucky. James was available. He was asked to come in for fingerprinting the next day and agreed with bad grace. Mrs Fox said that her husband would come in during his lunch break. Caroline said that she would come whenever it was most suitable for them and was told the morning preferably.

In the canteen, the three police officers were discussing the case. Frank would put his money on James Buchanan. Penny remembering that Caroline had giggled when told of her husband's death, plumped for Caroline. Neither she nor Salma had met James Buchanan. None of them thought that it was Bert Fox. As Penny said, he could have removed his son from the school rather than resort to murder.

They needed more clues.

CHAPTER 41

After some wet days, Friday was glorious. It seemed as if summer was coming back. At the police station, hopes were raised with the temperature. Frank had been told to take the three suspects for fingerprinting and was going to watch them signing their forms to find out whether or not they were right handed.

James and Caroline arrived together. James had planned this. He had called at Caroline's house just before 9 am, guessing rightly that she would have been called in too and would not have left before this.

"Get yourself ready, darling. Let's put on a united front."

He was secretly horrified at her appearance. In her dressing gown, with her hair unkempt, this was not the Caroline he had lusted after, had wanted for his partner, even for his wife. If he was to take her to the family wedding he would have to spruce her up a bit if he did not want to be embarrassed by her.

Not wanting to annoy him, Caroline dressed quickly and combed her hair. They went in his car. During the short journey, he reminded her of the supper they had had on the evening when David had been killed - pate and bread.

"You said 'dinner' by mistake remember, and remember too that you left to go to the pictures."

"Yes."

He preceded her into the station and enquired of the police constable at the desk where they were to go for fingerprinting. The man showed them into an interview room and Frank came along shortly afterwards with the equipment. They gave their fingerprints and Frank watched as they signed the necessary form. Caroline was left-handed, James right-handed.

They were told that Davenport wished to see them both in his room and the constable at the desk took them along.

"Just one wee thing to clarify, Mr Buchanan. What did you eat together on the night of David's murder."

"Pate and bread with wine, Inspector. I'm sure Caroline will have told you this."

"You said a meal Mrs Gibson, didn't you?"

"I may have said that once but I corrected myself. I was so upset at that time I didn't know what I was saying."

She smiled at him then looked across at Buchanan like a child hoping for praise, Davenport thought, remembering how his daughter looked at him when she had done something well.

Thanking them for their time, he showed them to the door then stopped.

"Mr Buchanan. Where were you this Tuesday evening?"

"At the opera in The Concert Hall."

"With whom?"

"With nobody, Inspector. Why are you asking?"

"There's been another murder Sir. Another teacher at the school has been killed."

Caroline told Davenport the arrangements for the funeral which was to be on Tuesday at Linn Crematorium at 10 am.

Back in James's car, he found out why Caroline had not been asked this question about her whereabouts the night of the second murder. She had already answered it the day before.

"And you never thought to warn me?" he said between clenched teeth.

"Did you need to be warned? Why would you want to murder another teacher at the school? We both know we were together on the evening when David was killed. We could admit to that you know," she said bravely.

"We're sticking to the original story. Haven't you realised you stupid woman that we could have committed the murder together?"

"I'm sorry, James. I didn't think of that. But we know we didn't do it."

"How do you know I didn't do it earlier in the evening? I don't know that you didn't."

"I had no reason to. I loved David," Caroline was crying now.

"Yes, loved him so much you were having sex with me!"

Caroline broke down completely at this and James realised that he would have to comfort her if things were going to go anywhere between them. He stopped the car in a lay-by then turned round in his seat and put one arm round her pulling her towards him. Soothingly he stroked her hair.

"Come on Caroline. I'm sorry. Let's go back to your house and you can make me a coffee before I go home."

Over the coffee he kept the conversation on pleasant things and Caroline relaxed. James turned the conversation round to the next day's wedding. He asked her what she had planned to wear.

"I've got a pale green trouser suit I bought for my cousin's wedding last year."

"Put it on and let me see it."

Caroline did as he asked and came down looking very smart in her outfit though her hair badly needed washing.

"It's smart Caroline but would you let me come upstairs and look through your clothes. I'd like you to look very feminine tomorrow."

Upstairs they went, Caroline feeling a bit nervous about him being in her bedroom but James was the perfect gentleman. He looked in her wardrobe and pulled out a summer dress with a short, floaty chiffon skirt in pale blue.

"Do you have white shoes?"

"Yes."

Caroline brought out stiletto- heeled white shoes.

"That would be perfect," he said and she began to warm towards him again. How nice it would have been if David had done something like this but he had always accepted her as she was, had never made any suggestions about her outfits.

They went back downstairs and soon James said he was leaving but would be back to collect her at 1.30 pm the next day.

He kissed her gently and told her to get a good night's sleep.

Later that same day Bert Fox came into the station to give his fingerprints. He was right-handed.

Even later, Mary Turner went into David's room in the admin. corridor to sort things out for Monday. She was a methodical woman and she wanted to be ready for her new job that day.

She decided to move a large cupboard across to the other side of the room and that was when she found a golf putter which had obviously fallen down behind the cupboard. Not realising its significance, she simply put it by the door to give to the head teacher to give to Mrs Gibson.

CHAPTER 42

Golf rather than crime was on the agenda for Charles Davenport and Fiona Macdonald on Saturday morning. Charles had taken Pippa to her aunt's at 10 am and had collected Fiona not long after that. They were into the third round of the Southside Police Mixed Tournament which was being held at Cathcart Castle Golf Club this time and were lucky to be playing their match quite early in the morning. It was a lovely day.

Charles had a handicap of 15. He seldom managed to get to the medal competitions monthly on Saturday mornings so his handicap had not gone down for some years. Fiona had only played in four medals and had a handicap of 34. Fiona went into the ladies' locker room to get her clubs and change. When she came out, looking smart in pale grey trousers and a pink polo shirt, Charles was waiting for her, wearing grey trousers. She laughed to see that he too had on a pink polo shirt. He had a good taste in clothes and was not afraid to wear pastel colours.

"They'll think we're twins," she told him.

"I'm flattered. You must be quite a bit younger than I am."

They were quite early so sat down on the bench in front of the clubhouse.

"How old are you Charles?"

"I'll tell you if you tell me," he grinned at her.

"Ok I'll be the dreaded 40 next March."

"I'll be 40 next April."

"So I'm cradle snatching!"

"No I prefer to say I'm your toy boy."

They both laughed together.

Their game was enjoyable and came down to the last hole like last time with both teams all square. It all depended on Charles's putt and he missed it, giving their opponents the match. He looked ruefully at his partner as they walked off the green.

"Sorry Fiona, I let you down there."

"I'm not bothered. I don't often win at games so I'm a good loser. Anyway we were lucky to get today off being in the middle of a murder enquiry and we might not be able to arrange a further round."

Their opponents treated them to a drink then the four went to get changed. Charles asked Fiona if she wanted to stay for a late lunch but Fiona, knowing that he would probably like to get back for Pippa, said that she had plans for the afternoon and would like to get home. They stopped outside Fiona's flat in Grantley Street. It was a busy street and there was nowhere to park so they didn't talk for long as Charles was blocking the street.

"We'll need to find that weapon, Fiona. I wonder if it was David's golf putter."

"Or the paperweight. We can't find either of them."

"I'll get Frank to look in the school grounds again on Monday. Maybe should have done that sooner but we've all been needed for other things."

"Thanks for the game Charles. You'd better go before a car comes down the street."

He waved and drove off.

The Bradford first eleven hockey team played their last match in the morning. Cathy and Mary had gone to see their head teacher on Friday to ask if they could still play this game as if they won they would have won the tournament. She had given her consent and had asked her staff if one would volunteer to go with them. Jan, having played hockey herself at school, said she would go rather than disappoint the girls.

Cathy elected herself spokesperson and gave the girls a pep talk about doing their very best so that Mrs Campbell would be proud of them.

"Maybe she can look down and see us," said one of the girls who was a churchgoer.

They won easily this time, the score being 4-1. Cathy had tried hard to be unselfish, even trying to turn herself round to pass out to the right wing as well as the left. Jan congratulated them and Cathy reminded them to take their sticks back to PE on Monday and rinse them carefully either at home or in the changing room showers.

"There's no Mrs Campbell to do it for us this time," she said looking sombre.

James had picked Caroline up at her house and had driven them both to the University Chapel for the wedding. The wedding went without a hitch and James was a delightful companion. Back at the hotel which was a large one on the outskirts of Cumbernauld, the guests had a long wait while photographs were taken. James was beginning to get impatient and was knocking back whiskies rather fast. Caroline had never seen him drunk and was not sure she wanted to. He left her at one point to "see to something". She did not question him about it.

At about 5 pm the line-up of wedding party assembled and the guests queued up to shake their hands before going into the restaurant. The tables were in a three-sided square with the guests facing each other at two large tables with the wedding party across the top. James was very quick to find their places almost in the middle of one of the large tables. She saw by the place names that they were seated side by side. A few minute later, a young man stopped across from them, looked at the name cards and said he was surprised that he and his wife were seated together and not across from each other as others were. He looked at James. James pointedly ignored him. Caroline gave the man a small smile.

"We're the same," she said. "I don't suppose it matters."

The meal progressed and the speeches started. Caroline was to her surprise beginning to enjoy herself. She found that she could even forget the funeral from time to time.

It was in the middle of the groom's speech that she felt James's hand touch her knee. She looked at him and smiled. Perhaps this was a mistake as his hand moved up her leg. Too scared to risk his anger and push it away, she simply froze. She was horrified when his fingers pushed in under her panty leg.

"James. Please stop," she whispered.

He bent closer to her and whispered in her ear:

"I want you commando. Go to the ladies' room."

In a daze she left the room, moving behind the folk at their side of the table, oblivious to the fact that the groom was still speaking and that some of the guests were frowning at her.

When she came back her panties were in her handbag.

Almost as soon as she was seated he had his hand up her short, full skirt and within minutes one of his fingers was inside her. She felt herself respond to his touch yet at the same time she was terrified that she would cry out. She almost did but he removed his finger as applause rippled through the room at the end of the speech.

"I see you still want me, Caroline," he whispered to her under cover of the sound. "When the speeches are over and the dancing starts, I'll meet you outside this room and we can finish what I've started."

She hoped that the speeches would never end, wondered if she could make an escape before the dancing started but knew that it would be worse if he had to come after her, look for her.

The bride and groom got up for their first dance and when that was finished and the guests got up to join them, James gave her a nudge. She got up and left the room, waiting outside for him to join her.

"Clever trick of mine moving the place settings," he said as he arrived. "Now where can we go?"

He opened a number of doors then finding what he wanted, he pushed her inside. It was a meeting room with a large table down the centre. James pulled her toward the table and pushed her face down onto it. He quickly lifted her skirt and in a minute it was all over.

She cursed her traitorous body for getting excited once again and he knew, damn him, for he smiled at her before taking her hand and leading her back to the main room where he swept her into a dance.

"You enjoyed that, darling. Didn't you? Let's do it again soon. Don't put your knickers on again."

The evening past in a daze for Caroline. He took her once more, in a store cupboard and she wanted to fight him but her body betrayed her and she found herself enjoying it.

At the end of the evening he drove her home. Surprisingly he did not come in with her but solicitously handed her out of the car, telling her that she had looked lovely and saying he would see her again soon.

Brave now that she was out of the car, Caroline said that she thought that maybe they should stop seeing each other now, not give the police any reason for thinking that they were closer than they had said.

"Caroline, Caroline, have you not learned that I am the one who will say when, if ever, our relationship finishes. I can't make up my mind if I want you, to have you to myself or if I have had enough of you. I know that we have at least one more experience to share but who knows what will happen after that."

He drove off.

Entering the house, Caroline felt uneasy once again. One more experience. She could only think of one other way he could take her and that was definitely not on the cards. Going to bed, she lay into the small hours wondering what to do.

CHAPTER 43

On Sunday, people spent the day in various ways. Caroline Gibson spent a long time in the bath. She had spent most of the night sleepless, trying to think of what the last 'experience' could be that James wanted them to share. As dawn broke she decided that it could only be one thing and she was determined that she would never let that happen. When she had shut the front door last night, the first thing she had done was shower and the second thing was to rip her dress into shreds and set fire to it in the bath. He had not been caring when he chose her outfit; he had merely been dressing her in such a way as to make his lovemaking easy. "Lovemaking," she thought in derision. "Love it certainly was not."

James had gone straight into a dreamless sleep. The next day he had gone to church as he often did. He bought the Sunday papers and spent the afternoon engrossed in them, especially The News of the World from which he gleaned some of his ideas for his sexual exploits.

Charles and Pippa went to Rouken Glen where they fed the ducks and visited the small waterfall which scared Pippa a bit. Being small, the fall seemed quite noisy to her. They had ice cream at the cafe by the pond, sitting outside and enjoying the better weather. They left at about 4pm to go to Charles's sister's where they were having their Sunday meal and at 7 o'clock, Charles drove them both home. Pippa went to bed before 9 o'clock after her bath, having been promised that she could read her Chalet School book for half an hour before lights out.

Penny had spent the morning with her mum then Mrs Price had gone out with Jack her man friend. Penny then went across the city to visit Salma. They often visited each other's houses and it was Salma's turn to be hostess. Penny loved being in Salma's colourful house and thoroughly enjoyed her meal with the family. Being an only child, she loved the busy-ness in Salma's house. This week, Salma's youngest sister had the idea of dressing Penny up in a sari and they had all laughed a lot when Penny tried to walk in it. Mrs Din had been shy of Penny at first but they got on well now.

It was Salma who suggested that maybe one week they could ask Frank to join them, perhaps to see a film or have a meal out. Penny was a bit doubtful but she wanted her two friends to get on together so said that she would suggest it to him next week and they got a newspaper to see if there were any films they would all like. There was one which looked a spy-type film so they opted for that.

Fiona did housework and the weekly wash and spent quite a lot of time thinking of Charles and of how well they got on. She had thought of one female friend who would enjoy a game of bridge and wondered if Charles would think of a male friend or if her friend could bring a partner.

The Fox family woke up late. Neil spent the afternoon cooking the evening meal while his parents watched TV in the lounge.

Fiona Donaldson went to church with her husband and son, then as usual had lunch at the golf club where she and her husband were members. Her teenage son hoped to join soon. Fiona was unaware that being left-handed, she was off the suspect list.

Geena and her flatmate May slept late, did some washing and cleaning then went out to meet friends for the evening at the local pub

The rest of the teachers of Bradford High met with friends and relations to whom they told the story of the double murder at their school and of how they had been interviewed by the police. The pupils also told their friends who were at other schools and basked in the glory of being involved in this exciting event.

One person thought back carefully over all the past events and decided that the police were not going to solve this case.

CHAPTER 44

"So Caroline Gibson and Fiona Donaldson are left-handed and Bert Fox and James Buchanan are right-handed. After what we heard from Martin Jamieson, it seems safe to assume that our murderer or murderers are right-handed as the head of David Gibson who must have been facing his murderer was bashed in on the left side and Irene Campbell who could have had her back to the murderer had her head bashed in on the right hand side. Davenport laughed.

"That sound very convoluted. Do you understand what I'm saying?"

They assured him they did.

"A tennis racket could have been used as a backhand stroke by a left-handed person," said Frank.

"Could the wound have been made by a tennis racket, Sir?" asked Penny.

"I'm sure that that wasn't the weapon used. It's not hard or firm enough. We still need to find the weapon but I think the golf club or the paperweight are our best bet."

"How could the person have got rid of the weapon, Sir? Surely someone would have noticed if they'd seen someone carrying a golf club with blood dripping from it?" said Fiona.

"Yes, unless that person was careful not to be seen at all."

"But a bit risky surely," went on Fiona. "Caroline could have explained away going to see her husband if she'd been seen. Likewise James Buchanan could have said he was arranging a game of something. Fiona could have been seeing him about her timetable or the please takes and Mr Fox could have gone back about his son but add a blood-stained weapon and their visits would not have been easy to explain away."

"I see your point. Well any other ideas?"

"What about putting the weapon out of the window and collecting it later?" said Frank.

"Good idea, Frank," said Davenport.

They looked at him expectantly.

"Back to the school I think. Frank, you and Penny scout around outside David Gibson's window. In fact look outside all those admin windows. You're looking for a disturbance of any sort rather than the weapon we were looking for last time. Salma, find out from Mrs Martin about Irene Campbell's home life. I want to find out if she was happily married or could have been having an affair with Gibson. She was after all the only woman, apart from the very young ones, who said she liked him."

The team were settling into Room 6 when the head teacher came to see them, bearing a golf putter.

"Inspector, this was brought to me by Mary Turner who is the Art PT but who will be acting depute head in place of David for the rest of this term."

"Where did she find it?" asked Davenport.

"She went into David's old room to get things sorted out for Monday, moved a large cupboard and it was lying down the back of it, completely hidden from view."

The team crowded round to look at the putter. It seemed clean.

"Fiona, would you have this taken to Martin Jamieson please. It seems clean enough but it might have been wiped clean by our murderer. It's bad that we missed finding it."

Mrs Martin had turned to go when Davenport called her back to ask if she knew anything about Irene Campbell's husband.

"Might he have discovered that Irene was having an affair with David Gibson and murdered them both?"

"I don't think that's very likely. Irene has been divorced for about six years. He left her for another woman so he hasn't got a motive, has he?"

When she had gone and Fiona had left, Davenport asked Penny and Frank to get moving on their search outside the admin. corridor windows.

"The paperweight is still missing and also look for bloodstains on anything outside especially David's office window."

Left to his own devices, Davenport went into the office and asked if he could see Christine Martin. June Grey phoned through and was told to show the Inspector in and bring some tea or coffee, whatever he preferred.

"I feel it only fair to let you know what we think so far," he said when they were both seated at a low coffee table.

"Thanks, Inspector."

"There could be a homicidal maniac trying to rid the world of teachers but it's unlikely. We've ruled out Mrs Donaldson as we feel sure that the murderer was right -handed and Mrs Donaldson is left -handed as is Mrs Gibson. Geena seems an unlikely candidate but we haven't completely ruled her out yet as she had some free time between 5 pm and 6 pm, as had most of our possible suspects."

"Do you want me to call her in and get her to tell us which hand she normally uses?"

"That would be a help, Thanks."

Christine went into the office and asked June Grey's assistant to get Geena for her and few minutes later Geena knocked on the door and was told to come in.

She looked frightened when she saw Davenport.

"Don't worry Geena. We just want to know one thing. Are you left or right handed?"

"Left handed, Mrs Martin. That's why I wear my watch on my right hand."

She held out her right hand to show them."

"Thanks Geena," said Christine Martin and smiled at the girl. "That's all we wanted to know."

Geena left, looking relieved.

"Who is right-handed, Inspector?" she queried.

"Caroline Gibson's man friend and Mr Fox, Neil's father and probably most of the teaching staff and pupils," laughed Davenport.

"Do you think the same person killed both people?" she asked him.

"I think so but the second one may have been a copycat killing. I wouldn't rule out a pupil for the second one either. Do you know of any pupils who might have wanted rid of Irene Campbell?"

"She was very popular with most of the kids, with the exception of those who didn't like PE like Neil Fox."

"Any other names? Neil struck me as a gentle big lad."

"I could get names from Irene's PT if you like."

When he nodded, she went across to the master timetable on her wall.

"He's got S2 just now."

She looked out of the window which looked onto the red dust tennis courts round which about fourteen young boys were running, supervised by a short, sturdy man in his mid-forties.

"There he is. Let's go out and speak to him now."

Davenport and Mrs Martin walked out of the school and across to the tennis area. Christine beckoned to the teacher and he came over to them.

"The Inspector wants to know of any pupils who might have hated Irene," said Christine.

"Irene! I'm sure no one hated her. The first years started off being scared of her sharp tongue but they all ended up liking her. She's such fun... She *was* such fun."

"No one then?"

"Well apart from Neil Fox who had to take PE and a few others in the Intermediate 1 class, all the upper school take PE because they like it. Irene never mentioned any other names in Neil's class as causing her any trouble."

"Could Neil Fox turn violent, do you think?" asked Davenport.

"No chance I would say. He's a big mummy's boy."

"What about second years?"

"There are a few who hate PE but I've never heard Irene mentioning anyone in particular. We share our S2 classes and there's no one I can think of who would hate Irene enough to kill her."

Davenport thanked him and he went back to his class who were slowing down with no one keeping an eye on them.

Christine Martin and Davenport parted company and Davenport went over to the window through which David Gibson would have looked. Frank and Penny were scrutinising the foliage there.

Frank straightened up when he saw his boss but it was Penny who excitedly called him over.

"Sir, we think there's stain on a leaf here. Look."

Davenport liked Penny. She never stood on ceremony when she was wrapped up in her work. He crouched down and looked at the leaf which she was pointing to.

"Break it off down at the its root, Penny and carry it carefully. I'll have it sent in to the SOC team and see what the stain is. Well spotted you two."

Maybe at last they were getting somewhere.

CHAPTER 45

The 18th of June dawned wet and quite windy. Charles Davenport, lying awake and with some minutes to spare before getting up, thought that the weathermen who had predicted wetter and warmer summers had got it right.

Fiona had asked his permission to go to David's Gibson's funeral and he had given her permission gladly as one of them really had to attend. Caroline, forgetting that she had told Davenport on Friday at the station, had rung him to say it was on Tuesday morning .She had been lucky to get it arranged so quickly but there had been a mix up over dates. A funeral had been booked in twice on the same day, so Caroline had been offered this day and she had jumped at the chance to get it over with. She had contacted everyone she could think of in case they had not seen the death in The Herald on Saturday. David's brother had been shocked as living in the North of England there had been no report in his newspaper of David's murder. After his shock, anger had come at Caroline for not telling him sooner. She had apologised profusely and offered him and his wife a bed for the night before the funeral but he had claimed business commitments that day and said that they would be arriving late so would go to an hotel and come to her house in time to go to the funeral and the following meal then get back down South. She was relieved. His wife was what Caroline had described to David as a "snooty bitch". She asked if David's two nephews would be coming and was told that they would not as they had not known their uncle well enough to disrupt their schooling.

Charles got up and after breakfasting, woke his young daughter. She got up quite happily which was unusual till he remembered that her class was having a trip that day. She reminded him as they drove to her school that she was to be picked up later that night, around 7 o'clock.

Fiona Macdonald rang Caroline that morning quite early. The funeral was at the Linn Crematorium at 10 am and she wanted to know if Caroline was OK. Caroline was quite calm and reminded Fiona that she was invited to the hotel afterwards for an early lunch. Her brother-in-law and sister-in-law were to accompany her to the funeral parlour and then to the crematorium so Fiona decided to go to the station first and then go to the crematorium, missing out the funeral parlour as she knew, from her visit, that it was a small place.

Martin Jamieson had been on the phone to let Davenport know that the golf club was not the murder weapon in either of the cases. The indentation on both corpses' heads had not been as narrow as the putter edge and there had been no trace of blood either. Vince Parker had reported that fingerprints on the handle had been those of David Gibson and no one else. There had been masses of fingerprints on the doors at PE and no blood on the area surrounding the swimming pool.

Davenport summoned his team to the Incident Room and informed them of this,

"I think we're looking now for the missing paperweight," he told them.

"Would that mean that the murder was unpremeditated Sir?" asked Penny.

"Probably, if it is indeed the weapon."

"I can't imagine someone carrying a paperweight about for days in case anyone else needed murdered," said Frank rather facetiously and received a glower from Penny and a severe look from his DCI.

"Watch your tone, young man," said Davenport. "You are however, quite correct. I don't see the paperweight being the second murder weapon..."

"...and Martin Jamieson said the two wounds looked similar," Fiona reminded him.

"We seem to be going round in circles again," bemoaned Davenport.

"Did Parker say anything about the blood on the leaf that was found?" asked Fiona.

"No. He's not had time to test that yet. Says he'll get back to me later this afternoon or tomorrow morning. He has another case on the North side of the city."

"Sir," said Salma who had been looking thoughtful. "Is it likely that the murderer, if it is the same person, would have taken away the paperweight? Would he or she not simply have wiped it clean and left it?"

"You're right. It would be a bit conspicuous to have carried it away especially if it had blood on it. So that means that another weapon was used the second time or else the paper weight wasn't the weapon after all. Or," he added, "one person used the paperweight and another used a different weapon."

"Or the murderer dropped the paperweight or other weapon out of the window," said Penny.

"Martin mentioned that the wounds were similar," Fiona reminded them again.

"If it isn't the paperweight and it isn't the golf club, what could the weapon be?" asked Penny.

"Well there could be a number of things at PE - handles of tennis rackets maybe, hockey sticks, high jump things. You know, the ones they jump over."

Davenport was searching his brain now for weapons.

"But there wouldn't be a hockey stick lying around David's room would there?" queried Frank.

"No but someone could have taken it with them if the murder was premeditated," said the DCI.

"Or someone on the hockey team wanted David Gibson dead. Or someone wanted him dead and went across to PE and borrowed a stick, "said Fiona. "Do we need now to interview some pupils?"

"Well if we're determined that a right-handed person killed both teachers, we're ruling out Fiona Donaldson, Caroline Gibson and Geena Carmichael. That leaves, out of the previous suspects, James Buchanan wanting Caroline for himself or Bert Fox, mad for revenge for the way his son has been treated."

"Or a pupil wanting revenge for some real or imagined bad treatment ?" said Frank.

"Or two pupils, one copying the other," said Salma.

At this point, Davenport, realising that they were getting nowhere, told them to get back to their various rooms, telling them that he would let them know when he heard from Martin Jamieson.

Fiona went back to her room and made herself a coffee before going home to change for the funeral.

Penny, Frank and Salma grouped together round Frank's desk to discuss what had been said.

"Well oh noisy one, Miss Din, what do you think?" asked Frank.

"I think, you who are past your sell-by date, Mr Selby, that it's James Buchanan. I smell a love triangle here," replied Salma.

Happy at seeing them tease each other with no rancour on Frank's part, Penny chipped in :

"Yes. I want it to be him too. He seems from what you said Frank, to be a cool customer and although no one saw him that night, he could easily have gone over to the school after his shopping or later in the evening after Mrs Gibson left his house."

"Do you think she did leave as early as she said?" mused Salma.

"I don't suppose we'll ever know unless she decides to tell us. What about you Frank?" asked Penny. "What do you think?"

"Well Penny Farthing, far be it from me to argue with both of you wise women," said Frank and the three of them moved off to their desks to see if anything else had come in for them. Crime did not stop just because murder had been committed twice.

Fiona arrived at The Linn only to find that the 9.30 funeral had not yet finished. The deceased must have been popular as there were cars parked all the way down the driveway. She could risk going up to the car-park but decided against that and stopped in the road before the gate to wait for the cars to disperse. Thus it was that she tagged on behind the hearse and the funeral car and saw Caroline sitting between her in-laws. They had to wait for the previous funeral car to leave, followed by the cars containing the mourners. Fiona got a space in the car park after this and joined the queue of people waiting to go in. The Linn was on a hill and it was a blustery day so it was a windswept group which eventually filed in. Fiona recognised Christine Martin and Phyllis Watson. Not seeing Stewart Wilson, she imagined that he would be in charge at school. Cathy Campbell was there with another teenager and what looked like his father as they closely resembled each other. The only other teacher was Alex Snedden.

The service was quite short. The 23rd psalm was sung, the minister who obviously did not know David, said a little about the deceased, the committal took place, there was a prayer and the last hymn, The Old Rugged Cross was sung and it was all over. The minister thanked them all for coming and invited them to come to The Busby Hotel and they moved out, shaking hands with Caroline and the other Mr and Mrs Gibson on their way.

Caroline was almost pathetically pleased to see Fiona Macdonald who promised to go for the post funeral lunch. Caroline had been crying. Her eyes were puffy and red. Her hair looked dull.

The man coming behind Fiona was tall and distinguished looking. She had looked round on hearing Caroline saying, "Good of you to come, James."

Fiona noticed that he held her hand for longer than was necessary and that Caroline now looked, if anything, apprehensive rather than upset.

David Gibson was at peace which was more than could said for his wife though no one present could have suspected that her grief was tinged with fear that she no longer had his protection.

CHAPTER 46

About twenty people came to The Busby Hotel for the funeral lunch. Caroline greeted them all warmly but with a lack of enthusiasm for James Buchanan, Fiona noted. He on the other hand kept close to her and managed to sit beside her at one of the tables. Fiona took a seat there too, as did David's brother and sister-in-law. David's brother said a few words of welcome and the staff then brought out plates of sausage rolls and sandwiches accompanied by tea and coffee. Buchanan declined the tea and coffee and got himself another drink from the bar. The first drink had been complimentary. If Buchanan had wanted to monopolise Caroline's attention, he was unlucky as David's brother wanted to know all about the murder. Fiona tried to help Caroline out. She introduced herself to them all and told them that the police were nearer to finding out who had committed this murder and the following one.

More than this she would not say and she turned the conversation to what Caroline was going to do now.

"Will you stay in the same house, Mrs Gibson?" she asked.

Gratefully, Caroline took up this change of subject.

"I think I'll stay for a while but I'll need to get something smaller now that it's just my salary coming in."

"David will have a pension surely from the education authorities," said his brother.

"Probably," replied Caroline. "That's why I'll not make a move right away."

The afternoon wore on and people started to leave. Caroline got up to see them off and then it was just their table left.

James Buchanan who had managed not to say who he was, now offered to take Caroline home. Fiona saw what looked like panic in the widow's eyes and stepped in:

"Actually Sir, I would like to take Mrs Gibson home. There are still some questions I want to ask her."

With that Buchanan had to be content though he looked thunderous, Fiona thought. David's brother and his wife said their goodbyes and Buchanan finally left too, telling Caroline that he would be in touch. He kissed her decorously on the cheek. Was it Fiona's imagination or did Caroline Gibson flinch?

Then it was just the two of them left. Caroline paid the bill.

"Do you want me to come to the station, sergeant or are you coming home with me?" she asked.

"I don't really have anything else to ask you. I just thought you would like to be left on your own."

Caroline's eyes filled with tears and she thanked Fiona warmly.

Fiona took Caroline's hand.

"If you ever want to tell me anything, you know where to find me."

"Well I ......No sergeant there isn't anything but thank you, thank you so much for coming today."

"Come on I'll take you home. You won't have your car with you, have you?"

"No I haven't."

As she got into Fiona's car, Caroline noticed a BMW parked at the end of the street and realised that James must have waited in the hope of catching her alone. She breathed a sigh of relief and determined to ask the sergeant inside for a coffee when they arrived at her home. Surely, if he followed her home, then he would leave on seeing her guest.

By the time Fiona got back to the station it was mid-afternoon, Vince Parker had reported back. The blood on the leaf was indeed that of David Gibson. Charles asked Fiona how the funeral had gone and was very interested in Caroline's reaction to the attentions of James Buchanan.

"I think she's scared of him, Charles."

"How does that fit?"

"Do you think he could be holding something over her?"

"What?"

"Maybe he knows that she didn't go to the cinema that night."

"He would only know if he'd been with her surely and if that's the case why doesn't she come clean. It would give them both an alibi."

"Not now it wouldn't. It would make it seem as if they had committed the murder together," said Fiona.

Talk turned to the blood on the leaf.

"So the murder weapon was put out of the window and the murderer walked down the corridor and out of the school without being seen," said Fiona.

"The only person seen was the head girl, Cathy Cameron. She'd been to see Gibson about her UCAS form. I think she waited at the office window in the hope that he would come out and give her a lift. Schoolgirl crush I think. Then there was the figure she saw leaving."

"Do you think we should see her again?" asked Fiona.

"Yes I do. Take Penny and go to the school now."

"And we know that Mr Fox came back on the Monday. He lied about that and he could have lied again about Tuesday. I think we should see both him and Cathy again."

Charles went to his door and called down the corridor:

"Constable Price, Constable Selby, my room please."

Frank and Penny arrived, looking alert and interested.

"Selby, I want you to go to the Fox house. He should be home after 6 pm. Bring Mr Fox in. Penny, get along to the school with DI Macdonald Ask Mrs Martin if you can have a word with Cathy Cameron the head girl. Mrs Martin might insist on someone else being in on the conversation but she might agree to waive that if there are two of you."

Fiona asked, "Anything special you want us to ask her Sir?"

"Ask her about hockey sticks. Has one gone missing to her knowledge? Ask her again about her wait for Mr Gibson. What made her give up waiting? Has she remembered anything else about the man she saw leaving the school?"?"

"What about the second murder?"

"While you're at it ask if she heard anything at the other end of the corridor. That other girl, Mary did."

When his staff had left, Davenport went along to talk to Salma. He told her where the others had gone.

"Fancy coming with me to see James Buchanan again, Salma?"

"Oh yes, Sir."

Davenport stopped at the desk to say that Mr Fox was to be put in an interview room when he arrived. Frank Selby could be told to go home. Making Mr Fox wait would not hurt.

Would anything come from this fresh lot of questioning?

CHAPTER 47

Later that evening, Charles interviewed Bert Fox. He had been left in the interview room, a cold empty room with only a table and four chairs round it for over an hour and he was nervous and blustering.

"You can't keep me in here. I've done nothing. I'll get my lawyer."

Davenport was all affability.

"Certainly, Mr Fox. Would you like to call him now? Or is it her?"

"I don't need one. I'm innocent. What do you want to know?"

Davenport switched on the tape machine which was a permanent fixture in this room and others like it.

"Tuesday June 18th. 19.16 pm. Present Robert Fox and DCI Davenport.

Mr Fox. When we first interviewed you, you denied having gone to Bradford High School to see David Gibson the deceased. Then you said you went on Monday. I am asking you now, did you return to the school on the following evening?"

"No I didn't. I've already said this."

"The school secretary heard voices coming from Mr Gibson's room. She heard a thump and clatter. I suggest to you that you paid another visit to the school. You had an argument with David Gibson and you hit him with a blunt instrument."

The man was ashen.

"I didn't, honestly. I didn't. I never went back to the school. My wife and my son asked me to leave things alone and I did."

"You have no one to give you an alibi, have you?"

"Surely someone at the pub will remember seeing me?"

"Yes but you could have slipped out. The school is very near your local pub isn't it? And on the second murder night you could have gone into the school before getting your fish suppers, Mr Fox."

If it was possible for the man to go any paler he did.

"That's all for now Mr Fox. Interview finished at 19.32 pm."

Davenport switched off the recorder.

"Go home Mr Fox. Think carefully about what I've said. You know where to find me if you think of anything else to tell me.

Bert Fox stumbled to the door then almost ran down the corridor.

Earlier, Salma had watched as Davenport tried to persuade James Buchanan to tell the truth about his relationship with Caroline Gibson. They were in his room at his chambers.

"He's a lawyer, Salma. He knows I haven't enough on him to bring him in for questioning but maybe he'll let something slip during an unofficial visit."

Davenport was skilful but Buchanan was a match for him.

"Are you sure Sir that your relationship with Mrs Gibson wasn't more than platonic?"

"I had only known her for a short while Inspector. I admit that I'd have liked things to - how shall I say - progress but on the evening in question we were merely getting to know one another over a light supper and some wine."

"You do realise that Mrs Gibson could be a suspect and that you could give her an alibi if you were to admit that she stayed much longer than 8.30?"

"I also realise that we could both be suspects if we had been together longer, Inspector so I would be foolish to lie to give her an alibi wouldn't I?"

Davenport got up to leave. Salma, feeling very daring, asked Buchanan if he would continue to see the widow.

"I may, sergeant. That will be up to Mrs Gibson," he said suavely.

Salma's gut reaction was to disbelieve this man. He was a smooth character but she did not find him attractive. She said as much to her DCI as they drove back to the station.

"I don't like him Sir. He gives me the creeps. Oh he's handsome enough but he's too cool. I wouldn't like to cross him."

Davenport was interested in the female slant towards this man. He felt he had lost out in their clash of words.

Fiona and Penny had found Cathy. They had arrived just before school ended for the day and Christine Martin had agreed to their speaking to her but in her room and with her present.

"Cathy. You said you were with Mr Gibson after school on the night he died," said DI Macdonald.

"Yes. I was."

"For how long?"

"For about ten minutes."

"Did you see anyone in the office when you went past?"

"The secretary was there but I don't think she saw me. She was typing on the computer."

"Was there anyone else along the corridor? The other deputes for example?"

"I don't think so. The doors were closed and if someone was in the doors were usually open."

"That's right," Mrs Martin confirmed. "We have an open door policy so unless an interview is really private, the doors are open when someone is in."

"Now Cathy, you said that you stayed at the office window before leaving. Why was that again?"

Cathy went red.

"I hoped that if Mr Gibson was leaving, he might give me a lift to the crossroads. He's done that a few times."

Mrs Martin looked uncomfortable on hearing this.

"I know that this is embarrassing, Cathy. Did you fancy Mr Gibson?"

"Yes I did. There's nothing wrong with that is there?" she asked defiantly. "Lots of us fancied him."

"Did he give you any encouragement?"

Cathy looked sideways at her head teacher.

"Well the last time I went to see him he said he liked my perfume and said I was a pretty girl. I was a bit taken aback when he came round the desk and put his arm round my shoulder. I might have fancied him but I didn't want to, you know, do anything about it. He was a married man. I was flattered though."

"Yet in spite of this you went back to see him that night on your own?"

"Yes I did," she said defiantly.

"Why?"

"I trusted him. He would never have done anything to harm me."

"And this time what happened?"

"Nothing. We just went over my form."

"How long did you wait at the office window?"

"I don't know. About ten minutes maybe, then I left thinking he might have had work to do."

"And you saw nobody else while you waited?"

"No. Only the janitor in his box and that man I told you about."

"Can you remember anything more about that man? Are you sure it was a man?"

"Pretty sure. No, I can't remember anything else. Sorry."

DI Macdonald nodded to Penny who took over, delighted at being included in the questioning.

"The following Tuesday Cathy, you say you saw Mrs Campbell at the poolside. Tell us again what she was doing."

"She was putting her fingers in the water."

"What did you say to her?"

"I asked if Mary and I could borrow four hockey sticks for a practice the next morning and she said yes. She said to take them now in case she was out of PE when we wanted them."

"Did you see anyone else?"

"Yes a fat boy, from fourth year I think. I don't know his name."

"Did you hear anything from the other end of the corridor?"

"No."

"The other girl did."

"Well I'm sorry. I didn't."

"What happened then?"

"We opened the cupboard where the sticks are kept and took four. I gave Mary two and took two home myself."

Penny had thought of something else.

"Did Mary go in with you to see Mrs Campbell?"

"No she waited outside."

Fiona remembered the other thing Davenport wanted to know.

"Cathy, do you know if any of the hockey sticks went missing recently?"

"Yes, one did. One of the team forgot to bring it in after a Saturday match but she brought it back a few days later."

"Who was it?"

"I don't know. Mrs Campbell just told me it had turned up."

"Thanks Cathy. Can we give you a lift?"

"That would be great."

Cathy went with them down to the crossroads at the traffic lights. She was subdued. She stopped before getting out.

"I hope you get the horrible people who killed my teachers."

"People? I wonder if she's right Penny. If she's wrong and it's one person I hope he or she doesn't kill again."

Fiona and Penny were silent as they drove back to the station.

CHAPTER 48

Martin Jamieson came into the station the next afternoon. Davenport took him into his room and poured him a coffee. Martin told him that Irene Campbell had been killed by the blow to the head, not by drowning.

"Thanks Martin for being so prompt again. So do you think the weapon was the same or similar in both cases?"

"Yes, definitely similar if not the same. It definitely was not the putter. The indentation was bigger in width, not much but definitely bigger."

"What about a hockey stick?"

"Get me one and I will see, though the dent would not be much bigger than the putter would make."

"Then how about a paperweight?" asked Davenport, thinking as he always did, how stilted Martin's perfect English sounded.

"I do not think so - too rounded, not sharp enough to cause the laceration unless it had something sharp on top and was held from underneath."

"We were told that David Gibson had a paperweight in the shape of a curling stone with a handle on it. I don't know its size though."

"Well that is possible but I could not say for sure unless I saw the thing."

Promising to let him have a hockey stick as soon as possible and the paperweight if it ever turned up, Davenport rang Christine Martin .She agreed to him borrowing a hockey stick and he said he would come over to the school to collect it.

He arrived as the bell was ringing to end the first period of the afternoon. The pupils, pushing and shoving each other in the foyer outside the office, stopped when they saw him and looked at him curiously. He saw Cathy Cameron in the distance and this reminded him to ask Christine about her when she, asking June Grey to make coffee, invited him into her room.

"I could do with a stiff whisky, Inspector, probably because Irene was so much more likeable than David, though I shouldn't say that I suppose."

Davenport accepted the cup of coffee from June Grey, agreeing with Christine that a whisky would be more acceptable in the circumstances. He asked about the head girl.

"I had a visit from Douglas Cameron, Cathy's brother," she told him. "He's her guardian as her Mum's been in and out of hospital and her father left home when they were young. Cathy's been having nightmares since the death of David and he asked if she could have counselling."

"Poor girl, she really must have had a crush on him. I suppose you get a lot of that sort of thing in a secondary school, young girls and male teachers."

"Yes and also older boys and young female teachers," she said.

Coffee cups drained, the two made their way over to PE. The PE Principal, when asked for a hockey stick, opened the door to Irene's staffroom and, pointing to a large cupboard, invited them to take whichever hockey stick they wanted.

Davenport counted them and asked if they were all there.

"Normally I couldn't have told you but Irene was so annoyed that one was missing last week and told me that she needed twenty-two for the primaries. She had to take one from my end of the department where I keep all the unused equipment. She got the missing one back, anonymously, so there should be twenty-two."

There had been that number when he had counted them, so if a hockey stick was indeed the murder weapon, then the weapon was in front of him. Davenport made up his mind to get one of the SOC team to the school to test all these

327

sticks although most looked very clean to him. He commented on this to the PE teacher.

"Oh, Irene would clean them I imagine after each match, either here or at the opposing school if there was a handy tap there. Don't think Cathy and her chums cleaned theirs though."

He pointed to some dirty ones.

Asked why Cathy and Mary had wanted some sticks for a practice, he told them that the first eleven had been determined to win their last match as they had a chance of winning the tournament and later on, after the murder they wanted to win it for Mrs Campbell.

"One of the English staff offered to go with them last Saturday and they did win," he added.

Davenport used his mobile to contact the SOC team and getting a time from them, he passed this on to both Christine and her head of PE.

There being nothing else for him to do at PE, he went over to the main building, to Room 6 where his staff were finishing up for the day. He told them about his conversation with Martin Jamieson and about having the hockey sticks checked. They in turn told him that nothing had happened that afternoon at school. No one had come to them with any information.

Back at the station, Davenport rang Soloman Fairchild on the top floor and was horrified to learn that Grant Knox had returned from a conference in London and wanted to see him.

"I told him you were at the school, Charles and he said he would wait until you returned. I told him about the second murder and naturally he's a bit...upset."

Knowing that Solomon would not denigrate his boss, Charles read between the lines and realised that Knox was probably furious that the first murder had not been solved and now another one had taken place. Realising that he would probably be late picking Pippa up at school, he rang his sister and asked her to go for Pippa and take her home with her.

He took the elevator to the top floor. He was not kept waiting but was told by the secretary to go straight in.

As usual, Knox did not ask him to sit and immediately launched into a tirade about incompetence and the unsolved murder.

"I go away for a few days and everything collapses. Fairchild told me everything was under control. Silly old fool. He should have retired years ago."

Davenport despised him for his disloyalty to his assistant but remained silent.

"So, who's in the frame for murder one and is it the same person who committed murder two?"

"I can't tell you that Sir but we think it's likely to be the same person."

"Likely!"

His ruddy face grew redder and he glared at Davenport.

"What do you want me to tell the press? That there's a teacher-killer roaming about and the police are baffled?"

"Could you not just tell them that investigations are on-going, Sir?"

"Trying to teach me my job, man?"

His voice rose. There was a knock on the door. He shouted, "Come in!" and Davenport was pleased to see Solomon entering.

"Sir, the men from the press are here, downstairs."

"Right, Solomon. You see them. You're good at platitudes. I've got an important dinner tonight with the Lord Provost. I'll see you again Davenport, next week. You'd better have some good news for me. Oh and no weekends off from now on for you or your team."

He rose from his desk and swept out of the room leaving Fairchild and Davenport looking after him.

CHAPTER 49

In the English department, Peter and Jan were discussing their new classes. They had taken their existing third year into fourth now that the timetables had changed. These classes were mixed ability ones for everyone except Alex who had the high fliers. Jan liked her class, though she had some really poor ability pupils. She was talking now about Neil Fox.

"Peter, do you have anyone in your new fourth year who gets grades 5 and 6?" Peter, who rarely assessed work except the specimen pieces for exam folders, said he did not have any really poor pupils.

"Neil Fox is so poor. He can't even manage a letter. I mean who writes, 'Yours sincerely' to a friend? And he has no imagination," said Jan.

"What about your fifth year higher class? Are they very bright?"

"Yes apart from the sixth year repeats. All of them except Cathy Cameron and Mary Baker who are trying for an A pass this time as they don't think they got that this time, are quite poor.

Peter knew Cathy from the admiring glances she gave him when they passed in the corridor.

"What's that girl Cathy, the head girl, like?"

"Well she's been off a couple of days recently but from what I've seen of her she thinks quite highly of herself. She doesn't seem to have any real girlfriends but the boys like her."

"I've got a boy like that. The girls all rush to sit beside him but the boys give him a body swerve," replied Peter.

The bell rang and they both went to their respective classrooms. It was time for their new fourth year. Jan handed back their friendly letters. She had graded them last night. She complimented some of her class, mainly girls, who had written full, interesting letters. When she came to Neil at the front, she tried to keep her voice low.

"Neil, this is awful son. It was to be a friendly letter telling your pal what you were going to be doing this summer, not a business letter. This wouldn't be worth putting a stamp on."

"Miss," said the boy behind who must have been listening very closely, "He doesn't have any friends, do you Foxy Face?"

Neil flushed an unbecoming shade of red. Jan told the other boy off for making comments, telling him that his letter had not been wonderful so he had no room to talk but the damage had been done and once again Neil Fox had been ridiculed by his peers.

Jan continued the lesson by reading some excerpts from the first chapter of "Of Mice and Men" which she had asked them to read at home last night. Lennie, big and not bright, was a character well-loved by his readers.

As the class filed out at the end of the lesson, Jan did not hear some of the boys chanting "Lennie Fox, Lennie Fox" at Neil as he left the room, shoulders hunched. Not even the thought of HE next period cheered him up.

Jan welcomed her higher class next. She had begun some relationship poetry and today was reading a poem called, 'Unto Us' which dealt with an abortion.

The atmosphere was hushed until it was spoiled by Cathy Cameron asking, "Miss. Have you ever had a baby?"

"No I haven't Cathy. I'm a Miss, not a Mrs."

"That needn't stop you Miss."

Cathy, annoyed at having a female teacher this year, was ready to annoy this young one and she looked round expectantly for someone to chip in with something funny. She was disappointed. All she met were frosty stares. Some of the girls had been almost in tears at the poem and the boys appreciated Jan thinking them old enough to discuss relationships, sex, marriage and abortion. Cathy had missed two of the best poems when she had been absent and had misjudged her fellow pupils this time.

Jan frowned.

"Cathy. You're sixth year now. You should be past the childish comments I think."

Cathy fumed and some of the girls smiled at each other. Only Mary felt sorry for Cathy. She too needed an A pass in English. She found English difficult being a science and maths person. She threw a sympathetic look in Cathy's direction but Cathy, mistaking it for a grin, thought that even Mary was against her here.

The lesson progressed with Jan starting them off on a Discursive Essay on the pros and cons of abortion. They would continue this at home, do a rough draft then be given a set time to do the final copy in class next week.

Some of the class had had Peter last year and were aghast at the pace of work expected from them by Jan in the dying weeks of this term. As they left the room, they grumbled a bit and Cathy, sensing that they maybe were not all in favour of the young teacher, decided to get them onside for some disruption during future periods.

Neil Fox, over in HE was still downcast over his teasing in English. Like Cathy, he blamed the teacher for his treatment.

Next door to Jan, Angus had kept back three boys who had disrupted his class. He had the Intermediate 1 class and most of these fifth years were not in the least interested in passing their exam next May. These three were hoping to leave at Christmas and wanted to have fun with this teacher who was so easy to rile.

One of them had had Angus last year and had shouted out:

"Where's your guitar Sir. Give us a tune."

"It's broken."

"Sing to us then Sir."

"Yes. Give us a song."

"La La La," trilled yet another.

Angus had told them to wait after class and was now attempting to give them a punishment exercise.

"Oh Sir, a punishment exercise."

"Ooh! Scary!"

As Peter and Jan came out of their rooms, Angus lifted his hand and Jan once again stepped in. The boy, who had had Jan the precious year and respected her, fell silent. Angus handed out the exercises and the boys ran off. Angus, feeling stupid at having been helped by this slip of a girl again and in front of Peter this time, asked her not to interfere again.

Jan, saying nothing, went off, leaving Peter and Angus to go downstairs together.

At Shawbank Police Station, Davenport had just received a call from one of the SOC team telling him that there had been nothing found on the hockey sticks. Feeling as if they were getting nowhere fast, he called in DI Macdonald.

"No blood on the hockey sticks, Fiona. They all looked clean to me when I saw them today but there was a chance I suppose."

"Surely any blood on one would have gone after washing. The club heads are smooth, no cracks for blood to seep into and if it was one used recently, well mud wouldn't help either."

"No paperweight either. Wonder if the murderer took it home. If we had a definite suspect we could get a warrant and search the house."

Davenport sounded despondent.

Fiona reminded him that they had a bridge game that evening. They had found another couple to play against as one of Fiona's friends played in another foursome and she had agreed to bring her partner.

"Well let's hope the fates deal us better hands than they have in our murder cases," laughed Charles.

Fiona liked that in him, the fact that he never stayed sombre for long.

"Oh, I meant to tell you, Fiona, Christine Martin invited us to attend prize-giving tomorrow evening. Are you free? It might be interesting to see some of our characters. She said that Cathy and Neil and Mary were getting prizes."

"Yes. I'm free."

Fiona adopted a camp pose as she used the line from 'Are You being Served?'

"Well I'll see you tonight then. Come earlier and we can squeeze in a quick drink together before the serious stuff."

On that note, Fiona left to collect her raincoat and Charles sat back to reread his notes on the hockey sticks and add the recent finding on them.

CHAPTER 50

Fiona went early that night to Charles's house in Newton Mearns. She had been before and liked where he lived.

He met her at the door, apologising for the weeds in his path.

"I never seem to get time for gardening," he grumbled.

Pippa, beside him, said cheekily:

"Daddy, you had plenty of time last weekend but you said that we so rarely got sun you were going to sit in the garden, not work in it."

"Minx! It's time you were helping your old Dad with the garden."

Laughing at them both, Fiona was led into the lounge where a gin and tonic was waiting on a small table near one of the armchairs.

"Hope I was right. Did you bring your car?"

"Yes but I think one drink is allowed, Mr Policeman."

"It sure is. Anyway if you decide to drink any more you can always get a taxi home."

Charles thought how pretty she looked. She was not beautiful, being a bit on the plump side but attractively dressed in a white pleated skirt with a bright yellow top, she was vivacious and her smile made him wish that he was alone in the house and could persuade her to stay overnight.

"Would she stay?" he wondered.

He had heard on the police grapevine about her abortive romance with an inspector at her last branch and wondered if she would be wary of setting out on another one, with another inspector.

However asking her to stay was not an option with Pippa here. Charles shelved his thoughts and realised that once again Pippa had homed in on an interested Fiona about her Chalet School books.

"Are you doing any more talks this year?" Fiona was asking, remembering that last school session, Pippa had talked twice on her books.

"We're doing group talks mostly this year," replied Pippa. "The teacher gives us a subject - a topic she calls it, and we sit and talk about it in groups of four. One of us is the chairperson and one takes notes and we all have to talk as much as possible - and listen too of course," she added.

"Did you tell Fiona that the new teacher you'll be getting next year is very old, Pippa?" Davenport teased her.

Seriously, the little girl said that her teacher was probably as old as her daddy was.

Fiona chortled at that and Charles retorted that she need not laugh as she was even older.

At that moment the bell rang and Charles let in their two opponents. Fiona introduced them to Charles and they shook hands. John was a stocky, fair-haired man in his late thirties and Kim was his opposite, being tall and dark and in her forties.

Thinking that Pippa might have finished, 'The Chalet School and Rosalie', Fiona had brought the next book in the series, 'Three Go to The Chalet School' and she handed it over.

"Oh, which three are starting the school? This'll be good. Thanks Fiona. I've only got one chapter left of the other one. Daddy wouldn't let me finish it last night."

Charles chased her off to her own bedroom, asking her if she would put the oven on for him at 9 o'clock.

"I've set it pet. Just put the kettle on at the same time."

He got drinks for the other two. John asked for a beer and Kim for gin and tonic, the same as Fiona.

For the first half hour, they sat and chatted. Kim was a secretary in a law firm and John was in the same church as Kim. Kim chatted away about her job though John was quite reticent about his work in the civil service.

"It's a boring job so I don't talk about it much," he said.

They moved over to the card table which Charles had placed in the centre of the room and the play began.

At 9.20 Charles who was dummy, went into the kitchen. The pizza which he had put into the oven earlier was almost ready to eat, as were the sausage rolls. He flicked on the switch of the kettle as it had gone off the boil and got out plates ready for the food.

"Charles. I've finished," called Fiona.

Looking flushed with pleasure, she told him that she had managed that rare thing, a grand slam.

"One more round then supper," said Charles, congratulating her.

This time it was Fiona who was dummy. She asked if she could do anything and Charles said she could put the food out on the plates and put boiling water into the teapot. "Does anyone prefer coffee?" he asked but they said they were happy with tea.

Charles went down one trick this time, and the other team scored a hundred points. They moved over to the settee and chairs to have supper. Charles called Pippa through. She was delighted to have been allowed to stay up late to help and have supper with the grown-ups and promised to go straight to bed after her slice of pizza.

The rest of the night passed enjoyably. Charles and Fiona in spite of their grand slam had lost but not by much and as they left, John and Kim suggested another game in about two weeks' time.

"Let's hope that our double murder case is solved by then," Davenport sighed.

They talked about the case for a little while. Unknown to her, Fiona thought the same as Salma and Penny. She thought that the murderer was James Buchanan. He could have killed David and noticed that he had been seen entering the school by Irene Campbell. Davenport thought that Bert Fox was the most likely candidate but wasn't ruling out Caroline and James together for the first killing and James for the second murder. Fiona agreed that Caroline seemed very nervous. Maybe the second killing had brought home to her the enormity of what they had done.

"What about Cathy Cameron? She had access to the hockey sticks. Wish we could find out who brought the late one back," said Charles.

Fiona could not believe that a teenager could commit a double murder but Charles reminded her of famous cases where a young person had been responsible for a terrible crime.

Fiona had had two more drinks so Charles phoned for a taxi and she agreed that she would come over the next morning before work to collect her car.

"I'll pay for this taxi," Charles insisted. "You can get the morning one. We're both to blame. I shouldn't have encouraged you to have another two drinks and you shouldn't have let yourself be persuaded!"

Laughingly she agreed and they went out to the taxi arm in arm.

CHAPTER 51

The only member of the police team to visit the school during the day on Friday was Davenport who wanted to ask a few questions about hockey sticks. Aware that they had taken up a lot of Christine Martin's time recently, though through no fault of their own, he telephoned first. June Grey put him through to Christine who was quick to reassure him that she understood his need to be at the school, questioning and interviewing. It would be fine for him to come again today. She would be free after 11 am.

Promptly at 11 o'clock, he arrived at the office window and knocked. June Grey's pleasant face looked out and she invited him in. She rang through to her boss and soon, Davenport was once again seated at the coffee table holding a cup of tea.

"Why all the interest in hockey sticks, Inspector?" Christine asked.

"Well, the golf club we, or rather your teacher, found in David's old room doesn't match the laceration on the head of either David or Irene, so we're looking for a weapon still. We thought about PE and what could be over there that could have been used and we came up with a hockey stick though there's a paper weight missing from David's desk too and it might have been used for the first murder. It's not really feasible to imagine someone carrying that about with them till the second murder."

"Why would someone have a hockey stick with them on the first occasion?"

"A premeditated murder, perhaps. Someone went into David's room with the purpose of killing him and took a stick with them or someone happened to have a hockey stick with them and David riled them so much that they used it. Or it was never a hockey stick."

"Cathy Cameron might have had a stick. No wait a minute, Irene asked her to find a missing stick but Cathy was off sick for the next two days and the stick just reappeared so it couldn't have been her. Did you ask the janitor if she had a hockey stick when he saw her?

"No but we think the stick or weapon was dropped out of the window because there was blood found on a leaf there and the blood matched David's so if it was Cathy she wouldn't have had the stick with her."

"When did the person retrieve the weapon from outside David's window then?"

"No idea. It would have to be cleaned too. Who else might have access to a hockey stick?"

"Well, the two hockey teams would and no one would pay attention to any girl or boy for that matter carrying a stick, especially as I'd tannoyed for one to be returned to PE. I don't suppose anyone would really notice a member of staff carrying one either."

She told him about Irene missing one stick for the primary school she was visiting on the Wednesday after the murder and he recalled Fiona telling him this.

Rising to his feet, he thanked her for his tea and before leaving thanked her too for the invitation to prize giving.

"My DI and I will come. It'll be interesting to see some of your pupils."

Back at the station, Frank was sitting at the computer when he was approached by Salma and Penny.

"Whoa! A deputation. Should I be scared?" he laughed.

"Salma and I wondered if you'd like to come to the pictures with us tomorrow night," said Penny.

Frank was taken aback. He knew that the two girls were now firm friends but had not thought that they would ever include him.

"That would be great. Will we eat out somewhere first? Make a special night of it? Where were you thinking of going?"

"To the Grosvenor in Ashton Lane in the West End," said Salma. "Penny and I've been going there quite often. You can even get a drink to take in."

"But you don't drink. Paki......Pakistanis don't drink."

Penny smiled. "I thought that too. I've learned a lot since meeting Salma."

"What's on?"

" 'White Fear'. It's a thriller with Brad Pitt."

"Well what about eating across the lane in that wee Italian place up the stairs first?"

They agreed to do just that. Salma would make her own way across town and Frank would take the bus with Penny from the South Side.

Frank was feeling happy and when the DI and DCI walked past the room they were talking in, he started whistling, 'Speed Bonny Boat' as his signal that he thought that Macdonald and Davenport were getting fond of each other.

Davenport stopped in his tracks and came into the room.

"Frank, that tune you've been singing reminded me. We've been sent two tickets for a Scottish Night at the church down the road from us here. You seem to like all things Scottish so you can go. It's not my cup of tea. Take someone with you. It's in the middle of July."

So saying, he turned on his heel and went off to his room leaving Frank open-mouthed and speechless.

Penny exploded with mirth and started doing a Highland Fling. Salma had a fit of the giggles. Then Frank saw the funny side of it too. He grabbed Penny and they started doing the Gay Gordons. Davenport hearing the mirth and revelry wished he could forget so readily the pressure they were under right now.

At about 6.45, Charles picked up Fiona. He had Pippa with him. She had declared herself interested in the prize giving as she would soon be going up to the 'big school' as he called it and he had let her come, warning her that she would have to sit still for quite a long time. At least it meant he did not have to ask his sister to baby-sit.

When they arrived, the hall was still quite empty so they got seats reasonably near the front.

Just after 7.30 the platform party filed onto the stage. Alex Snedden, resplendent in his academic gown, came on first and took a seat behind a table laden with books and cups.

There followed six people. Davenport and Fiona recognised Phyllis Watson and Stewart Wilson and rightly supposed that the other woman in academic gown was the new DHT Mary Turner. Christine Martin looked every inch the head teacher tonight, hair newly done, academic gown and her brightly coloured hood making her stand out among the others. The other two people, one on either side of Christine must be the speaker and his wife who would present the prizes. Mary Turner looked self-conscious and bit pink cheeked. She was not used to being so formally dressed.

The noise hushed as Christine rose and went to the microphone.

"This is a very special occasion for some of our pupils. It has been rather overshadowed by the unfortunate deaths recently of two of our teachers. I am not going to comment on that tonight. Tonight is for the boys and girls who have done so well this year. I now hand you over to Mr Wilson who is our MC for this evening. Mr Wilson."

Stewart announced that the choir would sing two songs and they stood up from the front seats where they had been sitting and sang heartily. Most of them were from S1 and S2, with a sprinkling of older pupils. This was followed by a few pieces from the brass instrument players - six of them plus their instructor.

Christine Martin was called on to give her review of the year. She did not touch on the events of the last few weeks but kept to matters of school importance, sporting successes and school trips featuring large.

"I would especially like to congratulate our first eleven hockey team who won the South

Side Schools' tournament and thanks too to Miss Stevenson who accompanied them to their last match, an example of Bradford staff rising to the occasion once again."

She took some time to relay the exam results which had come in at the end of August of the last year then she sat down and Stewart announced that the prize giving would now take place.

There were prizes for attainment and prizes for endeavour and prizes for sport. All the sports' prizes were handed out first then subject prizes starting with S1 and S2. Davenport noticed that Neil was standing at the edge of the stage and his name was called. He had won first prize for his third year HE. Someone in front of Fiona and Charles sniggered but not loudly and it was drowned in the applause from parents and the other prize-winners. Charles, looking to his right, saw Mr & Mrs Fox in the row behind looking proud.

Soon it was the turn of the fifth year. Their prizes were awarded on the strength of their prelim exams. Mary won for chemistry, physics and maths, Cathy for history. Finally there were only two large cups left. Stewart Wilson announced that the prizes for Citizenship went to the head boy, Gavin Smith and the head girl Cathy Cameron. The younger pupils clapped loudly for the two big pupils. The speaker kept his speech short and light. His wife graciously accepted a bouquet of flowers and it was all over.

On the way out of the hall, Davenport noticed Christine Martin standing with a young man. He went over to congratulate her and she introduced him to Cathy's brother. Davenport said that he must be proud of his young sister.

Douglas Cameron said that he was, very proud, especially as Cathy had not had a very good time at home recently with her Mum being in hospital.

At that point Christine invited Cathy and her brother to tea and cakes in the area outside the office and turning to Charles and Fiona asked if they would like to join the parents and prize-winners for refreshments. They declined, Davenport saying that as they had Pippa with them they would just get along home.

"I like the way they reward those who try as well as those who achieve," said Fiona as they drove to her flat.

"Is that what endeavour means, Fiona?" asked Pippa.

"Yes."

Knowing that Charles would want to get Pippa back home to bed, Fiona did not invite them up to her flat. They stopped in the middle of the street, finding no parking space as usual and Fiona got out, thanking him for taking her.

"Bye Pippa."

"Bye Fiona."

"Have a relaxing weekend Fiona."

"You too, Charles. Our last one for some time I expect, now that Mr Knox is back."

Charles grimaced.

"No doubt I'll be in trouble if he finds out that we've taken this weekend off."

CHAPTER 52

On Saturday morning, Charles took Pippa into East Kilbride shopping centre. She needed some new weekend clothes. Previously he had asked his sister to shop for these but he thought that Pippa at nearly ten was getting old enough now to choose her own clothes with a little help. Her mother bought her things when she went to stay with her down South during the holidays but she was growing fast and had already outgrown some of the things bought at Easter.

His daughter turned out to have expensive tastes. He had taken her into M and Co but she preferred the clothes in Next where they bought her new denims and two colourful tops. Marks and Spencer provided the new navy blue skirt for school and two more white blouses.

After that they went on a fruitless search in Waterstones for Chalet School books. Apparently they were not popular any more but the assistant said she could order some for them. Charles knew that Fiona would lend these books to Pippa but he also knew that his daughter was a saver of books as she had the whole set of Beatrix Potter and the whole set of the Mr Men books so he asked the girl to order six more. Pippa had their titles and numbers from the inside cover of her last one which was a more up to date version than the one Fiona had lent her the other night.

That done, they decided to have something to eat. There were many places to choose from but Pippa chose the muffin shop so they each had coke and a muffin. It was about 4 pm by the time they got home and Charles was glad that he was not going out that evening. He was tired.

At five o'clock, Pippa's friend Hazel rang. The girls spoke for some time then Pippa came through to ask if Hazel could come for a sleep-over that night. As Pippa had been at Hazel's some weeks ago, Charles knew it was her turn to play the hostess, so he said yes. At least it would give him a chance to please himself what he did in the evening.

Fiona had spent the day cleaning, washing and ironing. She sang as she worked. The case was causing problems but she was happy in spite of this. She liked the people she worked with and felt that she and Charles were getting along really well. It was a sunny day so after her domestic chores, she went for a walk in Newlands Park. Some people were playing tennis so she sat down to watch them, enjoying the sun on her arms. The sun made her think of the conversation she had had with Charles about holidays in the sun and she wondered if perhaps next summer they might go away, the three of them. She liked Pippa who was a clever, happy child. She was not fond of babies and had always preferred teenagers but Pippa was so easy to like.

On the way home she popped in for a DVD. She would be extravagant and send out for a Chinese meal later and watch the film while eating. Suddenly she was tired.

Salma met Penny and Frank at the foot of the stairs to the restaurant. They had their meal then they went across to The Grosvenor cinema. They went into the bar and Frank was amazed when Salma asked for a half pint shandy. He and Penny had spirits as they had no car to drive home. They took their drinks in their plastic tumblers into the cinema and settled down into the comfortable seats. Frank had not been here before and fancied coming back and trying out the sofas at the back. They all enjoyed the film and Frank thanked the girls for inviting him. He had enjoyed Penny's company as he had known he would but what surprised him was that he had also enjoyed being with Salma and had not once thought about being seen in the company of what he had always called a 'coloured person' until Penny had nagged him out of the habit.

Penny had some news for them, especially for Salma who knew her Mum. She told them that Mrs Price was going to marry her man friend Jack the following spring. They would live in Jack's house and Penny was to be offered the house they now lived in for half the selling price or the monetary equivalent. She was delighted for her Mum and she liked Jack. She had almost decided to put down a big deposit on a flat in Shawlands and use some of the money to go on a really good holiday the following summer. She asked Salma if she would think about coming with her.

Frank looked crest-fallen and Penny noticed that. Maybe if he and Salma continued to get along well, she would ask him to come along too.

Caroline Gibson, like Fiona Macdonald, had spent some time cleaning her house. She washed her hair afterwards and had a shower. She could not face her usual routine of going into Glasgow shopping - it seemed wrong to be enjoying herself with David dead. Also she would have to be more careful with money now. Funnily enough this did not bother her. After a life of selfish pleasure, she felt ready to settle down and wished so much that she could have felt like this when David was alive. They could have had a family. How she wished that they had had a child. She would have liked a part of David with her now.

Later in the day she began the sad task of sorting out David's clothes. There was a church in the vicinity which had a Nearly New sale every Wednesday. She would take the clothes there.

In the evening she rang Jane whom she knew was coming home that afternoon. Jane was indeed home and promised to come round the next evening.

The Fox family went to Silverburn. They always went shopping together on Saturdays and Neil enjoyed it as long as he was sure he would not meet any classmates who might tease him about being with his parents. Silverburn was not so likely to attract those who had no cars in the family and a lot of his classmates played football on Saturdays.

They went first into the massive Tesco and bought their week's supply of food. It was easy to see by their size that they ate a lot. Mrs Fox tried to buy sensibly but the salad items and fruit often rotted away unused, her menfolk preferring to tuck into hamburgers and fries, biscuits and cakes. She too had a sweet tooth and the trolley was full of confectionery items by the time they had reached the check-out.

They took the groceries to the car and filled the boot, then went back inside the shopping centre. Like Davenport and Pippa, they had lunch out and went home about three o'clock. An Indian take-away was their Saturday night treat and Bert Fox went out to collect it. Briefly he thought about the night he had gone out for fish and chips, the night when Mrs Campbell had died. Once again he was near the school and once again he met no one he knew.

James Buchanan played golf at his prestigious golf club near Bearsden. He was competitive and did not like to lose. He seldom did lose. This week his playing partner was a fellow lawyer, one Tom Kennedy who was also a member of this club. Tom was much less determined to win and did not mind when he lost eight up with six to play. They had lunch in the clubhouse, washed down with pints of beer. Tom was in the middle of an important lawsuit and happily chatted away about it while they ate.

James would have liked to discuss the Gibson murder with someone but wanted to keep his name out of it if possible so decided not to. He would have another chat with Caroline soon: make her see that it was in her own interests to keep to their story.

The staff of the school spent their free Saturday in various ways, playing sport, visiting relatives, lazing in front of the TV. Fiona and her family drove to Lomond Shores for the afternoon, Geena and her flatmate painted the kitchen and cleaned out the kitchen cupboards. Alex went fishing with his young son; Peter stayed in bed till three, then went out drinking in the evening. Jan had a driving lesson and went to the theatre with friends at night. Angus took his wife to visit her mother in a nursing home and went to a fiddlers' rally in the evening. Christine Martin and her husband drove through to Edinburgh to visit friends and stayed the night. Stewart and Phyllis were very busy with their young families, enjoying spending time with them.

The pupils did similar things. Mary visited her grandma in the afternoon and had a friend round in the evening. Cathy stayed in her room all evening playing CDs. She had visited her Mum in hospital during the afternoon. There was talk of her getting home the following week. In the morning she had risen late and had a late breakfast with her brother. They were very close though there was eleven years between them.

School was forgotten: two dead teachers were, for a while, forgotten too.

CHAPTER 53

It was communion at Newlands Church, a wealthy church on Glasgow's South side. James Buchanan was handing out wine to the right hand side of the congregation. He looked, as always, suave and smart and the older ladies in the congregation thought very highly of this young man who was always so polite and attentive to them. He paused now to smile at one of the younger women whose toes curled as she smiled back, thinking how handsome he was.

During the sermon his mind had been on other, more worldly things, such as what to do about Caroline Gibson. Should he finish with her now that she had lost her feistiness or should he continue his relationship? He had liked her independence and her nonchalance about her husband while knowing that he would never let her treat him like that. She was scared of him now which was a pity. As he had told her, he had one more experience for them to share but he was concerned that now that she had nothing to lose, she might not mind people knowing about them. This was why he always had affairs with married women as they needed to keep him a secret from their husbands so he could get away with treating them the way he did.

The last hymn was being sung when he made up his mind.

At the door he congratulated the minister on his erudite sermon and waited outside till his elderly mother came out. He always took her to church with him and knew that folk thought him an excellent son. She felt the same. She adored him.

He settled her in the car and asked her where she wanted to have lunch. He was delighted when she chose his golf club as although he would have to listen to her idle chat for a long journey, once at the club, he could leave her to go and talk to fellow players and the time would pass quite quickly.

As it often did, her conversation turned to him.

"James, Mrs Gillen was asking me why you had never married. Really dear, you would make such a good husband and father. Is there no one on the horizon?"

"Well, mother I am seeing someone at the moment. She's a widow with no children."

His mother was delighted and would never know that he had only told her this to keep her quiet.

Back at home, later in the afternoon he found himself wondering if indeed he should marry Caroline Gibson. She was beautiful, sexy and now malleable. Maybe it was time he had children and he need not be faithful to her. He could still have other women. If she knew what was good for her she would not complain.

Caroline had spent the day sorting out more of David's clothes. It brought tears to her eyes remembering how she had chosen them for him and how grateful he had been. Imagine James letting a woman choose his clothes! She thought about him now. She would not see him again and if he tried to force himself on her she would go to the police.

She stopped in the middle of the day and made herself a light lunch, then rang Jane to see when she was coming round. Jane said in the early evening. She had photographs to show Caroline and she wanted to know the up to date news of James.

Caroline went for a jog later in the afternoon once she had finished her clothes' sorting. Once again she missed David as they had usually accompanied each other on their runs. James was very fit looking and she wondered if he had membership of a gym or whether like David he played golf or perhaps squash. She realised as she ran, that she knew almost nothing about

James and vowed again not to wait around long enough to find out any more. What she did know, she did not like, although in all honesty she had to admit that he excited as well as frightened her. She wavered as she ran, wondering if perhaps she should continue seeing him. Maybe now that he could take time with her and did not have to snatch secret meetings, he might be kinder and more fun to be with. She would ask Jane what she thought as she was an impartial bystander.

Jogging into her road, she was looking forward to a hot bath and her evening with her friend. She did not recognise the BMW which was parked under the trees some way along the street.

The bell rang as she was towelling herself dry and without thinking she wrapped herself in a large fluffy towel and went to the door.

"Hello darling. Have I come at a bad time?"

James had waited just long enough for her to shower and knew exactly in what state he would find her. He was standing holding a large bunch of flowers.

Caroline clutched the towel tightly to her.

"As you can see, I've just showered. You've come at a really awkward time."

"Never mind. Show me into the lounge and I'll wait while you get dressed."

He sounded so unthreatening that she did what he asked, leaving him in her lounge and going upstairs to dress.

When she came back down, he was leafing through the Sunday Observer.

"Do you read this, Caroline?"

She sat down across from him.

"Didn't have you down as an Observer reader, Caroline."

"Why you should think I'm not I don't know," said Caroline offended. "I haven't cancelled David's paper if you must know."

"Well, I imagine that David was the brains of the family," he retorted. "Where's your Sunday Post?"

She decided to ignore that remark and he was pleased to see that some of her fighting spirit was back.

"Why are you here, James?"

"Can't an old friend come to see you in your hour of need?"

He crossed over to her chair and perched on the arm, putting an arm round her.

She stiffened.

"Don't even think of it, James. My friend Jane is coming shortly."

"How do I know that's true, darling?"

His hand was travelling towards the neck of her blouse when the doorbell rang and gratefully she pushed his hand away and got up to answer the door.

It was Jane. Caroline had never been so glad to see her friend.

"Jane. This is James. Do you remember him from your party?"

"Yes I do. One of my male friends brought you along, didn't he James? I believe you know Mark my boyfriend too."

"Hello Jane. Good party, especially since I met Caroline there. I'm pleased to meet you again."

James gave her a pleasant smile. He proceeded to be charming to both women and reminded Caroline that she needed to put her flowers in water.

When she went out to the kitchen, he started talking about her.

"Caroline's going through a really bad time right now, Jane. We both need to be around for her, take her out, and not leave her on her own."

Jane agreed, thinking how mistaken Mark must have been. This man was delightful, so caring and so, so handsome.

When Caroline came back in carrying the flowers, James rose saying that now that Jane was there he would get on home. He gave Caroline a chaste kiss on the cheek and when she followed him to the door, he said that he would see her again soon.

As soon as she came back into the lounge, Jane started eulogising about James.

"Oh Caroline, he's wonderful, so kind and considerate and what beautiful flowers!"

"Oh Jane, you don't know him."

Caroline went on to tell her friend what had happened at the wedding but she knew that Jane had been reeled in when she said that she wished that Mark was a bit more adventurous. He would only make love in bed and how boring was that!

In vain Caroline tried to show her friend how scared she was of James. Jane thought she was lucky and as the evening went on Caroline started to forget the bad parts of their meetings. It was nice to be going out with someone your friend found attractive and good to know that Jane envied her.

Jane showed her photographs of her holiday in Ibiza. She left at about eleven o'clock.

In his home in Newlands, James knew that he had made another conquest. Should he try to take Jane from Mark or continue with Caroline? He fell asleep in the middle of this pleasant dilemma.

CHAPTER 54

"Are we having a meeting this morning?" Frank asked Penny. He was arriving on time these days, determined not to give his boss any chance to be disappointed in him again.

"I don't know, Frank. Nothing's been said. Flora went along to Charlie's room just before you came in and she hasn't emerged yet."

At her use of the DI and DCI's nicknames, Frank started whistling one of his Charlie and Flora tunes then remembered where that had got him - an evening to spend at a Scottish night locally, and he stopped as if he'd been strangled.

"Penny would you come with me to that Scottish night?" he asked now.

"No way, Jose! I hate Scottish music and dance. Why don't you ask Salma?"

"She'll not want to come. What would a Paki know about Scottish stuff?"

"Frank. I thought we'd stopped you saying Paki and Salma is Scottish. She was born here and intends to live here all her life."

"I'm sorry. I didn't mean to say Paki. It just slipped out."

Penny knew that it was an improvement that he had actually apologised and smiled at him. "Ask her anyway. The worst that can happen is that she says no."

At that moment Salma came into the room and Frank, expecting the worst, asked her if she would accompany him to the local Scottish evening.

"It's not till quite late in July. I don't want to go by myself and Penny won't come."

He might be racist and sexist but he was very open, thought Salma, letting her know that she was second choice to Penny.

"Yes I'll come with you Frank. I haven't been to anything like that. There was a Burns' Club at school but I never went. I thought they might ridicule me, me being Asian, though I knew I was as Scottish as most of them."

"Thanks Salma. You're a pal."

Salma reddened. She was delighted that Frank was beginning to see her as one of them.

At that moment Davenport called to them from the door of his room.

"OK team, meeting in the Incident Room. Now."

"Come on team," said Frank mimicking his boss's habit of calling them 'team'.

Salma and Penny told him to be careful he wasn't overheard.

When they were all seated, some on chairs and some perched on desks, Davenport filled them in on what had happened on Friday.

"DI Macdonald and I went to the prize giving. Nothing helpful happened but it was interesting to see some of the pupils we know getting prizes. Neil Fox got a prize for HE, Mary went off with all the Science prizes and Maths too and Cathy got a Citizenship cup for being head girl and for History.

Now, about the hockey sticks, one hockey stick went missing. Cathy was to try to find it but she went off sick with a migraine for two days and by the time she came back, the stick had been replaced."

"Have they been tested for blood, Sir?"

Penny was impatient to find out more.

"I was coming to that, Penny. Yes we've had them tested and there was no blood on any of them. Seemingly Mrs Campbell always washed them and four had been used again and were covered in mud."

"But Sir," said Penny disappointed, "if one was used there must be some sign no matter how small the amount of blood or hair."

Davenport was about to retort sharply when he suddenly thought of something.

"You're right Penny. I'm wondering now if I told Vince the exact number of sticks. Maybe he didn't test the four which were taken away by Mary and Cathy. Frank, get on to Vince Parker and ask how many hockey sticks he tested."

Frank loped off to the main room to use a phone there. He was back in minutes.

"He says there were eighteen of them Sir."

"OK, Penny this is your pigeon. Get to the school. If there are four sticks covered in mud, bring them here. If all are clean, put all twenty-two hockey sticks into your car and bring them here. Frank, get back onto Vince and tell him that there were twenty-two sticks so I'm afraid they'll all need to be tested again unless Penny can narrow it down to four."

Frank and Penny went off..

"So Sir, you think it is definitely a hockey stick that's the weapon?" said Fiona.

"I'm not sure. It might be the missing paper weight. If it was held by its wee handle then the shape would be rounded like an Indian club hockey stick."

"Or," said Salma, "one teacher might have been hit by one weapon and the other teacher by the other weapon."

"Yes."

Frank came back and told Davenport that one of Vince Parker's men would be across as soon as possible to collect the hockey sticks.

"He's too busy to deal with it himself Sir. If you want the results quickly it had better be done by his assistant."

"That's fine by me."

"Anything else you want done about these sticks, Sir?" asked Fiona.

"Yes. I want someone to interview the two hockey teams today. Find out who brought back the missing stick. Fiona maybe you would do that."

Fiona left to get her jacket. It was a lovely day but she liked to look smart and felt she needed the suit jacket for that.

Left with Salma and Frank, the DCI asked what they thought of James Buchanan.

Salma said what she'd said to Penny and Frank earlier, namely that she suspected that he was the murderer and she found him intimidating.

"I think he wanted Caroline Gibson for himself. He seems a cool customer to me. I don't think he would let anything get in the way of what he wanted."

"I agree with Salma but they both might be in it together, Sir. Maybe they went to the school together and he dropped the weapon out of the window to her. She could have gone round the back of the school and met him at whoever's car it was," said Frank.

"But why did he or they kill Irene Campbell?"

"Well Irene did hesitate when I asked if she had seen anyone in school that night so she might have seen one or both of them and they realised that she had and killed her to stop her talking," said Frank.

"What if we find out that a pupil had a hockey stick?" asked Davenport. "What motive might a pupil have?"

"Hated the teachers for some reason." Frank said. "I know I hated some of mine."

Later that day they got the report from Vince's colleague. There was indeed blood, David Gibson's blood, on one of the hockey sticks, one of the four which Penny had found. There were lots of smudged fingerprints on the handle. Fiona returned, having asked Christine Martin to call a meeting of the two teams. She and the head teacher had gone over to PE to meet them. Not one of them had admitted to having returned the missing stick but the captain of the second eleven had said that she had waited in PE and counted all eleven sticks in so the missing one had not belonged to someone in the second eleven.

Fiona said that most of the first eleven girls had looked embarrassed as children will do when someone is accusing them of something and that Cathy had said that she was sorry she hadn't been as efficient as the second eleven captain.

"So - we don't know if one of the girls is merely unwilling to admit not returning the stick or if one of them used the stick to hit David Gibson with," said Davenport.

"Surely it's bit unbelievable that a teenage girl would kill a teacher or teachers," said Fiona. "Why would she do it?"

"Maybe she was reprimanded for something," said Charles, though he knew he did not sound convincing.

"Well Sir, at least we now have the murder weapon," said Frank.

"For at least one murder," Davenport reminded them. "Remember that the hockey stick was back before Irene Campbell was killed."

"Sir, is it feasible that the same hockey stick killed both teachers?" asked Fiona.

"Only if the person knew which stick was used first time."

"That would suggest that it was one of the girls then," said Penny.

Frank had had another idea.

"Sir, is there any chance that the hockey stick could have been left by one of the girls and another person found it?"

"Yes Sir, David Gibson might have found it and it was in his room or a pupil took it into his room and left it there," added Penny.

They might have found the weapon but the wielder was still far from obvious.

CHAPTER 55

Monday morning first two periods was Higher English for Jan Stevenson with her fifth and sixth years. She had started doing 'Brave New World' with them and had asked them to read some chapters over the weekend. Looking neat and tidy in a black skirt and pink shirt blouse, her short fair hair shining, she was at her door to welcome them.

"Good morning class. Sit down quietly and quickly and get out your books and notebooks please. As you're now Higher level, I expect you to take notes for yourselves as you did with our poetry sessions."

There was a bit of noise while they got all their equipment out on their desks. Cathy turned and winked at one of the boys. They had planned on a mild disruption of Miss Stevenson's lesson.

"Has anyone found anything in this fictional, brave new world that we have today?" asked Jan.

One girl put up her hand. It was Mary.

"Miss, their soma was like our valium."

"Good Mary. Soma was even stronger but it had the same effect."

"Test tube babies, Miss," one of the boys suggested.

"Good. Yes."

"How can you get a baby into a test tube Miss?" asked Cathy.

Some of the boys sniggered. Cathy was pleased. This was going nicely.

"Colin. Why did you snigger at that?" Jan asked one boy at the back, pleasantly.

"Well Miss, Cathy can't have read the chapters or she'd have known that was a silly question."

Cathy flushed.

"Have you read the chapters I asked you to read, Cathy?"

"No Miss."

"Then I suggest that you go into the library now and get them read. After that you can feel free to join in the discussions. Is anyone else in that position?"

No one else admitted to having failed to read the prescribed chapters so Cathy left the room, fuming.

At the interval she approached Derek, the boy who had agreed to help her and he said he was sorry but he had read the chapters and knew he could not help her out that time but to be patient. Their time would come and Miss Smart Alec Stevenson would be made to look silly.

With that Cathy had to be satisfied.

Mary came over to her.

"It's a good book, isn't it Cathy? Aldous Huxley wrote so long ago, yet he talked about things which are coming true now. I wonder if we'll ever get to the stage where 'mother' and 'father' will be swear words."

Cathy had been interested in spite of herself.

"Yes and we're getting to the point where parents can choose the sex of their baby so maybe in the future it will be possible for babies to be born with certain abilities."

Another girl chipped in.

"You know how there are tapes to play to learn languages? Well, I've read further on and they play tapes to the babies while they sleep and it gets them interested in certain things, like flowers so those babies want to be gardeners."

"It would make things so easy if you could decide that a certain number of children would grow up to be scientists or doctors wouldn't it?" said Mary.

"Don't you think Miss Stevenson is good? I loved the poetry about relationships and the birth of babies and then this book which deals with the same things," Mary went on, full of enthusiasm. Cathy began to have some doubts about making fun of the teacher if the class liked her so much. She would meet up with Derek and see what he thought.

Their next period was PE and after the interval they went off to the gyms wondering who would be teaching them for the last few weeks. It turned out to be quite easy as the PT also had fifth and sixth years so the number being small he had joined the two classes up and he got them to play badminton in a knock out competition which was fun.

As he was talking to them, the man thought how true it was what one of his colleagues had once said that if you died, all the class would want to know was who was taking them now !

In room six, Penny was reading her latest novel, one by Elizabeth Elgin about the people caught up in the Second World War. They were taking it in turns to man the room in case anyone thought of something to tell them. Frank was taking over from her in the afternoon.

There was a tap at the door and Christine Martin came in with a cup of tea for her.

"Can you tell me if you're any further forward?"

Penny thanked her and told her that blood had been found on one of the hockey sticks, David Gibson's blood. She did not think that the DCI would mind her telling that.

Meanwhile, back at the station, Davenport had received a call from Vince Parker and he called Fiona into his room to tell her that he had asked Vince to double check the hockey stick in case it had been used twice and Vince had tested the stick himself and he had found another blood type on it. This had been matched to Irene Campbell's blood group.

"Sorry Sir. My assistant is new and was satisfied with one specimen. I'll be reprimanding him, Sir."

"That's Ok," said Davenport. "We all have to learn."

He wished sometimes that Parker could relax a bit. He was so serious and pedantic at times, unlike Martin Jamieson with whom he could share a joke.

"So the same weapon was used both times," he told Fiona now.

"I wonder why the paperweight has vanished then," said Fiona.

"Maybe David took it home for some reason."

Charles decided to phone Caroline Gibson right away and luckily she was at home.

Fiona heard his side of the conversation.

"Mrs Gibson, DCI Davenport here. Can you tell me if David brought home a paperweight shaped like a curling stone with a wee handle?"

He listened.

"Sorry, can't tell you how big," he replied.

There was another pause.

"You're sure? Thank you. Sorry to have bothered you."

He hung up.

"No Fiona. She has never seen anything like it."

"Have you any information about Irene Campbell's funeral?

"No. Will you phone her son for me? Here's the number."

Fiona went into her own room and phoned Irene Campbell's son who told her that his mother had always said that she wanted to be buried next to her parents in Newton Mearns' Cemetery and the funeral would be on Wednesday at 3 pm. There was to be a service at Mearns' Parish Church first. Fiona thanked him, told him that one of the police team would be there and rang off, going back to tell Charles who said that he would go himself. It being near his home, he could go home for lunch and go straight on to the funeral.

If only they could find a motive for the two killings. Until then, there would always be the worry that there would be another victim. On impulse, Davenport rang Christine Martin to ask her to warn her staff to be very vigilant.

Christine sent a pupil round with a circular right away.

CHAPTER 56

A quiet smile was on James Buchanan's face as he contemplated the evening ahead. He had had a successful day in court, getting a verdict of not guilty for his client. The man was guilty - he was sure of that - but his skilful reasoning had convinced the jury of the man's innocence. It bothered him not at all that now a rapist would be going free. He had no patience with the woman who had crumbled under his cross-questioning. It had been pathetically easy to make her stammer and contradict herself. The rapist, looking cocky and smug, had thanked him and swaggered off, probably to boast to his friends.

James whistled as he showered and changed. He had decided in the early hours of last night that he would see Caroline Gibson one more time then would transfer his attentions to her friend Jane who had been so obviously taken with him. She, unlike Caroline, had a partner, so would want to keep his attentions secret after she had had sex with him. It was so easy after the first time, as they felt guilty and did not want their partners to know what they had done so he could get away with anything. Caroline, on the other hand, had no one now and might feel able to spill the beans. He was a methodical man however, and always went through a number of sexual manoeuvres with his women. Caroline had one left and he was loathe to forego it, as of all his exploits, this one gave him the most pleasure.

Thus it was that at a minute to eight, he was walking up the pathway to Caroline's front door. He did not see the beautiful roses in the front garden or smell their scent. He was on the scent of his quarry.

Caroline answered the door then wished she had pretended to be out and not answered.

"James. How lovely to see you. Sorry but I'm going out shortly."

"Where are you going?" James asked pleasantly.

"I'm going out with Jane."

"Seeing Jane again? Her boyfriend must be very understanding."

"He is."

"Like David. How lucky you both are or sorry, you were."

The sarcasm was so obvious that Caroline blushed.

"I don't think you're going anywhere my dear. Surely you're not scared of me."

Saying this, he moved past her into the hall and she could do nothing except shut the door and follow him into the lounge.

"How about a drink for both of us? Mine's a whisky and soda." James said and Caroline went into the dining room to the drinks' cabinet and poured him a whisky. Suspecting what was to come, she did not know whether to fortify herself with a stiff drink or stay sober. Choosing the latter and pouring herself a diet coke, she hoped that it was not a mistake.

When she returned to the lounge, he had taken off his jacket and loosened his tie.

They sipped their drinks and he asked her how she had been since the funeral. She told him then he went on to ask if she had heard any more from the police. He seemed pleased when she said that she had last spoken to them at the funeral.

He had by now finished his drink and asked for another one. She made it very strong, hoping that it would at least mellow him if not make him forget the sex which she was quite sure he had come for.

"Trying to get me drunk, darling?" he drawled. "Why are you afraid of me now? You were the one so keen on a physical relationship if I remember rightly."

Caroline felt her cheeks redden.

"I'm not afraid of you," she lied. "It's just that I feel guilty about what I did, cheating on David and now he's dead."

"So come here. He is dead and you don't need to feel guilty any more."

Reluctantly Caroline went over to sit on the settee beside him. As usual it took only some kisses before she wanted him and she made no protest when he began to undo her blouse. She tried to undress him but he stopped her and soon she was naked. He picked her up in his arms and carried her out of the room but instead of heading for the stairs to the bedroom, he made for the kitchen.

"One more little experiment my love," he said. She shivered but with no clothes on she was in no state to rebel.

It was soon over.

Trying to keep some dignity, she straightened herself and walked into the lounge where she dressed hurriedly.

"And now you can leave, James. I am not an animal like you, so find another animal to play your dirty games with."

She walked to the door and threw it open.

"Goodbye Caroline. I was finished with you anyway," he said cruelly. "I've left you a memento of our time together."

When Caroline shut the door she was shaking. She felt sore and used. She walked into the dining room and poured herself a strong gin and tonic.

She drank it in the lounge and gradually her composure came back. He had finished with her and this made her feel better.

Deciding to have a bath to cleanse herself of him, she went into the kitchen to clean the glasses and saw the jar of Vaseline on the work surface - the memento of their time together!

That was the last straw. She went into the hallway and took down her jacket. As she drove down the driveway, anger had taken over from her revulsion and she drove quickly to the police station.

The policeman at the desk told her that all the people on the case had gone home but if she did not mind waiting, he would ring the detective inspector.

He ushered her into a waiting room and rang Davenport at home.

"Mrs Gibson, would you mind talking to DI Macdonald? Mr Davenport has a young daughter and he can't leave her?"

Caroline was pleased. She would rather talk to the woman who had befriended her recently. She was taken into a small room, brought a strong cup of tea and two digestive biscuits and she took them gratefully.

Fiona Macdonald found her there half an hour later and took her into her own room, switching on her electric fire as in spite of the month it was a chilly night. Fiona was in jeans and a sweatshirt and somehow this made it easier for Caroline to tell her what she had to say.

She started with the first date, sparing herself nothing as she detailed what had taken place. She told how she had, in spite of this, seen James Buchanan again and told how she had thought that she was in control that time only to find herself on the receiving end of a punishment session.

She came to the night of David's murder and her voice trembled.

"David told me he was golfing so I rang James and arranged to meet him. He came for me at home and I followed him to his flat in my car. We had supper, pate as I said and wine. I left to go home. He followed me, attacked and raped me."

Fiona gasped.

"We decided to keep quiet about our relationship as it gave us both a motive for killing David. We were together till about 10 pm, from about 7 pm. I'm sorry I kept quiet but by this time I was too scared of him to disobey him."

Fiona told her that what she had done was a crime, withholding evidence, but reassured her that now that she had told the truth, she was sure that Davenport would overlook the fact.

"Why are you telling us the truth now?" she asked Caroline and, looking down at her hands, Caroline told her the story of what had happened that evening.

"Sodomy as well as rape," Fiona said and wrote in her notebook.

She asked Caroline if she felt safe going home on her own and Caroline told her that James had finished with her now.

"Do you believe him?"

"Oh yes," Caroline said bitterly. "He told me last time that he had only one more experience to share with me. No doubt he has another victim in his sights."

"So it's being finished with that has made you come forward," said Fiona. "You want revenge?"

"No, it's not that," replied Caroline and went on to tell Fiona about the 'memento' left by James this evening.

"That was the last straw."

Caroline, agreeing to come in the next morning to sign her statement, left for home and Fiona went into her own room to write up what she had just heard. That done, she rang Davenport at home.

Could James Buchanan have murdered David before he saw Caroline that night? Had he gone in to see David to tell him that he wanted his wife, been laughed at and taken up the hockey stick which was at hand? It was unlikely but possible.

Another interview with Mr Buchanan was called for.

CHAPTER 57

Frank could not sleep. He had woken up around four am and something was worrying him.

He wished he had his notebook at home. The birds started singing, a sound he had seldom heard at this time before. He was up, shaved and dressed by seven o'clock.

The sergeant at the desk was amazed at the sight of PC Selby running in at 8 o'clock.

"Frank where's the fire?"

"I can't stop. I want to check something."

Frank opened his desk drawer and took out his notebook. The DCI had all the typed up reports in his room but surely he would find what he was looking for in his notebook - if he could read it!

He frantically turned the pages till he came to the interview he and the DCI had had with James Buchanan. Yes here it was. James Buchanan had said that Caroline Gibson had not long been a friend. He was sure that Penny had said something about them being old friends.

Impatiently he waited for Penny to come in and when she did, he asked her to look up her notes where sure enough she found that she had noted that James Buchanan and Caroline Gibson had been, according to Caroline, friends from their "single days". One of them had lied.

When Davenport came in, Frank and Penny went immediately to his room and told him of the discrepancy in the statements. He said that he remembered James Buchanan saying words to the effect that Caroline had only been his friend for a short time.

At this point Fiona Macdonald arrived. Davenport told her what Frank and Penny had told him and she laughed.

"I remember she told me only a few days ago that he was a recent friend."

Seeing Penny's puzzled face at her laughter, she asked Davenport if she could call Salma in and when Salma arrived she told them all about her visit last night from Caroline Gibson and what had transpired.

"So we have it confirmed what you two have told us. She lied when she said he was an old friend and he was certainly more than a friend. A pity we didn't pick up on this earlier but never mind." Fiona sounded rueful.

"Yes, good work Frank.," said Davenport. "If she hadn't confessed to the DI last night, this would have helped us. She's coming in this morning to sign her statement then I'm going to call in Buchanan. They now have alibis for later in the evening but he has a motive for killing David. He could have wanted Caroline and killed to get her."

"How would he get the hockey stick, Sir?" asked Salma.

"That's the trouble, unless it was in Gibson's room and he riled Buchanan and he picked up what was at hand."

"Sir, the set of fingerprints on the desk wasn't Buchanan's or Caroline Gibson's," said Penny.

"No but he maybe didn't touch the desk."

When Caroline came in, Fiona told her about the discrepancies in their statements about the length of time she and Buchanan had known each other and said that they would use this first when they were questioning James later that day, only using her evidence if this failed to get the truth from him. Caroline thanked her. She had had time in the small hours to wonder what James would do when he heard that she had gone to the police and told them the truth about the night of the murder. Surely he would not be so stupid as to get his revenge on her for this. She sincerely hoped that the police evidence would be enough to get him to tell the truth.

She was unlucky. Being a lawyer, James was not fazed by the fact that Caroline had said he was an old friend then changed it to a recent friend. He said that she had made a mistake about the meal they had had and about his reasons for not going to the cinema so this was just another small mistake she had made or else Frank had written down the wrong thing. Frank, sitting with Davenport in the interview room, bridled but said nothing.

Davenport then had to tell him that Caroline Gibson had come to the station last night and confessed that they had been together till around ten pm on the night of David's murder and that far from being platonic friends they had been having a sexual relationship which she obviously wanted kept from David. This in turn gave Buchanan a reason for killing David.

"I didn't want the silly bitch permanently," Buchanan. "She's an airhead who only thinks of make-up and clothes. Why would I want rid of her poor mug of a husband? She said he had forgiven her for another affair and he would probably have forgiven her again if he found out about us."

His opinion of David Gibson was patently obvious. The look on his face said it all.

Davenport knew that he was going to get no further with this man and ended the interview. He switched off the tape.

"I wouldn't think of going to see Mrs Gibson, Sir. She has been told to contact us if you do and if she does contact us, I'll suggest that she makes an official accusation of rape and sodomy."

Buchanan gave a thin smile and left the room.

CHAPTER 58

In the Incident Room later that day, Davenport brought his team up to date on his meeting with James Buchanan. If what Caroline had said about them being together till 10 pm was true then if they had murdered David together it would have been later as Buchanan was still in chambers at 6 pm. Caroline could still have done it earlier, by herself. The janitor had been in school between 7.30 and 8.00 and it seemed unlikely that David would have stayed on in school as late as 8 pm, with a friend to meet at the golf club.

Davenport ventured the opinion that the murder had taken place after 4 and before 6 which let out James Buchanan. Fiona, who had come to like Caroline, said that she could not see Caroline bashing David's head in, especially having heard about the type of sex James was involving her in. She imagined that Caroline would have felt safe in her affair only knowing that she had the comfort of David to return to should things start to go wrong or pall.

Who did that leave then?

Someone in the school who bore a grudge, a pupil or a teacher or someone in the Fox family who certainly did have an axe to grind?

Davenport reminded them that Bert Fox did not have much of an alibi and that he had only supplied the one of being in the pub after 6 pm. What about earlier? They would have to check with his work.

Then there was the second murder. There was the possibility that Irene Campbell had seen David's murderer but she could not have seen Caroline or Buchanan if they were not guilty. She could have seen Mr Fox and he did not like her either. Could Irene have seen a pupil? It was possible. Both Neil Fox and Cathy Cameron had been late in school on both nights.

Cathy had said that David was alone when she left his room after helping her with her UCAS form. She had been seen by the janitor waiting at the office window. Would she have waited there if she had killed the teacher? On the other hand it had also been her who had seen Irene Campbell just before she was murdered. There was of course the nameless person Cathy had seen leaving the building. Surely that pointed to Bert or Neil Fox who both often wore tracksuit bottoms.

Mary had heard a noise at the other end of the PE department but Cathy had not. Surely if she had been guilty she would have grabbed onto that piece of information with both hands and supported the idea that there was someone else present at that time?

Neil Fox had been seen in PE by both girls but surely it was a bit unlikely that he would kill two teachers just because they made him take PE and also he must have known that any other teacher replacing these two would do the same.

Was there any other teacher who bore a grudge against these two teachers?

And what about the weapon? Was it indeed lying there in David's room? Had it been picked up and used in an unpremeditated way?

Davenport had reread all their notes over the weekend at home and the only teacher with a possible weapon had been Angus Scott. He had been in the office with a guitar. However, the blood had been found on a hockey stick, both types of blood belonging to both victims.

Davenport turned to what still had to be done.

They needed to fingerprint Neil Fox and Cathy Cameron and maybe Mary.

"Does anyone know Mary's surname?" Davenport asked at this point. Nobody did but it would be easy to ask June Grey.

"Fiona, will you do that, please? Tell the three pupils concerned to bring an adult with them to the station as soon as possible and we'll see whether they are left or right handed too."

Bert Fox would have to be asked his whereabouts between 4 and 6 pm on the evening of the first murder.

"Frank, you see to that. You'll have to wait till he's home from work today."

The DCI asked if anyone had anything to add to what he had told them.

Penny had one question.

"Sir what about Mrs Fox? We've never even mentioned her."

"True, Penny. Probably because she has always seemed so reasonable but you're right. If we're considering female pupils, we should surely think about Neil's mother too. Frank. Ask Mrs Fox to come in for fingerprinting along with her son. We can't leave any stone unturned. And check whether she is right or left handed while you're about it."

"What about the other women, Sir - Fiona Donaldson and Geena Carmichael?" asked Salma.

"Neither has an alibi for the early time of 4-6 pm but Fiona Donaldson is left-handed so I'm ruling her out and so is Geena."

There being no further suggestions, Davenport dismissed his team.

Salma, Penny and Frank gathered round Penny's desk.

"I did so wish it could have been James Buchanan," said Penny. "From what you've both said he seems a nasty piece of work."

"Yes, he's a cool customer," said Frank and Salma agreed. Neither had liked Mr Buchanan.

In his room, Charles was voicing this same opinion to Fiona.

"I'm sorry that Buchanan seems to be in the clear."

"So am I. After what Caroline Gibson has told me, it would be nice to have him put away. I know she was cheating on David but she's showing remorse now, unlike him."

Later that evening Mr Fox was interviewed. He had been at work up till 6 pm on the night of David Gibson's murder and he shared an office with another man. This could easily be verified and Frank was asked to do that the next day. Mr Fox came in with Neil and they were fingerprinted. Mrs Fox had a part time job and had been serving in Morrisons that afternoon up till 6.30. Neil had a key and had let himself in to his house as he always did on his mother's late days. He had been late of course, having had to do detention. It was now not necessary to fingerprint Mrs Fox.

Cathy came to the station with her brother. Her mother was back home but was not up to a police station visit. Mary, whose surname was Grant, came with her father. Neil was left-handed but Mary and Cathy were right-handed.

It was the next day before the results of the fingerprinting were known.

Cathy's fingerprints matched the unknown set on the desk. No one else's did.

"Of course she was with David Gibson that night. We know that and as she was filling in a form she would have leaned on the desk," said Davenport, irritated that he had not realised who that set of fingerprints belonged to.

It was the day of Irene Campbell's funeral so Davenport went home to change into his best suit and black tie. Fiona was going too but she had come to the station in a black suit and white blouse. She asked the others to complete any reports they had to do so Frank went off to his desk, Penny promising to help him if she was needed. She had nothing else to do herself and offered to get tea and coffee for Frank and for Salma who was writing up a telephone call she had had from a woman who had called about a man whom she thought was stalking her. Fiona was busy in her own room, typing up her conversation with Caroline Gibson about her meetings with James Buchanan. It read like a Jackie Collins' novel, she thought. Penny asked her if she too wanted a drink from the canteen and Fiona thanked her but said no. She was used to the coffee from Davenport's own coffee machine and would get herself one from that if she needed one.

Another funeral, hopefully the last, she thought, as she went out to her car.

CHAPTER 59

Davenport had changed into his suit, crisp white shirt and black tie. He did not intend to take his car to Mearns Church as he lived so near to it. He had arranged to meet Fiona at the church door and she had agreed to drive him home from whichever hotel was being used afterwards.

When they went in, the church was very full and they took a seat quite near the back, grateful that they did not have to go forward to nearer the front.

The service was short and moving. The minister obviously knew Irene so his eulogy was personal. In the front row, a young man and woman were sitting very close together. She had her arm round him. It was clear that she was the elder and had been used to taking care of her younger brother. They must be Irene's son and daughter. In the seat behind, on his own, was a man in his late forties. From his isolated position, Fiona gathered that this was Irene Campbell's ex-husband. It was clear that his children were not on good terms with him as even at this sad time, they obviously did not want him near them.

The congregation rose to sing the final hymn, "Abide with Me" and then they remained standing as the family filed out.

Davenport and Macdonald waited as everyone else exited the church and were in the last car out of the car park. It was a short drive to the cemetery.

Unlike at the crematorium, more than one funeral could take place at one time and it was important to follow the funeral cars. Fiona stopped her car in the street outside. Davenport got out and was gazing out over the myriad of graves, noting that some were well-tended and some neglected. He strolled across to one near the gates and read the inscription. It was the gravestone of a child. She had been only seven years old and Charles wondered what she had died of. How awful to lose a young child, he thought, knowing how devastated he would feel if anything happened to Pippa.

The hearse and the funeral cars arrived and they got back into Fiona's car and followed the procession as it slowly wound its way down a number of driveways, coming to a stop as near as they could to the mound of fresh earth which was to be Irene Campbell's last resting place. Remembering the bright-eyed, cheerful young woman he had seen at school, Davenport found it hard to think that she was dead. If this was how he felt, how terrible her family and friends would feel.

The cars slowly emptied, their occupants making their way to the graveside. Fiona was old enough to remember when women were not expected at gravesides and was glad when Davenport hung back under some trees, leaving space nearer to the grave for Irene's relations, neighbours, colleagues and friends.

From where they stood, Charles and Fiona could see who was there and realised that Christine Martin must have been given permission to close the school as there were many teaching and non-teaching staff present. They recognised faces from the interviews they had held recently.

Fiona found that it was easier to work out who had not come and discovered that she was not surprised to find Peter and Angus from the English Department missing as was the PT of technical who would not have known Irene very well. Was she being cynical to think that Peter and Angus would see this as some extra free time from school? Geena was there too and June Grey and so too was the janitor and some women who could be cleaners. Charles knew that Irene, more so than other members of staff, would meet the cleaners as she often stayed on late for extra-curricular activities. Christine had told them what a dedicated teacher Irene had been.

The slim figure of Fiona Donaldson was standing next to Christine Martin and Fiona remembered that these two were friends and fellow members of the badminton team. No doubt Irene had played too. Jan Stevenson was behind them, on her own. She was younger than they were and would not like to push herself forward. Davenport was glad when Alex Snedden joined her.

Cathy Campbell and Mary Grant were standing with some other girls. Cathy's brother had come with her and another woman was there, presumably the mother of one of the other girls.

Far back as they were, the police officers could not hear the words of the funeral service but both had attended enough funerals in the course of their work to know what was being said. They saw the young man and woman move forward and throw a handful of earth each on the coffin. They turned away and again the young woman's arm was round the young man's shoulders. The mourners moved away from the graveside and Davenport left Fiona's side and approached the two young folk.

"Sorry to bother you at this time but I'm DCI Davenport. I'm in charge of the investigation into your mother's death."

The young man was sobbing but the young woman was dry-eyed.

"I'm Melanie Campbell, Inspector and this is my brother Fraser."

They all shook hands. Davenport could see the boy trying hard to compose himself.

"Please find the monster that killed my Mum," Melanie said.

"I'm sorry to ask this but do either of you know of anyone who disliked her at all?"

"Mum! No one disliked my Mum," the boy almost shouted. Some of the mourners turned round at the sound.

"What about your father? I believe they were divorced."

"My father is a fool!" said the girl. "He went through the usual male menopause. Fell for a younger woman. It was not because he hated Mum. He wanted to stay friends with all of us, Mum included. Stupid man! Wanted to have his cake and eat it!"

The bitterness was at odds with the fresh young face and Davenport thanked his lucky stars that he and his ex-wife had parted amicably, even if only for the sake of Pippa.

"Well if you think of anyone at all, please let us know," he said, handing her a card with his phone number on it.

Once again Fiona followed the cars of the other mourners to a local hotel. They often felt as if they were intruding but this was a good chance to see friends and family unofficially.

The first to leave were the pupils. It would be a bit of an ordeal for them. Cathy had been at the crematorium for David Gibson's service and committal but this burial must surely have been more upsetting. The girls were subdued and left it to Cathy's brother to approach Irene's son and daughter to give his condolences and thank them for their hospitality. Davenport noticed that Irene's ex-husband had not come back to the hotel. He probably knew that he was not wanted.

The teachers sat at two tables, about twenty of them. As they left, only one went up to the family table, not wanting to overwhelm the two youngsters. Christine spoke for all her staff and Davenport who was approaching, heard her tell Melanie and Fraser how much she had valued Irene as a colleague and as a friend.

Fiona Donaldson tapped Davenport on the arm.

"Are you any further forward with finding who committed these murders, Inspector?"

Hating to have to give her the stock answer but knowing that he could not go into details about the case, Davenport assured her that they were doing everything in their power to find the identity of the murderer or murderers and with that she had to be satisfied.

Charles let his DI thank the family for their hospitality. He walked out of the hotel and stood in the warm sunshine. He would need to get back down to Shawlands to pick up Pippa from his sister Linda's. School would be closing in a few days' time for the long summer holidays. How he hoped that the case would be closing soon too.

CHAPTER 60

Fiona had spent yesterday evening with a friend from college days. Instead of going out somewhere as they usually did, they had decided to just stay in so Fiona had invited Susie across to her house, promising her a take-away supper. They had just cleared the table of all the packaging and debris of the meal when Fiona remembered that she had been going to ask Susie, a well-travelled woman, about the Far East places she had visited.

"Do you think a nine year old is too young to appreciate a holiday over in the Far East, Suz?"

"Well my nephew went at ten and he thoroughly enjoyed it. The people are extremely friendly."

"This child will be eleven by a year in September. She's a bright kid."

"Well I would say she would enjoy it. Malaysia is a vibrant place. Penang is my favourite spot. It's not a beautiful island but it has so many different nationalities living on it. The food is so varied and they even have a McDonalds!"

"What about the hotels?"

"There's a strip of beach called Batu Feringgi and the hotels along there are good. There are expensive ones, reasonable ones and downright cheap ones. Only problem is that there are jellyfish in the sea. Why are you asking?"

"It's for a colleague of mine who has a young daughter. He would like to go somewhere where the heat is humid and not dry. I said I would ask you."

"And does this colleague have a wife as well as a young daughter?"

"Yes but they're divorced, amicably I believe. His wife usually has Pippa for the holidays but Charles says that she would let Pippa go away with him at any time."

"Fiona Macdonald, is there something you're not telling me?"

Fiona blushed.

"I think he might ask me to go with them. He's a good friend, nothing romantic. I couldn't face that yet, so soon after...."

Susie having supported Fiona through her break-up knew to stop teasing her friend.

"Well the Far East is somewhere you must see at some time and yes, I'm sure the young girl would enjoy it if you think she could stand the long journey."

"Oh give her a Chalet School book and she would sit for hours!"

"Chalet School! Not another fan, Fiona. You must just love that."

"I do. I'm not usually much good with young children but I find it so easy to get on with Pippa, perhaps because we share that interest and she doesn't seem to mind sharing her Dad with me, occasionally."

The evening passed quickly. Fiona told her friend about the case they were working on and Susie told her about her next holiday, in August. She went with a schoolteacher cousin from England and they were going to Switzerland this year, a new venture for them.

At 10.15 Fiona's phone rang. She went into the hall to answer it. It was Davenport.

"Sorry to phone you so late, Fiona. I need help. I was tucking Pippa in tonight and she calmly announced that she was having a boy called Ronald for a sleepover at the weekend.

I tried phoning her mother then remembered that she was on holiday in France and she refuses to take her mobile with her. What will I do?"

Fiona's silvery laugh came down the phone.

"Oh, you poor soul. Has Ronald asked his parents yet do you know?"

"Oh never thought of that. They'll probably say no."

"Mind you they're only kids. Would it do any harm?"

"That's what I was wondering. I don't fancy having to explain why it's OK to have Hazel but not OK to have Ronald. Who is he anyway? I've never heard of him."

"Surely you must have heard about him, Charles. He was the class bully until he met Pippa who stood no nonsense from him. She told me about him ages ago, think it was the time I picked her up from school."

"Maybe she has talked about him and I just haven't listened carefully."

"Well what are you going to do?"

"Think I'll wait and see if he's allowed to come and if he is, I'll set up the tent in the back garden and give them both sleeping bags. Make it different from sharing with Hazel."

"Good idea."

"Hope I didn't disturb you."

"I'm with a very old friend, a college friend. She's the one I was going to ask about Pippa and The Far East. She thinks Pippa would enjoy it, especially if she'll read for the long journey."

"Good oh. Right, talk to you about that tomorrow if we get some free time. Ask her when is the best time to go. Thanks for listening to me. 'Night."

"'Night, Charles."

Fiona had Susie in fits of laughter when she told the story of Pippa and Ronald. Susie did not bring up the subject of how Fiona was getting on with this Charles but she had been given some food for thought. She told Fiona that apart from the rainy season from September to November, any other time was fine to visit Malaysia.

After Susie had gone, Fiona sat for a while thinking about the possibility of holidaying with Charles and his daughter next summer. She knew that Pippa was going to be with her Mum for the whole of the school holidays this year and wondered if perhaps she and Charles might get some days away. Hopefully this double murder would be solved soon and they could take a well - deserved break.

CHAPTER 61

Jan Stevenson had wondered when she first met her in her new Higher English class, why Cathy Cameron had been chosen as head girl and in fifth year too. Jan had not been in the school when the staff had chosen Cathy and Gavin. Gavin was serious and studious and respected by his peers surprisingly, maybe because at times a wicked sense of humour came through unexpectedly. When Jan had asked why Cathy had been chosen, she had been told that Cathy had been suggested because she had been so good at sports and PE and a total opposite to Gavin. No other sixth year or fifth year girl stood out for any reason and the suggestion, by Irene Campbell, had been debated for some time until Fiona Donaldson had said that it might give the girl something to take her mind off her mother's illness.

Jan found her immature and today Cathy was giving her more reason to think this of her.

They had been discussing a close reading passage about equality for women in occupations and Cathy had asked what a woman should do if she worked on the roads and was asked to strip to the waist in hot weather. The boys had all sniggered and Derek had shouted out, "Bet you would do it Cathy!"

"Would you do it Miss?" asked Cathy, looking innocent.

As the class had been given this passage to read over at home prior to this lesson, Jan smelt a rat. She thought that Cathy and probably Derek had planned this disruption between them. She could not let this continue but how to stop it?

"As I've used my brain and got a good job this isn't likely to happen to me Cathy. Perhaps if you took your lessons more seriously you might also get a job that doesn't pose you such difficult problems." Her voice was dripping with sarcasm but not anger and she seemed quite calm.

Some of the girls burst out laughing and Cathy knew that it was her they were laughing at, not the teacher. Even some of the boys whom she had hoped would help her disrupt the lesson were laughing at her, instead of at Miss Stevenson.

She had been beaten and she knew it.

"Well done Miss. Sorry. My sense of humour lets me down at times."

Jan smiled back, finding herself attracted to this girl for the first time. She could take a laugh at herself.

The lesson continued without a hitch.

The next period for Jan was her fourth year class. She had asked them to prepare a solo talk of about five minutes on their hobby. Things were going reasonably well until it was Neil Fox's turn. Jan was prepared to hear him give some excuse why he could not do it and was pleasantly surprised when he came out to the front with his notes.

He had chosen to talk about cooking and his enthusiasm for his topic began to show through. Everything was going well until one boy called out:

"Fanny Craddock's got nothing on Fanny Fox!"

The class burst out laughing and Jan could not get them to stop. They had been quiet for an unusually long time listening to talks and this was the signal for them to stop behaving. Neil was red to the tips of his ears. He slunk to his seat. Jan, thinking that it might be better to diffuse the situation with humour, said,

"Very clever, Scott. Remind me to nominate you for comedy turn of the year."

The class quietened down. Jan did not see the look of despair that Neil sent her. It seemed to him that his teacher had sided with the class.

Next door, Angus was having his usual bad time with his fourth year even although the class was small, it being so near the end of term. He would have given them a free period but the head teacher was adamant that all classes would work up till the last day. His guitar was still not fixed and this was how he usually kept his poor classes quiet by playing the guitar and then using the song as a poem. He had tried asking his class to bring in the words of some modern pop song but all he had received was a song where one phrase was repeated over and over again. He had resorted to trying to interest them in a Keats's poem - he knew nothing more modern - and had failed miserably, none of them being at all interested in 'Ode to Autumn'. One boy sitting near a window had opened it and thrown the poetry book out into the playground. It was not often that Peter stirred himself to help another member of staff but his peace had been shattered by the roar of noise which emanated from the room across the landing. He opened his door and was halfway across when the swing doors opened and his head teacher came through, having seen the book flying through the air as she was on her way across the playground.

"It's OK Peter, leave it to me."

Peter went back to his own class.

Just as Christine Martin opened the door, Angus was grabbing one boy by the collar. He had one fist raised.

"Mr Scott !" she called out.

Angus lowered his fist. The boy started blustering:

"Mrs Martin did you see that? He was going to hit me. I can report him for grabbing my collar, can't I?"

Christine told the boy to go downstairs to the office and wait for her, then turning to the class she reminded them that they needed to listen to their teacher if they wanted to pass their exam next year.

She asked Angus quietly to come to see her at the end of school and walked out.

She was lucky to be able to convince the young trouble-maker that it would not do his street cred much good if he needed help to defeat the elderly man. She felt sneaky resorting to those tactics but did not want an assault case to come out of the incident.

When Angus came to see her, she asked him why he had decided to stay in teaching after his sixtieth birthday. He obviously did not enjoy his work. She told him how nearly he had come to a court appearance and Angus agreed to think over his future. How she hoped that he would decide not to return after the holidays!

CHAPTER 62

It was a beautiful day for the second last day of school before the summer holidays. Davenport hoped that Mary and Cathy would still be in school as he wanted to check with them about one more thing, the noise which had been heard at the other end of the PE department on the day of Irene Campbell's murder.

At around 10 o'clock he tapped on the office window. June's grey head appeared almost at once and she gave him a cheery smile.

"Mr Davenport, come along in. It'll be Mrs Martin you're after. She's just popped along to science but should be back shortly. Are you in a hurry?"

Davenport went into the office and found Geena sitting there.

"Morning, Geena. Not busy today?"

"It's the last but one day for the staff Inspector. I don't go on holiday for a while yet so plenty of time to get everything done with no interruptions."

"I don't go on holiday either till August," said June. "I miss the staff in some ways but like Geena, I get through a lot of work for the new session when they're not here."

Davenport accepted a cup of tea and sat chatting to them till Christine arrived back then he went into her room, taking his cup with him.

"Any further forward, Inspector?" Christine wanted to know.

"Well we've eliminated some folk because they're left-handed: Geena and Fiona for instance. I'd like to talk to Mary Grant and Cathy Cameron if they're in school, to clear up one little point. Do you know if they are in?"

Christine got up and went into the office. She came back to tell him that both girls were indeed present that day. It was easy to check up in these days of computerised registration. As there would be little work being done on the last day she did not mind using the tannoy and she called for them both.

Cathy arrived first. June brought her into the room. Davenport asked her to sit down across from him at the coffee table.

"Cathy, just one thing: on the day you went to get the hockey sticks from Mrs Campbell, are you sure you heard nothing from the other end of the PE department?"

"Well, I've thought of that and I think now that I did hear a noise."

"You said you hadn't before."

"I know but there was a small noise. I remember now wondering what it could be."

Davenport thanked Cathy and she left.

Mary was brought in soon afterwards. She looked nervous.

"Sit down, Mary. Don't be scared. I just want to ask you about the noise you said you heard coming from the boys' end of PE on the night Mrs Campbell was killed."

"Yes Sir."

"What did it sound like?"

Mary looked a bit sheepish.

"Well Sir it was Cathy who said she'd heard a noise so I told you there'd been a noise but when I thought about it later, I didn't hear anything myself. Sorry Sir."

Davenport assured Mary that it was OK and she too left.

Charles looked thoughtful.

"So first of all Mary has heard a noise and Cathy hasn't. Now Cathy says she heard something and Mary didn't."

"Does that mean there was or wasn't a noise, Inspector?"

"I'm not sure. Thanks Mrs Martin, for your help again."

After he got back to the station, Davenport called his team into the Incident Room. He told them about the discrepancy in the statements of the two girls. As he usually did when puzzled, he pulled at his left ear lobe. As he did not realise he was doing it, he saw nothing cheeky in the fact that Frank immediately did the same, getting a nudge from Penny.

"There's something not right here, folks," Davenport shared with the others.

"It sounds as if Cathy told Mary there was a noise. Mary didn't hear it but mentioned it as if she had. Now Cathy is supporting Mary but didn't remember it before," remarked Fiona.

"But she must have if she told Mary about it, Sir" said Penny.

Davenport had been thinking.

"Right team, I've had an idea. Here's what I propose to do."

Davenport was back in the school before lunch. He asked for and got Mary Grant again. The news she gave him was interesting. Back in Christine Martin's room, he asked her permission to try out a theory he had. She was a bit reluctant but when he assured her that there was no danger for anyone she agreed.

Davenport spoke that day to Mary again and to Jan Stevenson. They promised to do what he asked.

That afternoon, in English, Jan kept her Higher class hard at work though as it was her last time with them this term. She had been going to give them a free period; in fact she had promised this the day before. There were some grumbles. Mary, sitting next to Cathy whispered to her that it wasn't fair and asked Cathy if she could persuade Miss Stevenson to let them off work now."

Cathy rose to the occasion

"Miss, you promised us no work today. Can we have the rest of the period off?"

"Really, Cathy!" Jan snapped. "I thought yesterday that you had grown up and here you are acting like a child again. Do you want to pass the exam with a high grade this time?"

Cathy was astonished. Miss Stevenson was usually so controlled.

"I only asked, Miss," she replied.

"You only asked. Notice the 'you'. No one else asked. They are adults you see, unlike you."

The period progressed and eventually the bell rang. The class trooped out. Mary apologised to Cathy for getting her into trouble.

"It doesn't matter, Mary. I think Stevenson's got it in for me."

In the afternoon, Jan had occasion to tell Neil Fox off for loitering in the corridor.

"Get a move on Neil. If you go any slower you'll stop."

He felt a bit aggrieved as it was after all nearly the last day and even teachers were more lax then. He made a face at Cathy Cameron who was passing. She smiled at him.

"I know. She went for me today too."

Jan stayed in the staffroom the whole of lunchtime and was busy all afternoon with S1 and S2 classes. Knowing that she would have no time tomorrow to prepare for next session, she told her friend in the science department that she was staying on for a while after school and not to wait for her as she usually did. She went down to the staffroom and made herself a cup of coffee, taking it back up to her room.

CHAPTER 63

There was a tense atmosphere in Shawbank Police Station. Charles and Fiona were having a coffee in his room, trying to take their minds off things. They had not been able to face lunch. The other members of the team were in the canteen having lunch and discussing what had been planned for this afternoon. No one was hungry and even Frank had left his favourite meal of egg and beans congealing on his plate. Davenport had thought up a strategy for flushing the murderer out into the open but they were all very aware that it could fail or worse still go horrible wrong.

Lunchtime over, they met in the Incident Room. Even Penny was silent and Davenport chased them off to their own room with instructions to get on with routine work and be ready to leave promptly at 3 pm.

At about ten minutes to three, his phone rang and it was Knox's secretary to tell him that Knox wanted to see him right away. Charles groaned inwardly.

"Sorry, Wilma, something important has come up. Tell him I'll come up later."

She gasped and he hung up.

If his instincts were wrong, he knew that he would be in big trouble for this; on the other hand if he was correct, he would be able to give Knox the name of the murderer.

It was very quiet in the corridors of Bradford High School. The school had emptied quickly as it usually did. Jan got up and opened her door. It was quite stuffy in her room. She had a copy of "Whose Life Is It Anyway?" in front of her. The set of new books would hopefully arrive during the holidays but she had her own copy from her university days and she wanted to make some notes for her Higher class to use the following year.

She heard the swish of the swing doors and looked up. It was Cathy Cameron, heavily laden.

"Cathy, you look like a packhorse. What are you doing with all that stuff?"

"Clearing out my locker along in the common-room, Miss and taking home all the things I won't need for next year."

"Is that your own hockey stick then?"

"No Miss. It's the school's stick, the one I always use. Pity I won't need it next year."

"Why not?"

"I'm giving up hockey. I want to work harder for my exams next year."

"Good for you Cathy."

"So you believe me too, do you?" Cathy's voice had changed. "Mrs Campbell believed me."

"Why shouldn't she?" Jan looked down at her book. "Is there anything I can help you with Cathy? I'm quite busy as you can see."

"She was silly to believe that I would accept Mary being captain of the first eleven."

"Oh is that why you're giving up hockey? Nothing to do with working harder."

Jan sounded disinterested.

"I don't think Mary will be back next year."

"Why not? Look Cathy, I really must get on. Do you want me for anything?"

Everything after that seemed to happen at once. Jan looked up as the hockey stick was coming down then the descent stopped as the stick was grabbed from behind.

"Let it go. She's got to die. She's got to die. No one makes me feel small. No one. I'm Cathy Cameron. I'm..."

"Cathy Cameron, I'm arresting you for the murder or David Gibson and Irene Campbell and for the attempted murder of Jan Stevenson..."

Jan did not hear the rest. She had fainted across her desk.

Salma led the girl away, handcuffed. Cathy was still claiming her right to kill her English teacher then the rant changed.

"Get your hands off me Paki. Do you not know who I am black bitch? I am Cathy Cameron."

Frank, listening to this diatribe was horrified. He had come into the room with Salma and Davenport but had not been needed to control the girl, Davenport being more than a match for her.

Hearing the racism spew from the girl's mouth as Salma led her down the corridor, he realised that this could have been him talking a few months ago. How awful for Salma to have to listen to that! Getting Davenport's permission, he sped off after them.

Charles turned to Jan who had come round.

"Sorry Inspector. I don't know what came over me."

"Do you feel well enough to come down to the head teacher's room? The rest of my team are there and I want to let them know what has happened."

Jan said that she was fine and they set off along the corridor. In the distance they could still hear Cathy's voice.

Fiona and Penny were in Christine Martin's room and looked delighted to see them both. Davenport asked Christine if she had anything stronger than tea or coffee for Jan and she produced a small bottle of brandy which she kept in her desk, for medicinal purposes only, she assured them.

Fortified by the brandy, the colour came back into Jan's cheeks.

"I did what you said Mr Davenport and sent Cathy with a note to my friend in Science telling her not to wait for me because I would be working on in my room after school finished."

"She's good at reading notes," said Christine. "She was the one I gave the note to telling you all to be careful after Irene was killed."

"What made you suspect Cathy, Inspector?" asked Jan.

"I first started to suspect Cathy when I found out that a hockey stick was the murder weapon. Then today I discovered that she had planted the idea of a noise at the other end of the PE Department in Mary's head. She had been seen with a hockey stick on the day of David Gibson's murder. No one admitted to having returned the missing stick. Why not? Because it had been used to murder David. Who saw Irene Campbell just before her death? Cathy Cameron. We only had her word for it that Irene was still alive when Cathy returned to Mary. Even if she did not kill her then, Mary went for the bus home. She told me that today. Cathy could have come back. Neil Fox could have gone by then."

Penny was too eager to wait.

"Why did she kill them Sir?"

"I imagine that David rebuffed her advances that day or the day before. She had seen him twice about her UCAS form. Either she went in intending to kill him on the Tuesday or she just happened to have the hockey stick with her and he knocked her back then."

"And what about Irene Campbell? What did *she* do?" asked Penny again.

"I asked Mary about that today. Irene replaced Cathy with Mary as captain of the first eleven team for next year. Cathy appeared to be OK with that, even saying that she intended to give up the sport to concentrate on her studies next session."

"That's what she told me upstairs," said Jan. She sounded scathing that I believed her too. Her voice was chilling. It took me all my time to appear to be busy with my work."

"I noticed the change in her voice too Jan," said Davenport. "That's when I knew that I was right. The contempt in her voice for Irene Campbell and yourself was so strong."

"And she would have killed me because I made her feel small in front of her English class today?"

"Yes. I found out from Mrs Martin who taught Cathy today and that's why I asked you to belittle her."

"I'd done that the other day when she tried to disrupt the lesson. Maybe it was one time too often."

"Or maybe she had decided to kill you before what happened today, Jan."

"She apologised so nicely yesterday too."

"Yes I'm sure Irene Campbell thought she had taken her demotion very well too and David Gibson probably had no idea of what he'd done to her."

"No, David walked over peoples' feelings on a regular basis so I'm sure he didn't spare a second thought for how she would feel when he rejected her advances, as I suspect he did," said Christine. "I found it hard to believe that he had encouraged her."

"She was very clever, standing outside the office window and not hurrying away," said Davenport. "She knew she might have been seen, so made her presence obvious later on. She dropped the hockey stick out of the window and collected it later, inventing a migraine to keep her off school and returning the hockey stick while she was supposedly off. She lives near the school and would know when the coast might be clear."

"Yes she often walked her dog through the grounds. I've seen her," said Christine. "She could have brought the dog to give her cover. The janitor would be used to this and think nothing of seeing her with a hockey stick either."

"When I asked her if she'd seen anyone else that day, she took the chance to feed us the story about seeing a man in tracksuit bottoms going out through the swing doors. That of course made us suspect Mr Fox who when not at work wears a tracksuit," said Davenport.

He got up to go and Fiona and Penny rose too.

"Thanks for helping us out, Jan. It couldn't have been easy," said Davenport.

"I knew that there were three of you next door, in Peter's room and anyway I knew what to expect so could probably have defended myself if I'd had to. Sir, she said that Mary wouldn't be coming back to school next year. Did she…"

"…intend to kill Mary too. Yes, I think so," said Davenport, looking sombre.

Davenport, Fiona and Penny left, Davenport offering to come to the school the next day to inform the staff. Christine Martin thanked him gratefully and offered to run Jan home, an offer which she gratefully accepted.

CHAPTER 64

Davenport went to Cathy's house. Her mother, looking very frail, answered the door but luckily Douglas was in and appeared behind her. Telling his mother that this was one of his friends, Douglas took Davenport into the lounge, asking his mother to make coffee for them as this would get her out of the way, and knowing what he had to tell the man, Davenport thanked her and off she went to the kitchen. There was no easy way to tell the man about his sister so without any beating about the bush, Davenport told him that Cathy had killed two teachers and tried to kill a third.

Douglas looked stunned.

"I'd like to see her bedroom please, Sir," said Davenport.

Douglas Cameron led him upstairs and opened a door which said on it, ' Cathy's Room. Keep Out!'

The first thing he noticed was that the walls were covered in photographs. Nothing unusual in that, as most female teenagers put up pictures of boy bands and Pippa had up pictures of ponies but these photographs were all of Cathy by herself. She stared down at him from every wall, as he went to the bureau and opened the top drawer. It was full of photographs as far as he could see. He lifted the top one and saw that it was a picture of Cathy's brother. It had been cut, presumably to remove Douglas from a shot of him and Cathy. Davenport pulled down the flap of the desk and opened the small drawer there. There was a slim line diary. He took it out and quickly flipped to the date of the first murder. The girl had written at the end of that day's space, "Killed DG." It was the same the next week, just the bald entry. "Killed IC". Reading the next few days' worth, he noted where she had written simply, "Mary???" and when Jan Stevenson had annoyed her. There was one comment, "She'd better be careful."

Davenport showed the entries to Cathy's brother. The man looked stricken.

Davenport went on to tell him what had just happened at the school.

"I'd like you to come to the station, Sir. We're holding Cathy there."

As they turned to leave the room, Davenport's eye was caught by an item on the desk top - a little curling-stone paperweight. The last piece of the jigsaw fell into place. Cathy had taken a memento from her victim. Beside it on the desk was a whistle on a ribbon. He felt sure that that would turn out to belong to Irene Campbell. He wondered what she would have taken from Jan Stevenson.

They apologised to Mrs Cameron for leaving without drinking her coffee, and went in Davenport's car to the station.

As he approached Interview Room 1, Davenport could hear Cathy's high-pitched voice. The man beside him stopped and ran his hand through his hair in an attitude of despair.

"That sounds just like my grandmother," he said. "I don't know if I can do this."

"I'm so sorry Mr Cameron but I need to have you with me because of child protection guidelines. I can't question Cathy without a member of her family present. Would your mother maybe do it?"

"Douglas Cameron stiffened and squared his shoulders.

"No, my mother certainly can't do this. She's just out of Leverndale Hospital, Inspector. She takes bad depressions. She couldn't cope with this. No way."

Davenport stopped.

"You said there that Cathy sounded like your grandmother. What did you mean by that?"

"My grandmother, Mum's mother, lived with us when I was small. She had megalomania I found out when I was older. She was OK when

441

under sedation, Mum told me later, but if she stopped taking her pills, she became full of her own importance. Even when the Dr was called I remember hearing her tell him off for calling her by her first name. "My name is Mrs Fraser. Who do you think you are, calling me Agnes?"

"What happened to her?"

"She ended up in Gartnavel Royal. I never saw her again, though Mum visited her from time to time."

"What about your father?"

"I think he left because he couldn't stand living with Gran and with Mum who took fits of depression."

"How did this all affect Cathy?"

"She was too young to know about Gran, She was about three when Gran went into Gartnavel. She blamed Mum for Dad leaving. She was his little doll. He spoiled her rotten."

"Does your Mum have megalomania too?"

"No. She lost my little baby sister - it was a cot death - and she's had spells of depression ever since."

They walked on and went into the interview room. Davenport switched on the tape, made his usual comments and nodded to Fiona to stay with them, out of sight at the back of the room.

"Cathy. Tell us what happened on the day of Mr Gibson's death."

"Why should I? Who the hell do you think you are? I demand to go home."

"Well you see, we're all confused here and need someone clever like you to help us out."

Cathy preened.

"Oh, OK. He fancied me, I know he did."

"Because he put his arm round you once?"

"He didn't do that but I knew he wanted to and would do it if I gave him any encouragement. He was unhappy at home. I know he was."

"So what happened that evening?"

"I went to him with my UCAS form and when it was finished I leant forward on the desk and tried to kiss him."

Her colour rose.

"What happened?"

"He laughed. He laughed at me."

"So what did you do?"

"I had my hockey stick with me so I hit him with it. He fell forward, hit his head on the desk and fell onto the floor."

She giggled. The sound was eerie in the almost empty room.

"I leant over the desk and I knew he was dead."

"And you were very clever with the hockey stick weren't you?"

"Yes"

She stopped giggling and said solemnly, "I *am* clever. I opened the window and dropped the hockey stick out then closed the window. I went down the corridor and waited for a few minutes outside the office window till I saw the janitor.

I told I was waiting for David but I wasn't. He'd had his chance and he'd blown it, stupid man."

Next to him, Charles felt the man's shoulders move. He heard his intake of breath.

"There was no other man going out by the other swing door, was there?"

"No."

"What happened with Mrs Campbell?"

"Stupid Mary. I walked her to her bus stop and I went back. Mrs Campbell hadn't been bending over the pool the first time I saw her but she was now. I hit her with one of the hockey sticks, the one I call *my* stick. It has a notch on the handle. I like to keep the same stick. She fell over. I pushed her into the pool."

"Why Cathy? It was a clever move but why did you do it?"

"She made Mary captain of the hockey team. Mary! She told me I was too selfish a player. How dare she?"

Cathy's voice was rising. Davenport leaned over to switch off the tape but Cathy was continuing:

"I saw Campbell on the night of David's death when I was going into the school to meet him. I thought she might have recognised me."

Davenport opened his mouth to say something but she was continuing:

"I took round the circular to the staff telling them to be vigilant. I had a good laugh at that. Stupid lot hadn't a clue."

"Was it you who had the clever idea of texting to Mrs Donaldson from the PE department?"

"Yes, the text came through from Mrs Donaldson asking where the silly cow was so I texted back that I wasn't feeling well and just to go on without me or something like that."

"So you decided next to get rid of Miss Stevenson. What did she do?"

"I wanted Peter for my teacher next year. I know he fancies me and anyway the silly bitch thought that she could embarrass me in front of the class and get away with it!"

"Oh, Cathy." Her brother was almost in tears.

"Was Mary going to die too?" asked Davenport.

"Of course she was. How else would I get back to being captain again? I've been getting friendly with her and was going to get rid of her during the school holidays. With Mary out of the way they would plead with me to be captain again. I hoped to make you suspect her with the noise thing but that went wrong. Silly bitch!"

"Cathy."

Her brother's voice was full of pity.

"Don't cry, Douglas. They all had to die. Just like Marion."

"Marion. Who's Marion?" asked Davenport.

"Oh no," Douglas Cameron said brokenly. "Not Marion too."

"Well, Mum was taking too much time with her. I did it for you too, Douglas. Mum was neglecting you too."

"Your baby sister?" whispered Davenport.
"Yes."
"Davenport had heard enough.
"Interview with Catherine Cameron ending.
5.16 pm."

CHAPTER 65

They were in the local pub. Davenport had just bought the first round ever for his team. Fiona, knowing that she was going back to his house for the evening, had a gin and tonic. Frank looked at her in surprise. He had thought her too straight-laced for alcohol. He realised that maybe he should not prejudge people.

Penny and Salma had shandies, Frank himself had an orange juice. He had decided that he was going to take the girls out for a drink later and he would drive and let them drink. Davenport looked a bit surprised but he too was going to be the driver so he had a diet coke.

Cathy Cameron had been found not guilty that day, in late August, on the grounds of diminished responsibility. She had stood in the dock and proudly confessed to two murders and an attempted murder. She had never shown any remorse.

It was some months since the events at Bradford High School.

Fiona had been seeing quite a lot of Caroline Gibson and could tell the others that she no longer saw James Buchanan who had moved on to Jane, her friend, in spite of Caroline's attempts to dissuade her from seeing him. Jane had chosen to ignore her warnings and they had lost touch.

In another pub on the South Side, Christine Martin was buying drinks for her management team. They had been discussing the trial. As it had taken place during the school term, only Christine and Stewart had attended, as had Irene's son and daughter and Caroline Gibson.

Talk turned now to school affairs.

Angus had retired from teaching. He had handed in his resignation on the last morning in June, much to Christine Martin's relief. His replacement was a young woman who was conscientious and hard-working. She and Jan were fast becoming friends. Mary Turner had applied for and got the permanent post of DHT at Bradford High. Christine thanked her now for picking up so quickly the work that had been left unfinished by David Gibson.

David had not deserved to die but the admin. corridor was a happier place without him.

Irene was sadly missed by staff and pupils. Even Neil Fox missed her and he was still being forced into doing physical exercise by the new teacher. His father was not complaining to the school and Neil had his kit with him every day. Mary had replaced Cathy as captain of hockey and as head girl, Christine having discovered that the quiet girl was popular with her peer group.

Charles raised his glass:

"To my team," he said and caught a grin from Frank to Penny. He wondered if a romance was starting up between these two.

Christine raised her glass:

"To my team," she said and caught a grin from Stewart to Phyllis who had noticed this new phrase creeping into their boss's speech.

The paths of police officers and school teachers had crossed for a brief time. They would probably never meet again.

Made in the USA
Charleston, SC
22 September 2011